Like The
Ocean Moves

Like The Ocean Moves

BOOK ONE OF THE TORCHBEARER SERIES

Liz Mitchell

ISBN: 1546642781

ISBN 13: 9781546642787

Dedicated to A, B, and H

Acknowledgements

The vast web of support and encouragement I have received over the many years I've been writing helped book one of the Torchbearers series evolve from dream and hope into solid reality. Words can't capture the appreciation I have for my husband Brian, who has taken care of our children while I closeted myself to dream, pray, and write. My parents have cheered me on since elementary school, when I first began writing the stories that played out in my imagination. Their unwavering support of not only my ambition to write, but the degrees that helped get me here, can't be underscored with enough gratitude and love. My brother, Jon Hofmann, has spent many hours being my number one beta reader, telling me what works and what doesn't. I value his opinion perhaps more than any other critic I'll ever have.

A huge thank you goes out to Roger Hodges, whose support and encouragement acted as a tremendous springboard toward this avenue of success for Like The Ocean Moves. Along the way Gary Chapman and Dan Madigan joined the list, adding their support and expertise as well. Gary, in particular, has been a great encourager and fount of wisdom in this project. Thrown into the mix were other beta readers: author Karissa Knox Sorrell, the Rudd family, my uncle Dr. Robert Bowles, and Randy Hargis. More thank-yous go to Dean Glascock, Scott and Laura Beth Russell, former professors and mentors from the University of Evansville and Murray State University, fellow MFAers, Generations Church, Jack and Berta Pitzer, Franziska Heiland (my little German sis), Melanie Hofmann for photography and inspiring the cover art, and many other family members and friends. An additional note of gratitude and respect is owed to the memory of Sgt. W. Patrick Rudd, Company B, 3rd battalion, 75th Ranger Regiment, Fort Benning, GA.

My acknowledgements would not be complete without my honest, heartfelt thoughts about the truth of Like The Ocean Moves. Before I wrote a word of this book, I prayed each time and asked Holy Spirit to be part of my words, to breathe life into them, to make this book what it should be to further the Kingdom of God within and among us. I believe that he honored that prayer and that what you read in these pages is a good story, a fictional story, but one that brings Heaven a little closer to us. I invite you, my reader, to engage not only the characters, but the One who inspired them. Perhaps you too were born a Torchbearer.

More information on how to support first responders can be found via the Patrick Rudd Project and www.patchofvalor.co.

Endorsement for Like The Ocean Moves

"Every genuine work of art has at its core, a good story. Every painting. Every song. Every poem. Every book. We are drawn to them because, at our cores, we are each a story being written every day. **Like The Ocean Moves** is not a good story. It is a great story brimming with rich characters, plot twists and intrigue. Liz Mitchell has written a book that encourages, challenges, excites and captures the reader. It makes me want to be a better son to my Father God. It makes me insanely desirous to see Heaven. It makes me want to be an author. It makes me want to be a Torchbearer."

Gary Chapman

Gary Chapman has long been one of the most respected singer-songwriters in Nashville. For nearly four decades, Chapman has seamlessly blurred the musical lines of contemporary Christian, pop, country and southern gospel, racking up an impressive list of awards including seven Dove Awards, five GRAMMY nominations and writing credits for legendary artists such as Kenny Rogers, Alabama and Wynonna. Chapman is also widely remembered as the host of TNN's popular "Prime Time Country" television series and the "Sam's Place" concert series and radio show at the Ryman Auditorium.

Gary and wife Cassie adopted a baby daughter, Eva Rose in 2013 and remain very close to his son Matt and daughters Sarah and Millie, who've since spread their wings for school and successful careers respectively. *"Family is everything to us"*.

Once a week, Chapman sings live from his living room and tells the stories behind a different classic hymn. *"These timeless songs were the only thing that gave my father peace in his final days. When he was struggling, I would just take out my guitar and play the songs that I had learned as a child for him at his bedside. Singing those hymns I grew up with helped me remember what music is really for."* After a long struggle with Parkinson's and Cancer, Gary's father went to be with the Lord in peace like a preacher should, Easter morning at sunrise. **"A Hymn a Week"** has grown into a global, loving community. https://www.facebook.com/ahymnaweek/

Gary's broad experience in music and television keeps him in demand and qualified for just about every facet of the creative process. He claims he has **"taken recreation to an artform"** and enjoys hiking, fishing, boating, scuba diving, skiing and pretty much anything you can have fun doing outside. He soloed an airplane when he was 12 years old and has been a licensed pilot of fixed wing and rotorcraft his entire life. He and Cassie love to travel and are always ready to see what's around the next bend in the road.

Foreward for Like The Ocean Moves

Christian suspense novel.

Christian suspense novel?

I never really knew what that was. Of course I had an idea what it should be.

Just by the name of the genre I thought I knew what I was in store for when reading Liz Mitchell's **Like The Ocean Moves.**

I thought wrong.

Let me tell you going in what I thought **Like The Ocean Moves** was NOT going to be.

I didn't think it would be nerve-racking. I didn't think it would be well written. Nor did I think it would be gripping.

It was NOT supposed to be suspenseful. It was NOT supposed to be thrilling. It was NOT supposed to be exciting.

That's what I thought. And once again writer Liz Mitchell proved me wrong. Very wrong.

Like The Ocean Moves is a book that hits hard. A right hook to the Solar Plexus that knocks the wind out of you. Leaves you gasping for air once you find yourself trapped in the story with characters you can't help feel for. Relate to. Envision yourself as. She creates people. The people that we want to be. The people we should be. The people we fear we may become. The people we loathe. And the people we love. Real people.

In other words she creates the world as it is. She holds up a mirror and you can either look away or stare into the reflection and question who is looking back at you.

But that is what good storytelling does. It creates questions; sometimes more questions than answers. Sometimes those questions are the ones we always wanted to ask; sometimes they are the questions we were afraid to think about. And we may not find the answers we want but we may find the answers we need.

Mitchell writes with a conviction of both a devoted Christian and a dedicated artist, she has created a story that is powerful both in plot and in passion. Like a seasoned tightrope walker she carefully moves along the line between the worlds of the celestial and terrestrial. Leaving herself open perched up high, in the spotlight carefully taking each step with measured poise.

She writes with a style that is both personal and prescient at times. Her subject matter is upsetting. As it should be! Because it's a subject matter that needs to be addressed. Has to be addressed!

But can a book be both upsetting and uplifting? Unsettling and inspiring? Angering and enlightening?

The good ones can. The good ones take us to places we don't want to go. Places we don't want to know exist. Places we'd rather not think about let alone visit. Places we need to see. And Mitchell takes us to those places. Because that is the destination of providence, the last stop of humanity.

Mitchell becomes a tour guide of the human condition, in both the psychological plane and spiritual domain where she takes you on a trip where both faith and fate intersect at that place called life, the crossroads where one way leads to the temporal world and one towards a heavenly realm. One direction towards destiny and one towards divinity, one path well worn for most, the other unexplored for many. But both within our reach.

Like The Ocean Moves is a story that moves between redemption and retribution with a stopover in repentance. It's a story that moves from the darkest of the dark to the brightest light and away from the banality of gray indifference.

Mitchell creates a place where both the pious and pitiful live side by side; the devout and devious are shoulder to shoulder, a place where the good, the bad and the unimaginable all collide and explode into a firestorm of emotions. Emotions that are all too real.

She deftly moves us between the soulless desolation that is prevalent in this world to the miraculous salvation of the next, never letting us forget that faith, true faith, is something that is both inexplicable and unexplainable but always unwavering.

She shows that decadence is offset by decency, desperation negated by deliverance, that in the end it's the warm glow of salvation that guides us through the blackness of doubt.

She writes about virtue lost and innocence regained. She writes from a place that lies between the mind and the heart – the soul.

Does Liz Mitchell have a voice? Yes. One that is both a whisper that can be heard in the deafening silence of apathy and one that is a shout that can be heard over the din of moral destitution. Her voice resonates, her faith is resilient, her message is rewarding. And her words become a beacon, a light that will lead you through the bleakest of nights towards the dawning of a new day. She illuminates the path towards a better place. It's up to us to get there.

Dan Madigan
August 2016

Madigan is a screenwriter, author, documentarian, and director of live television. He worked for Vince McMahon and the WWE writing and directing their live shows **RAW** and **SMACKDOWN**. Madigan also wrote WWE Films first **"See No Evil"** which launched that series franchise. He wrote the international best seller **'MONDO LUCHA A GO-GO"** for Simon& Schuster Publishers, the ultimate tome on professional masked Mexican wrestling. Madigan then wrote the documentary **"VIVA LUCHA LIBRE"** based upon his book. From there he stared in the PBS special **"TALES OF MASKED MEN"**. As a road manager he toured the world with such acts as **BLOOD, SWEAT & TEARS** and **Chuck Negron** from **THREE DOG NIGHT.** He lives in California with his wife Karen and son Kane and two cats.

Chapter One

The heavy police presence at Sweeny Elementary School had not yet amassed in Amy's second grade classroom. She hadn't had time to check emails and no one had interrupted her ninety minute reading and writing block, so catching the reflection of so many blue uniforms in the Plexiglas of the library widow made her stomach flip-flop. She dropped off her students for enrichment time and headed to the lounge. She had forty-five minutes to use the bathroom, eat her peanut butter and jelly sandwich, grab another hot cup of coffee, call and make an appointment to get her son's teeth cleaned, and make copies for afternoon math time. In the back corner of the lounge Mr. Jackson cursed and fumed at the Xerox machine, stating colorfully that it had jammed for the fourth time in thirty minutes.

"Amy, have a seat." Teresa, her closest friend through her eight years of teaching, patted the chair next to her. "Want some of my chips?"

"That would be great. How's your day?" Amy said over a mouthful of salt and vinegar chips. "And what's with the platoon of policemen in the lobby?"

"I don't think policemen come in platoons."

Amy unwrapped her sandwich. "You know what I mean."

"You haven't heard?"

"Apparently not."

"Do you know that sweet little girl, Katey Johnson? She's in first grade with Jonas."

"Yeah. She's our neighbor. I saw her this morning. Why?"

"You saw her? When?"

"She was waiting for the bus this morning when we left the house. What's going on?"

"Amy, she's missing. She didn't get on the bus. Her backpack was in the street and no one knows where she is."

Amy felt the blood run out of her face and gooseflesh raise on her scalp. The peanut butter got lodged in her throat and she forced it down with a swallow of coffee. "But I saw her. She was where she always is."

"You need to go the main office right now. The police are there questioning people. Didn't you read the email?"

"Who has time to read emails? Are you serious about this?"

"I'm serious." Teresa took her three-digit addition sheet for afternoon math practice from Amy's hands. "Go now. I'll make your copies. How many?"

Amy stared at her sandwich. She'd seen Katey. She couldn't be missing. Quickly she replayed her morning inside her head. She was making lunches for herself and Jonas when he came out of his room in his favorite Batman t-shirt and green sweatpants that didn't match at all. But it was Friday and she was running even later than she normally did, so she didn't send him back to change. Instead, she grabbed their lunchboxes, her purse, and her bag of graded papers, juggled her monster-size coffee thermos, and followed Jonas out the front door. She was busy trying to balance it all and lock the door while Jonas spoke with Katey. She'd been waiting in her usual spot in her front yard near the sidewalk. Jonas had asked to bring her along. Amy's throat closed up with the memory. She had told them both no. She knew she was running late and didn't want to take the time to let Katey's mother know her daughter would be riding with them. Despite the cold February temperatures, Amy had left Katey standing in the yard, her *Minnie Mouse* backpack hanging down to her knees. She had backed out of her driveway a little too fast, narrowly missing a large SUV, and hightailed it to work.

She had seen her. Spoken with her. Surely no one had taken her in the short time between Amy leaving and the bus arriving. There must be some mistake. Either way she should go to the office and talk to an officer. "Make thirty copies," she said to Teresa. "Someone always messes up and needs a fresh sheet." She threw the rest of her lunch in the fridge for later and grabbed her coffee. Throwing a thank you over her shoulder to Teresa as she left, Amy walked quickly toward the front of the school.

Outside the main office the scene was systematic, cold, and frightening. Uniformed officers and men in suits stood talking with teachers and custodial staff. Some recorded the conversations while others took notes. Katey's teacher, a first year straight out of college, pulled tissues out of the box she held under her arm, swiping at tears as she described Katey's personality, likes and dislikes. Amy's principal, Mrs. Richards, looked like she'd been chain-smoking and drinking *Red Bull* all morning. Two more officers blocked news reporters with cameras from entering the school. They seemed to be rolling tape anyway.

Amy had no idea what to do. She tried to make eye contact with Mrs. Richards to alert her that she needed to speak with her. But Mrs. Richards was busy with the police and didn't seem to be aware of anyone else. Amy thought separating an officer from the pack might work, but they were all grim and serious with their questioning. The atmosphere was charged with stiff tension and Amy felt her calm façade shrivel.

A tap on her right shoulder made her jump and toss her cup of coffee all over the floor.

"I'm sorry, ma'am. I didn't mean to startle you."

The man bent down, pulling a wadded *McDonald's* napkin out of his pocket to wipe up the mess. "I'm Officer Yates, one of the detectives working Katey's case."

Amy picked up the empty cup and stuck out her other hand, now shaking from too much adrenaline and caffeine. "Amy," she said, grasping his hand. "Amy McEwan." It briefly registered in her mind that he looked familiar. Something about his slate gray eyes and the crooked line of his nose.

They both stood and regained their composure. "I suppose you're aware of the situation," he said.

"Yes. I just found out. I really hadn't had time to read my emails today."

He smiled. "I'm sure you had a few other things to occupy your time."

Amy tried to slow down her breathing and steady her hands. "Yes," she smiled in return. "Always."

"Do you know Katey Johnson?"

"Yes. We're neighbors."

"You live next door to the family?"

"Yes."

"I'm going to need to ask you some questions."

"I saw her this morning," she said, blurting out the thing she'd come to the main office to say in the first place.

"You saw Katey this morning?"

"Yes. In her front yard. Waiting for the bus like she usually does."

"Did you talk to her?"

"Yes." Guilt swept over Amy as she recounted how Jonas had wanted Katey to ride with them this morning. He'd invited her and Amy had disinvited her, worried about the extra minute and a half it would have taken to get her mother's permission. Tears spilled over with the sickening realization that she could have stopped it all, could have prevented a kidnapping this morning, if she'd just slowed down.

Officer Yates pulled a package of tissues out of a different pocket than the *McDonald's* napkin had appeared from and offered it to her. "Please come with me. I need you to tell me everything you remember. Every last detail."

He led Amy into an emptied classroom across from the main office. Once there, Amy started her story, locking the door, turning around, Jonas talking with Katey, pulling out of the driveway, and—"That SUV was there."

"What SUV?" Officer Yates' dark eyebrows rose and his pen poised above the small notebook in his hands.

"A maroon SUV. It was parked across from my house. It's not usually there."

She'd never seen a group of people move so fast. In the blink of an eye the whole room was full of police officers taking down every word she said about the maroon SUV. But that's all she could remember. No other distinguishing characteristics. It was big. It was maroon. She'd almost hit it backing out. No, she'd never seen it before. No, she had no idea who owned it.

Officer Yates thanked her, left quickly, and was replaced by a long line of new interrogators. She told the same story over and over, inwardly berating herself for not paying more attention, for not taking the time to put Katey in the car and bring her to school. Would it really have mattered if Amy had been two minutes late for hall duty? She felt foolish and angry that she hadn't slowed down, hadn't fully taken in the situation. How many times had she called Jonas back inside because someone was walking down the sidewalk that she didn't recognize? Her mother made fun of her for it. Said she was over-protective of Jonas and needed to relax. She told Amy she would make him a "mama's boy" and he would grow up too dependent and not able to make it on his own. But her mother wasn't a part of their daily lives in Nashville and she didn't know what it was like to be the single mom of an active, inquisitive little boy who never met strangers. To him, everyone was someone he could be friends with. That's why he and Katey were so close. She was shy and quiet and according to her parents, hadn't had many friends until Jonas came along. When the two of them had moved in, his bubbly, talkative personality had helped her blossom and begin playing with other kids in the neighborhood. She'd begun talking to strangers.

By the time school let out for the day, Katey's disappearance was all over the news. Her amber alert included the maroon SUV, but no one had called in with any solid leads. No one else in the neighborhood had seen the SUV parked outside Katey's house. One other person thought they had looked down the street this morning and noticed something out of the corner of their eye. But like Amy, that neighbor swung her car around and drove to work without another thought about strange vehicles hanging around.

All the teachers had been interviewed one by one. None of them knew anything more. Several of them had taken turns covering Amy's class for the rest of the day while she talked with police officers and detectives,

FBI agents and school board officials. She'd told the story of her rushed, selfish action so many times she thought once more would surely push her over the edge into a complete emotional break-down. The only thing she wanted to do was go home, cry for a while in a hot shower, and binge on vodka and chocolate. She hadn't had a drink in probably six months. Single moms don't go out much and Amy didn't spend money on little luxuries, including the goods for a drink or two. But the grocery store she shopped at had a liquor section. She'd stop there on the way home, get a frozen pizza for supper, and buy a treat to take the edge off her worn nerves.

The last person she talked to was Mrs. Richards, who'd weathered the storm of police and reporters as well as possible. If she'd looked like she'd been on a *Red Bull* streak earlier, Amy thought she now appeared to have put her finger in an electrical outlet and charged herself a few volts shy of a personal lightning strike. After reassuring one another that surely the police would find Katey, Amy had collected her purse from the only locking cabinet in her classroom and headed to the gym to pick up Jonas from after-school care.

"Mommy!" Jonas ran to her and wrapped his arms around her waist, hugging her tight. He smiled and said, "I met police officers today. They came and asked me all about Katey. Then they gave me candy and pop!"

Amy felt a surge of anger. She should have been there when they questioned her son. It did not seem at all appropriate that he should have been questioned without her there to hold his hand and help him. On the other hand, she thought, he seemed to have managed just fine. Even if he had felt nervous, candy generally fixed everything in Jonas' world.

"Were they nice to you?"

"Yep."

"Did you tell them everything you could think of about how awesome Katey is?"

"I sure did. And I told them she might come over and play today. She does lots of times on the weekends."

Amy's stomach clenched. They hadn't told him why they were asking about Katey. And why should they? It was her job to tell him. But not here. Not now, in front of all the other kids who might not understand why mother and son would both be crying.

Chapter Two

At the grocery store, Jonas was still sniffling. Amy had explained Katey's disappearance the best way she knew how, and promised him that the police officers who had talked to him were trying really hard to find her. But that was little comfort to both of them and in the end, she'd resigned herself to not being able to fix it. She always wanted to fix the broken things in Jonas' life. It was part of being a single mother, being everything to him every moment of every day. She wanted his life to be as perfect as possible because God knew she'd done her part to screw it up before he'd been born.

Jonas was an accident. She met his father when she'd landed her first big gig in Nashville. She was an elementary teacher by day, wannabe country music star by night. She'd auditioned to be a back-up singer for an up-and-coming act. Greg was the drummer. He was tall, ridiculously handsome, had washboard abs and a knack for making her laugh. He was everything her parents had told her to stay away from, so naturally she hadn't needed much seducing. They had only dated for three months when she found out Jonas was on the way. The timing was impeccable. That up-and-coming act got up and went and took Greg with them. He'd let her go so fast she'd hardly had time to know much more than his name. He'd seen Jonas once, wished them both well, and sent a check every couple of months. He said he didn't want the courts involved. Couldn't deal with possible publicity. So he sent money and she took it, staying quiet and raising their son on her own.

But tonight was one of those nights when being a single parent left bruises on her heart. She didn't know what to say to make it better for her son or for herself. She couldn't fix this one. But, she decided, she could splurge and buy a few luxuries they didn't normally have.

"What do you want for supper, Jonas? Frozen pizza?"

"No." He wiped his nose on his Batman shirt.

"But you like pizza."

"Not the frozen kind. The cheese is gross."

She shrugged her shoulders. He was right. "What sounds good then? You can have anything you want."

"French fries."

"Fries. Got it. What do you want with the fries?"

"Ketchup."

"What else? Chicken nuggets? Maybe some fish sticks?"

"No. Just ketchup."

Amy started to argue. Normally, she would insist on some kind of protein to offset the fries. Or at least some veggies. But what did it really matter in the grand scheme of things if her kid had French fries for supper tonight? At least he would be with her, under her roof, an arm's length away.

"Okay. French fries and ketchup."

"What do you want, Mommy?"

Amy thought about the ready-made chicken salad croissants in the deli, the mixed greens salads with lowfat dressing packets lining the refrigerated shelves. "Ice cream."

"With chocolate sprinkles?"

"Definitely with chocolate sprinkles." And, she thought to herself, a little bottle of something just for Mommy. Maybe after a glass of wine or a vodka and orange juice, her mind would stop fixating on the messes she couldn't change.

After finally locating the chocolate sprinkles, Amy headed for where she thought the liquor aisle was. No luck. She tooled around the aisles, hunting a sign that said *Jim, Jack and José are here for you!* But no sign was jumping out anywhere. She finally waved down a bald guy in a green smock.

"Excuse me. Could you tell me where the adult beverage section is?"

"Well, it used to be in aisle two."

"That's where it used to be?"

"Yeah. But it's not there now."

"I see. Where is it now?"

"Oh, we got rid of it. Not enough sales."

"Are you serious? The one time I want to buy alcohol and you don't have it?"

"Nope. We don't have it." The guy looked her over. She watched his face take her all in, from her teachery tennis shoes with her gray work pants, all the way to her red hair, no doubt frizzed out into a clownish A-frame shape around her head. "You look like you've had a bad day, lady."

"You could say that."

"Listen," he leaned his bald head closer, revealing teeth sorely in need of a dental hygienist. "I know a guy. He works at *Beers & Such* on the corner. He could hook you up. Take the edge off, you know?"

Amy couldn't believe her ears. She pointed at her son. "Do you see him? He's six. Do you really think I'm going to take my kid to a liquor store and find a drug dealer? Really? Are you brain-damaged?"

He looked completely offended and held up his hands. "Geez, lady. I was just trying to help. And for the record," he eyed the security camera over his left shoulder, "I did not offer you drugs. I offered to put you in touch with a friend."

"Unbelievable." Amy wheeled her cart around and stormed down the aisle. All the decency in the world, she decided, had been flushed down a toilet the size of Texas.

"Mommy, why is he brain-damaged?"

"Never mind. Let's just get our ice cream and go home."

When Amy turned the corner onto Iroquois Lane, she felt stupid for not considering the consequences of living next door to the Johnsons. The press was everywhere, including her front yard. Police officers in uniform and plain clothes were talking to neighbors while K-9 units sniffed and searched every leaf and corner of every house on the street. As she pulled into her driveway, a swarm of reporters approached both sides of the car. She would have given her right leg for a garage.

But Amy was spared from having to fend them off by Officer Yates, who materialized beside the car and ordered them all to give her space. She was thankful, as Jonas immediately began crying with so many lights and people around. Yates opened the door for her and asked, "Can I help you in?"

"Yes. Carry our stuff. I'll get Jonas."

She surprised herself by giving him orders, even if he was in plain clothes. But she desperately wanted to get in the house and draw the curtains as quickly as possible. Yates collected the lunch boxes, the backpack, the purse, and the grocery bags and walked them to the door. The reporters did what he asked and let them pass without a word. Jonas hid his face in her neck and held his own weight against her body as she tried to shift him to unlock the front door.

"Do you need help?" Officer Yates asked.

"I've got it." Amy replied, swinging open the door and flipping on the lights.

He closed the door behind them and locked it. "When I walk back out, lock it again. I'll have a talk with them when I leave so no one should bother you tonight, but just in case, take extra precautions. Reporters are first-class jerks."

Amy blew out a breath, glancing out the front windows. "I understand."

Jonas popped his head up. "Can we make fries now?"

"Yes. Why don't I turn on some television for you while I heat them up and talk with Officer Yates?"

Jonas nodded and took his shoes off before plopping himself on the couch with a bounce. "Can I watch *Spongebob*?"

"How about *Mickey*?"

"*Ninja Turtles*?"

"Fine." She closed the curtains in the living room first, blocking out reporters and cameras and flashing lights. "There you go, kiddo. I'll call you to the table when supper is ready."

"Is it really supper if it's just fries and ice cream?"

She saw Yates smile at that. "Well, tonight it is. But don't get used to it."

She gave him a kiss before turning to Yates, who still stood by the door, holding all their stuff. "I'm sorry. Let me take that."

"Just point me to the kitchen."

"This way." She led him around the corner and into the eat-in kitchen, turning on more lights as she went. On top of the table twitching his tail lay her cat. She shooed him off and spoke over her shoulder. "Just put our bags on the table. I appreciate your help."

"It's not a problem. That's a huge cat. What's his name?"

Amy smiled, still trying to place his familiarity. "Dog."

"Are you serious? You named your cat Dog?"

"Yep. Jonas wanted a dog, but they're a bit more work than what I wanted. So we settled on a cat."

"But you had to name him Dog."

"You got it."

Officer Yates aimed a crooked smile her way, making her stomach flutter. She realized then she had not allowed a man in her house in a very long time. His presence was business only, but it made her nervous. More so because she couldn't remember where she'd seen him before. He was in jeans and a white button-down with an understated brown sports jacket. Amy appreciated his handsome, clean-cut looks, but hated noticing him at all. She averted her eyes and washed her hands under a stream of scalding hot water instead.

John cleared his throat, stepping around the large black and white tom cat and placing the groceries on the table. "When I saw your car pull in I walked over. I didn't know how you would handle having so much attention focused on you. Did they tell you to expect that?"

"No."

"They should have. I'm sorry."

"It's okay. Katey's father's career as a songwriter has recently taken off into the stratosphere. I should have expected more than a little media interest. I've just never dealt with a situation like this before."

"I wouldn't think so."

Amy put the ice cream away and set the oven at four hundred to bake the fries. When she pulled out the chocolate sprinkles, she set them down and made herself look at him straight in the eyes. He was lean and dark and his gray eyes held hers firmly. She noticed a tattoo on his right hand, just above the joint of his thumb. A black Celtic cross that finally sparked a memory.

"I've seen you before. At a church service. Weren't you the pastor?"

He nodded, another smile aimed her way. "That's my side gig."

"Oh," Amy was surprised. The two professions didn't go together easily and the thought of having a pastor in her house did not ease her tension. But the inclusion of pastor within the scope of Officer Yates somehow made him seem less like a stiff suit and more like a real person. "How'd that happen?" she asked.

He shrugged. "I went to seminary and joined the Army as a Chaplain. Served a few tours, came home, tried life in the pulpit full-time, but it just didn't fit. So I became a cop instead and preach when God asks me to fill in."

Amy took in his words, measuring him as pastor, soldier, police officer, and man. Something in his steady gray gaze softened her resolve to hold herself apart from him. She wanted to trust him. She wanted someone to tell her that everything was going to be okay. Before she could talk herself out of a moment of vulnerability, she took a deep breath and asked him what she really wanted to know.

"Is Katey going to be okay? Tell me the truth."

He tightened his jaw but didn't look away. "I don't know the answer to that."

Amy nodded. "But something bad is probably happening to her as we speak, isn't it?" Her palms were starting to sweat and she could feel the tears coming up in her throat, choking her words and making them squeak out in a tiny, hot breath.

Yates still didn't move. "It's probable. But I don't know anything for sure." He didn't move any closer, but she saw his body relax a little. "I've been in constant prayer for her," he said. "I'm not going to stop praying and I'm not going to lose hope. I'm going to work hard and have faith and get her home."

Amy took a few deep breaths and got control of herself again. Tonight was not a night for a good cry. At least not until Jonas was sound asleep.

When his breathing was slow and steady and he was quiet under his superhero blanket, she could sneak into the bathroom, turn on the shower as hot as it would go, and cry for as long as she wanted. But not yet. Yates was right. She couldn't change Katey's reality in the now, but she could certainly pray for her future to be changed.

"Can I call you Amy?" Yates asked.

"Of course."

"Amy, you and your son are the last known people to have seen and talked with Katey before her disappearance. It's really important that you tell me if you remember anything else about this morning or anything in recent days or weeks that has seemed suspicious to you."

"Officer Yates, I promise I have told you everything."

"John."

"I'm sorry?"

"Call me John."

"John, then. I can't remember anything else. I've been going over it in my mind all day. I was in a hurry. I had hall duty today and I'm perpetually slow in the morning. I'm always running late. Today was no different. I should have listened to Jonas, though. I should have put Katey in the car with us. She rides with us sometimes, especially on cold mornings like today. But I didn't do it." Amy picked up the bottle of sprinkles and slammed it on the counter like a hammer. "Why didn't I just slow down? Ninety seconds. That's all I would have needed to tell Angela I was taking Katey with me. Ninety seconds. But I said no. I said no and I left and I barely noticed that stupid SUV sitting right there, waiting for her. I just didn't know!"

Tears escaped her eyes again and for the third time that day, John Yates pulled a tissue out of his pocket and handed it to her. "I didn't mean to upset you, Amy. I just need you tell me if anything else pops out in your memory."

She wiped her nose on his tissue. "Do you buy stock in tissues or what?"

"Ninety-nine cents a package at Walmart or free at a drive-thru."

Amy smiled despite herself. "Thanks."

"No problem."

"I promise I will tell you anything at all that I remember. That's what all the other officers and FBI agents kept hounding me about today. They asked me eighty thousand questions to try to help me remember other details. But honestly, I've told you everything."

"It's okay. I believe you. But the brain works in strange ways. When you're not trying to remember, something might come to you. So here's my number." He pulled a card out of his back pocket with his name and contact information on it.

"Use my cell. Day or night. I'll be working this case twenty-four hours a day until Katey comes home. Call me about even the slightest thing. Something that doesn't seem important to you at all might help me put all the pieces together."

Amy took the card. "I'll try to remember more."

"Not just you. Jonas, too. He's been questioned, as you know. But kids are different. They remember things in unique ways. You need to talk to him. Ask him about what he's seen, who he's seen, who they've played with, when they've played, everything. I think he'll talk more freely if I'm not around." He paused. "But if you want, I could stay and make the fries. Help you talk to him."

Amy stiffened her shoulders at his offer. She did not want a man in the house, no matter how genuine or helpful he might be. She had wanted his reassurances, but she would not allow familiarity to grow between them. "No. I'd rather talk to him alone."

"I understand," he nodded. "But if he says anything at all that is more than what we know so far, like a stripe on the van or someone new he's talked to recently, I need to hear about it immediately."

"Okay. I'll call you."

"Even if it's in the middle of the night. Promise?"

"I promise."

Katey – Part One

It was so cold! The wind bit my ears and made my legs tingle under my jeans. I wish Ms. Amy had let me ride with her to school, but she's always in a hurry, Jonas says. My momma is, too, whenever we go somewhere. So I didn't tell her I was freezing out there. As soon as her car pulled away I looked up and there was D.D. standing beside a big maroon truck with the door standing wide open and heat blasting out. I got so excited I ran right over and jumped in. The heat felt good and he smiled, took my back-pack, handed me a sausage biscuit and an orange juice and told me he had a big surprise for me.

Then D.D. shut the door and we took off lickety-split. I ate my break-fast and brushed off the crumbs so I would look nice for D.D.'s surprise. He told me I didn't have to go to school. Instead I would get to go on va-cation. I smiled at him in the mirror because he loves me and it was cozy in the heat. And I got sleepy. So very sleepy.

Chapter Three

John Yates leaned back against the desk in his office and stared at the time line on his white board. After leaving Amy McEwan, he'd gone to work organizing all the pieces of information his team had collected. In the center of it all he'd taped a picture of Katey's smiling six year-old face. He had to find her. Something in her blue eyes held him steadfast and touched the core of his heart. All the cases he worked on touched him in some form or fashion, but he had learned to disassociate himself from most of the victims, purposefully distancing himself from them so that he could do his job without becoming too emotionally involved. But Katey had blasted through all his defenses and held his heartstrings like a pair of reigns. And every time he thought of Katey, Amy was right behind her.

Amy McEwan was fiercely independent and clearly did not have any problems taking care of herself and her son. Her coworkers had all spoken highly of her, praising her professional work in the classroom, her love for her students, her volunteer work in the after-school adult education program, and the loyalty and courage she showed by raising her son alone. He had asked about Jonas' father, trying to get a good picture of the Johnsons' neighbor and the comings and goings of her household. Her coworker and friend, Teresa, had blown off the question, stating that he had never been in the picture.

That knowledge had surprised John. Amy was gorgeous with red hair that hung in curls and framed her heart-shaped face and green eyes perfectly. She was tough and smart, and had made him smile more than once even in the midst of so much turmoil and angst. How could anyone let her go? Then there was Jonas, with bouncy blonde curls, energetic and spunky, all boy down to the dirt under his fingernails. John would give anything to have a son like Jonas. Once, he almost did. Almost.

John turned when he heard the click of his supervisor's office door. "Yates," Chief Anderson said, "go home. Get some sleep while you can."

He reluctantly agreed, knowing he wouldn't be much use to Katey or anyone else running on empty. He'd grap a sandwich on the way home, shower, and turn in. Four to five solid hours of sleep would buy him another sixteen or twenty to work. He grabbed his keys and following his chief out hoping some solitude would allow him to stop thinking long enough to fall asleep.

Chapter Four

Amy talked to Jonas about Katey again over supper. He dipped his fries in ketchup while she pumped him for details about their play time. They'd played outside a couple of times in the last few weeks, but it was still February and even in Nashville, too cold most of the time for outside play. She asked about strangers and people that might have been watching from their car windows. But nothing seemed to kick his memory off any more than all the questioning she'd been through had done for hers. After two scoops of chocolate ice cream and three spoonfuls of sprinkles, Jonas said his belly was about to pop.

"Mommy, I'm done. Can we watch a movie?"

"Sure. I'll just throw this stuff in the sink." She thought about their neighborhood, swarming with news crews and police officers, about the Johnsons, out of their minds with worry and fear.

"Hey, Jonas, you want to sleep in my room tonight? We can snuggle up in my bed and watch a movie on my TV. How does that sound?"

"Awesome! But can I pick the movie?"

"Sure."

"Yes! *Minions*!" He sped down the hallway toward her bedroom. "Last one in pajamas is a rotten egg!"

"Wash the chocolate off your hands and face!" Amy cleaned up the kitchen and double-checked the locks on the front and back doors. Before turning out all the lights, she peeked out the curtains and saw that the news crews had left for the night. No doubt they would return in the morning.

Snuggled up in her bed, it didn't take long for Jonas to fall asleep. She turned off the movie and held him close, brushing back his hair and looking at the way his blonde eyelashes curled against his cheeks. Her heart was so full of love for her son and anguish for Katey, the tears started before she could tamp them back down. Along with the emotion her tears brought, her thoughts turned to God, spurring the prayers she had been thinking all day.

Praying and going to church happened occasionally, but not consistently. She'd grown up as a preacher's kid and hated every minute of it. Her entire childhood had been lived on display for her father's flock and their small community in western Kentucky. Good, bad, or ugly, everyone had known about every little thing Amy did or didn't do. She was never able to meet their expectations. Never pretty enough, never clever enough, never proper enough. She'd been slapped with a ruler by a Sunday school teacher for using bad language after accidentally stapling her finger to her Noah's Ark craft. Her mother's friends mocked her in front of their daughters for her clownish red hair and pimples during her teen years. During her senior year in high school, Amy had fallen for a boy in math class. His father was the town's only tattoo artist and the boy already had two of his own design inked darkly on each tight bicep. He designed one for her with angel wings and a red rose, then drew it in the center of her back so that she could look at it in the mirror. She told him there was no way she could come home with a tattoo. When her parents saw the drawing on her back they'd assumed she'd really done it. Her father's slap against her cheek still stung, years later, as did the words disappointment, slut, and failure.

By the time she graduated from high school, she'd had enough of rules and regulations, hypocrisy, and constant condemnation from others anytime she put a toe over their lines of propriety and orderliness for how young women ought to behave. She'd chosen to leave town and attend school at the University of Tennessee and finally settled in Nashville, ready to spread her wings. It wasn't until after Jonas was born that she'd given any thought to her relationship with God. Since then she'd explored it off and on, praying when she needed help, attending church every couple of months. It wasn't that she didn't believe in God. She did. But she'd never really known him the way others seemed to. God had been formed in her mind as a stern task master, unbending and distant. She'd met other Christians who talked about God's love and joy and how wonderful it was to worship him and feel him filling up their hearts with himself. But Amy had no frame of reference for any of that and no idea how to make the God in her mind seem loving.

Tonight, however, she needed that love. She needed it for herself, for Jonas, and most especially for Katey. That sweet girl's life depended on his love, on his nearness, on the truth of his realness. If God really was who he said he was, he could save Katey. He could remove her from the danger she was in and put her right back in her parents' arms. As Amy prayed, she wasn't sure if she was asking for the possible or the impossible. But she prayed anyway, holding Jonas in her arms, tears sliding down her face in anger at the situation, at her own negligence, and that's when it happened.

It was like a seam split open in the middle of her bedroom, as if a curtain had hung there unnoticed, disguising a fuller reality. One second everything was normal, in perfect order. The next, her room was flooded in a brilliant light that hurt her eyes and at the same time, warmed and comforted her. She put her hand up to shield her eyes and realized that within the light was a figure. Terror flooded her body and she pulled Jonas tightly to her chest and screamed, "No! Get away! Don't take him!"

But the figure stepped forward, revealing herself. She was tall, at least six feet. She wore red and gold armor and carried a broadsword at her waist. Her hair glowed like sunlight on daffodil petals and her eyes were the deep purple of sunset against full clouds. Wings, a good two feet taller than herself, stretched up above her head. She emitted power, strength, grace and beauty. She was smiling at them in a way that immediately comforted Amy. Inexplicably, she felt that she knew this being, had always known her, even though she'd never set eyes on her before. The word angel crowded Amy's conscious thoughts as she tried to wrap her mind around what was happening.

"Amy," the angel said, "please don't be afraid. I promise I won't hurt you or Jonas. I would never do that. Do you believe me?"

Amy listened to her voice. There was more in its tone than just the timbre of a normal voice. There were layers of sounds within it, like flowing water or a spring breeze or a harp's chords strummed. It was strange and somehow familiar, and comforted Amy's fear. She found that she did believe this large and beautiful creature standing in her bedroom.

"Yes," she said, "I do believe you."

"Good," she said. "That's a beginning."

"Are you an angel?"

"Yes," she said, still smiling. "I am your angel, in fact. Father God has given me charge over you since your conception. I have always been at your side."

"Like a guardian angel?"

"Just like that," the angel said.

Amy took that revelation in and while she did not relax, she no longer felt afraid. The light had dimmed behind the angel, but still lit up Amy's bedroom like midday sunlight. Her mind raced from question to question before she finally settled on one. "Why are you here?"

"You prayed for help and Father God sent me. I am here to take you and Jonas back with me to Heaven."

"Back to Heaven? Are you serious?" Amy's voice hushed to a whisper. "Are we dead?"

The angel laughed, and the sounds of water and breeze and music heightened in her voice. "No, no. Your bodies are still very much alive."

"Then why would we go to Heaven if we're still alive?"

"That is an excellent question. I wish I could tell you everything right away to set your mind at ease. But it is not my place. Someone else would like to talk to you about the Father's plans. So if you are willing to trust him and trust me, I will take the two of you there."

"There," Amy echoed, "to Heaven?"

"Yes."

"You're really serious?"

"I would not have revealed myself to you if I weren't serious. I had not planned to do so until your body expired. But Father God's plans are sometimes surprising and far more interesting than anything I can imagine as his servant."

Amy looked down at Jonas and realized he was fully awake and staring open-mouthed at the angel. "Mommy, it's an angel."

"I know."

"She's in our house! This is so cool!" Jonas sat up in the bed and laughed. It was a full-belly, hold your sides laugh she heard all too rarely from him. Before she could stop him, Jonas crawled to the foot of the bed, just a couple of feet from the angel. His excitement was uncontrollable as he bounced up and down.

Sudden fear seized Amy once more. She thought of all the horror stories she'd heard of people being hoodwinked, of the news crews and flashing lights that had been just outside her door a few hours before. The angel might be real and might mean no harm. But she absolutely would not let Jonas out of her reach.

"Jonas," she grabbed his arm and tried to pull him backwards. "Stay away."

The angel remained still, but the light around her began to emanate from within her as well. She focused the bright lavender of her eyes on Amy and the illumination of her entire being grew to encompass her. In the warmth of the angel's light and presence, she felt the strength of her fear and anxiety break and lose its control over the direction of her thoughts.

"How did you do that?" Amy asked.

"It's love, Amy. I'm just directing love toward you. Remember the scripture you read as a child."

The words came to Amy like she'd heard them only yesterday, instead of twenty years before. "Perfect love casts out fear."

"That's right," the angel said. "You don't have to be afraid of me or the One I represent."

Jonas scooted out of Amy's grip and began to bounce on the bed again. "What's your name?"

The angel never relaxed her warrior's straight posture, but her gentleness with Jonas softened everything about her. "Harbor."

"Harbor? That's a strange name."

"Jonas, that's not very nice to say," Amy said.

Harbor did not seem bothered. "My real name is something you cannot yet understand because it is in an angelic language. One day, when you come to Heaven for eternity, you'll be able to learn it. But for now, it is easier to translate it into something you are familiar with. So you can call me Harbor."

"Okay. I can do that." Amy watched him interact with the angel, incredulous that he should act as if talking to a warrior angel in her bedroom was an experience they had all the time.

Harbor refocused her attention on Amy. "It's time to make your choice. Will you come with me? Can you trust what you know of Father God more than your fear of the unknown?"

Amy tried to peek past the angel into the light. Was there really an open doorway to Heaven in her bedroom? What would she find there? Who would she find there? Why did Father God want her and Jonas to come now? It was true that she had just been praying, but it wasn't something she did often. In fact, she didn't necessarily consider herself on intimate terms with God. Had he really listened and responded?

Amy's inner questioning was interrupted by Jonas, back in her lap, begging to go with the angel. "Please, please, Mommy? Let's go with Harbor."

She decided to be honest. "Jonas, I don't know. I'm scared."

He took her face in his hands and kissed her forehead, as she had done with him so many times before. Her heart soared with love for her son. Then he squashed his nose against hers and giggled. "Mommy, let's go have an adventure."

There was no fear in her son. There was only trust and joy and love. Amy also felt love and joy emanating from Harbor, who stood still, hands outstretched to the two of them. She made her decision.

"Let's do it, Jonas. Let's have an adventure."

Chapter Five

Amy took Jonas in her arms and stood up beside the bed. Anxious feelings tumbled through her like a freight train, making her heart knock against her ribs. But she fastened her eyes on Harbor, who held out one hand. Amy took a few deep breaths and stepped forward to take it.

She was engulfed in light. It flooded her, warming her whole body until it felt liquid and pure, weightless and strong as steel. Her conscious mind was swarmed with emotions, all linked with happiness and unfathomable joy. It felt as if she was reliving a thousand moments of delight in one instant: the electric excitement of a summer thunderstorm, the sensation of splashing feet in sea foam, scents of roses and lavender, riding within the tumbling roar of a rollercoaster, all while floating through the light like a butterfly in a breeze. She could not yet see anything beyond the light, but she could feel and receive more than she ever thought possible, as if all that she was accelerated into an expansion of herself, until Amy began to include her surroundings as part of herself. When that happened, Amy's eyes focused. The light dimmed until she saw everything. Until she saw Heaven.

Before her stood a wall of epic proportions. Twelve layers of jewels: sapphire, emerald, amethyst, and others that made the outer wall of New Jerusalem. Its ephemeral weight created an aura of an impenetrable, dominant, and completely delicate fortress. Within the wall was a large gate, the size of a skyscraper, made of translucent pearl that reflected the light of the jewels in the wall, creating thousands of colorful prisms. Leading up to the gate was a rolling meadow of flowers. Not just one type of flower, not even twenty. But flowers of every kind on earth bloomed around her in what seemed to be an eternal spring, allowing each aroma to drift and sway on the light wind that made her red curls dance around her head. Amy recognized roses and black-eyed susans, sunflowers, azaelas, hibiscus, iris, and every kind of lily imaginable. As her gaze roamed and took in the details of New Jerusalem, she realized under her feet stretched a pathway that shimmered gold in the light.

Amy couldn't stop the thought from coming out of her mouth. "The streets are really made of gold? That wasn't just something some poor guy made up to make himself feel better about dying?"

"It is written in scripture, dear one." Harbor said. "Of course it's true."

"It's all true? All of it?"

The angel smiled, the translucent feathers in her wings lifting in the breeze blowing through the fields of flowers. "Yes."

Amy marveled at everything, much like Jonas, still in her arms and squealing with happiness. "Mommy! We're here! We're really in Heaven! Do you see this stuff? Do you see those colors? Are there new colors in those rainbows? That door is huge! Can we go in it? I want to see Jesus! I want to meet everyone!"

His excitement was contagious and Harbor seemed to feel it, too. "Jonas," she said, "there is more to Heaven than I can show you while you are here now. Your visit is very special. Not many people come here before their bodies stop working, so your stay with us will be short. But I promise to let you see as much as possible if you will promise to take the knowledge back with you and help other people believe as you do."

Jonas looked at her and reached out his hand. Harbor took it and they shared a solemn shake. "Deal."

Again Harbor laughed and Amy was once more taken aback by the many layers of sound in her voice. Then she heard a new sound. It was like a trumpet, but less shrill. It blew one long blast high above her head. She craned her neck up the tall face of the jeweled wall as Harbor pointed at a gold tower to her left. "It's a shofar," Harbor explained. "A ram's horn. That angel is Azure. He is a lookout between the two dimensions."

Far up in the golden tower, Amy could make out the figure of another angel. His wings were halfway open as he leaned down and waved. Amy waved back and asked, "Why is he waving? He seems happy to see us."

Harbor rested a hand on Amy's shoulder as she led her forward. "I've been with you a long time. You were not aware of my presence, but I have stayed with you through long, dark hours of fear, confusion, anger, and pain. You have been wounded by many moments in your life. Some were your own doing. Some were inflicted on you by believers who know King Jesus and acted outside of his authority. Your pain is real and fresh. But here things are different. You are loved, Amy. You are so loved. No one here will condemn you for anything. No one here will hurt you, point out your flaws, or say something ugly. While you are here, you are our honored guest. You are a human in the last days, allowed to see the halls of Heaven in your flesh, returning to earth shortly for important work. You are a hero, Amy. And Jonas is the biggest hero of all."

Amy would have let that sink in longer had she not found herself passing through the tall gates of luminescent pearl. What lay beyond them took her breath away. An entire kingdom stretched farther, wider than her eyes could take in. The buildings were white and shimmered in the light. There were all sizes and shapes of buildings, all grand and beautiful, intricately detailed with spires and turrets, arches and bridges that connected one great work of architecture to the next. It was a kingdom of wealth and glory, where every soul was privileged and no one lacked anything. It was not a loud place, but not silent and gloomy, either. She could hear the business of communication and life happening, the low rumble of people talking and living among the castles and manors before her.

The cityscape seemed to lie not only beneath her feet at the precipice of the gate, but also at the foot of a tall promontory in the center of New Jerusalem. Amy inexplicably knew, just as she knew the name of the city, that at its center was the Holy of Holies. The Throne Room of God. It was a massive structure, many football fields in length and width. Its tall columns reminded Amy of pictures she'd seen of Greece's Parthenon. But this structure was different, larger, and pouring out of it was that lovely light that had enveloped Amy as she entered Heaven. It lit everything. There was no sun, no moon. The light from the Holy of Holies bathed the streets of Heaven in a warming glow. Across the distance she could see streaks of colors and flashes of lightening coming and going from within the open alcoves of that central sanctuary. She could hear singing and what seemed like a hundred of each instrument playing, along with low-pitched rolls of thunder. That is the sound of worship, Amy realized. She thought of the hymns she'd heard as a child and the contemporary songs she knew, all seeking to imagine and portray in words what she was seeing with her own eyes. The reality humbled her and she knelt down, putting Jonas down beside her. As she knelt, love like she'd never known flooded her heart, mind, and body. She was moved to love in return, offering up the darkest corners of herself.

Painful scenes from Amy's life played out in her mind's eye. She relived them briefly, feeling each sharp edge of grief she'd lived through already. Once more she felt the injustice and cruelty of her parents' snap judgments of her inadequacy. She felt the loneliness and rejection of her father's cold shoulder and the years of his silence since she'd told him he was going to be a grandpa to a boy who had no father. She relived the day Jonas was born, experiencing the pain of labor beside indifferent nurses who sent her home to an empty house, a newborn in her arms. The fear, the anxiety, the loneliness, the rejection pricked her once more before being soothed and replaced with a deeper sense of peace than Amy had ever known. Suddenly those defining moments held no sway over her any longer. The pain of always measuring up short of everyone's expectations ceased. Instead she felt love. Love that completed her, filled the empty spaces, allowed her to be whole and free for the first time. The feeling of acceptance grew larger, pulling from her more and more of her painful memories. She released them one by one from a place inside herself she hadn't even known was there, locked down in a weighted darkness that had held her back from this place, from the possibility of this moment, for far too long.

As her emotions steadied and she opened her eyes once more, Jonas was beside her, standing on tiptoes, arms outstretched toward the Holy of Holies. She watched him worship, knew that even in his silence, he was somehow giving and receiving love within the Throne Room, now just a short distance from where they stood.

He opened his eyes and looked at her. "Mommy, you're better now?"

"Yes, honey. Better than I've ever been."

"Good. He said you would be. And he said we would get to hang out with him in a little while."

"Who said that?"

"Jesus." Jonas smiled. "Only here he isn't just Jesus. He is King Jesus."

Amy nodded. She looked where she knew he was and nodded. "I can't wait."

From behind she heard Harbor's voice. "That will be soon, dear ones. But not quite yet."

Amy stood in awe as Harbor came forward flanked by more warrior angels. There were seven of them in all. Each one stood straight and tall like Harbor, some reaching eight feet high or more, their wings at least two feet above their heads. All wore the same gold and red armor as Harbor. In the center of the breastplate on each one was a gold lion, teeth bared, claw stretched forth in a vicious strike. She knew again, without being told, that the insignia was the Lion of Judah, another name for Jesus. In her mind she'd always associated the term with the lions she'd seen on television and in zoos, trained and lazy, snapping their tails at flies and taking naps in the sun. But she realized the real Lion of Judah was nothing like that. If he was aligned with these warrior angels, all carrying swords as big as she was, he would not be defeated.

Suddenly made aware of her own appearance, she looked down and realized somewhere between her bedroom and Heaven, her pajamas had been replaced with a pair of jeans, her favorite green t-shirt, and her comfy blue Sketchers. Jonas sported jeans and a gray *Batman* t-shirt that matched his shoes. It seemed an insignificant detail, but it boosted her confidence enough to raise her eyes back to the row of impressive angels before her. Amy had no idea how to greet such awesome creatures, so resplendent in strength and beauty. She bowed to them, but Harbor stopped her immediately. "No. Do not bow to us. We are servants of the King, just like you."

Amy stood back up and smiled instead. They all smiled back, breathtaking and frightening in their beauty. They looked like humans but on a grander scale. Harbor stepped over to the angel on the far right side. His eyes were sharp and white like a glacier in sunlight. His hair, also white, flowed down his back. His skin, dark and beautiful like polished onyx, gleamed in stark contrast. "This is Quill," Harbor said. "He is an intelligence gatherer and will help with communication during our mission."

Quill knelt on one knee and looked at Amy. "It is my honor to serve you, Princess."

She laughed. "Oh, I'm not a princess. I'm just Amy."

"You're wrong, Princess. As a daughter of the Most High, you are certainly a princess. And now we will help you to be a warrior as well."

Amy was startled by Quill's words because as much as she wanted to laugh them off and make another joke, the conviction in his voice caught at her spirit and reminded her of the sermon she'd heard John Yates preach the first time she'd met him, when his gray eyes and Celtic cross tattoo had caught her attention and helped jog her memory for their second meeting. He'd been a guest speaker that Sunday morning. The topic of his message had been the lineage of Christ and the importance God placed on who his earthly family had been. John had discussed the believer's lineage in Christ, making him or her part of the royal family of God, essentially creating a kingdom of princes and princesses, a kingdom of rulers for the coming age. Quill confirmed John's message. Her belief in Jesus as God's Son and her acceptance of him into her heart made her an heir with him. She really was a princess.

The angel beside Quill stepped forward and knelt as well. "This," Harbor said, looking directly at Jonas, "is Shake."

Amy watched Jonas, as Harbor did. "Hey, wait a second," Jonas said, coming to stand directly in front of the angel. Even though Shake was kneeling, Jonas barely reached the angel's chin standing on his toes. "I know you."

Shake smiled and took Jonas' hand. His eyes, blue like the pictures Amy had seen of the Mediterranean, brightened until they shone with an inner light. "Yes, we have met. But only in that place between dreaming and waking."

Jonas knitted his eyebrows and seemed to think hard about Shake's description. Then he shoved a fist in the air. "Yeah! I remember! That scary shadow man kept coming in my room, messing with my hair and making my bed squeak. You came and kicked his butt and he left. You went ka-pow with your fist and swung around with your sword and..."

Amy was shocked. She remembered the shadow man phase. At least she thought it had been a phase. All the experts said kids having bad dreams and night terrors was a normal part of the growing experience. But as she watched Jonas and a massive warring angel named Shake re-enact what seemed to be a pretty fantastic fight with the "shadow man," she was forced to consider the possibility that the experts had no idea what they were talking about.

Amy stepped toward the angel as they finished up their show with high fives. As she neared, Shake got up from his knees and bowed low toward her. "Princess Amy, it is an honor to serve you." He cut his blue eyes toward her son, still whooping and throwing punches in the air. "As well as Prince Jonas."

"Are you my son's guardian angel?"

"Yes."

Amy paused, grateful for all the things this angel had done for her son without her ever being aware. "Was the shadow man a demon?"

"Yes."

"Why was he in my son's bedroom?"

"He had been assigned to bring fear and anxiety to Jonas, to rob him of rest and weaken his body and mind."

Amy had no idea what to say to that. Demons in her house? What more did she not know about the unseen world of angels and demons that had surrounded her all her life? How could she have been so ignorant of it all?

"Thank you," she said. "Thank you for fighting it off."

Shake bowed once more and moved back into the line of angels. Harbor introduced the rest as Fuente, Baum, Ruckus and Thistle. Each was fierce in strength and beauty and each pledged loyalty to Amy, promising to serve her.

"I appreciate each one of you," Amy said. "But I really have no idea why you need to serve me at all. Why have you brought us here?"

Harbor nodded. "I think it is time to discuss our business. For that, we will ask that you come with us and allow Jonas to be escorted to a different part of Heaven. He has different things to learn, of equal importance, and all central to our goals."

Amy looked at Jonas, now giving all the angels high fives and fist bumps, his excitement uncontainable. She found, however, that she could not give her consent so easily. Fear gripped her still and she did not want to let him out of her sight. Not even when she knew he would be taken care of by literal angels.

Harbor came close and whispered, "Trust, Amy. Let go of your fears. I give you my word that Jonas will be safer than he has ever been."

Amy nodded. Her fear was ridiculous and she knew it. So she grabbed her son up in a bear hug and kissed the top of his blonde head. "Have fun, honey. I'll see you in a little while. Won't I?" she asked Harbor.

"Of course." Harbor nodded and motioned to someone behind Amy. She turned to see another angel coming forward. This one was not a warrior. Her beauty was stunning, so precious and pure, looking at her face was like witnessing the birth of a dawn. Her hair was a soft pink and it floated like corn silk in the breeze. She bowed to both Amy and Jonas, bringing tears to Amy's eyes.

"I am Brisa," she said, smiling in a way that filled Amy with complete peace. "May I escort Prince Jonas to his next appointment?"

Amy could not talk. Brisa's grace and beauty, her gentle response, humbled Amy. She kissed Jonas once more and nodded at Brisa, who embraced Jonas before leading him away, around a tall fountain in a courtyard of Honeysuckle, and out of Amy's sight.

Katey – Part Two

I fell asleep in D.D.'s big truck and woke up here. I haven't seen D.D. I call for him but my throat is scratchy and my tongue feels too big for my mouth. My head hurts and I am so sleepy. It's cold in this place like it was cold outside. Dirty light shines in from small windows up high and it looks like somebody's basement. I see old cans of paint on wooden shelves and big tools hang from nails in the walls. There's a bathroom with no walls in the corner and a bed in the middle.

I can see all of it through the bars of my cage. Why did D.D. put me in a dog kennel? It's too small for me. I can't stretch out and I can't open the door. I've banged and banged on it but it's chained shut and my fingers won't fit through the tiny key hole on the pad lock. I try to yell for him again but I can't get the words out over the pain in my head and my too big tongue. I twist and scoot and look around some more. More cages. More kids, just like me. How many of us are there? They are all sleeping, except one. She looks back at me. Her big brown eyes stare right at me. She puts her finger to her lips to make me hush and I know. It doesn't matter if D.D. is here or not. He lied. He lied to my momma when he said he was better. And he lied to me. This is not a vacation. And I am not going to be okay in this place.

Chapter Six

John Yates could not sleep. Eyes open or shut, his mind would not stop whirling in the scant details of Katey Johnson's case. With no license plate information to go on, he had pulled all maroon SUVs rented in the Nashville area in the last three months. In the morning he would begin working on local auto mechanics and body garages to see if anyone had worked on or painted a maroon SUV. Of the hundreds rolling along the highways of the U.S., he had to find the right one. The one that, at least as of yesterday morning, carried Katey Johnson.

He'd looked for suspicious vehicles dozens of times. Sometimes he could track them down with ease. Modern technology was a gem not to be wasted. Last week he'd traced a car thief to his latest heist and nabbed him by activating the *STAR* system in the car. With a few key strokes John turned off the engine from five hundred miles away, thirty seconds before local law enforcement officials showed up with the handcuffs. That had been a fun day.

But his instincts told him the maroon SUV would not be that easy to track. It would have no modern amenities. This kidnapping had been planned, staged, and perfected. He would not tell Angela and David Johnson that their daughter was likely hundreds of miles away at this point, gathering speed and distance as the hours clicked by. He would not tell them she was probably hungry and cold, bleeding, broken. He would not speak of the human trafficking growing at alarming rates all across the nation, including in suburban life in Nashville. He would not bring up the heinous acts of Hell committed against children like Katey in the underground sex trade. He would not tell them any of that unless he had to, unless the guys working the internet angles of Katey's case found her angelic face in some pervert's posted videos or pictures. By then it might be too late.

Sometimes John Yates loved his job. He loved the rush, the feeling of accomplishment when things went right and he completed what he'd been trained to do. But laying in the dark, reworking possibilities over and over in his mind, was not something he enjoyed. This part of the job haunted him, drove him to the breaking point as the case pushed forward and he pushed himself, working around the clock, even when he didn't have to. But that's why he had become a cop to begin with. He'd left his comfortable pastorship in Indiana because he needed more. He wanted to go the extra mile. He wanted to be the one to fix the problems, to bring back the ones who were taken away.

He'd seen too many taken. He'd known going in to his job as Army chaplain that death would greet him day and night. He had gone in eyes open, thinking he was fully prepared. But how can a man be prepared to walk through Hell and carry the light of Heaven at the same time? He'd gone in to the war zones with the infantry, the Green Berets, the Rangers, to kneel over the men who lay in pools of blood, their bodies filleted and massacred by IEDs and bullets that shredded their internal organs. He'd held their hands, prayed with them, prayed over their bodies, sent them Home with the sound of his voice. He'd prayed with their brothers and sisters, still covered in blood and the ever-present sands of Iraq. He had offered them peace. But when it was all said and done, that was the one thing he chased after for himself and could never grasp.

John thought he had found it with Candace. She had been on the hiring committee that had snapped him up as their full-time pastor in the Presbyterian church he'd applied to. Rural Indiana. Nothing bad happens there, he'd thought. He met her, fell in love with her, and married her in six months. She'd gotten pregnant immediately and he relaxed into his post-war life, content and happy.

And then it had all been ripped away, a desert mirage of peace. It was raining that night. The baby, she'd said, rubbing her third trimester bump, wanted ice cream. He had offered to go, but he was working on a sermon and as usual, she'd dismissed his offer with a smile. *Do what you need to*, she'd whispered in his ear. *We'll be back in a few minutes.*

He'd continued working, not realizing an hour had gone by. When a knock on the door broke through his concentration, he'd assumed it was Candace, arms full of groceries she'd decided to get while she was out. Instead two Indiana state police officers stood on his door step with apologetic looks on their faces. She'd been involved in a car accident, they'd said. A kid, high on meth, had led officers in a high speed pursuit. The kid had lost control of his truck and t-boned her sedan. It was a driver's side impact. And just like that, Candace and the baby, a boy they were going to call Sam, had been taken from him.

His whole life flipped on its edge and ran sideways for the better part of a year. He'd quit pastoring, began drinking heavily, making a regular habit of all-night tirades, pacing the floors of his house and yelling at God. On one particular night, the last one, he'd decided, he'd had enough of it all. He'd been awake for thirty-six hours, physically, mentally, and emotionally broken and spent. He'd hurled every insult and shouted every cruel and indecent thought at the God he knew heard every word. He relived it all. He felt the wetness on his knees while kneeling in the puddles of blood pooling beneath the soldiers whose bodies gaped open, having made the ultimate sacrifice for their country. He recalled the ones who had been able to say one last word, one last confession, one last proclamation of love. He closed his eyes and breathed in the scent of too many flowers, too many people packed into the sanctuary of his church as he said goodbye to Candace and the son he would never meet. Wanting to be free of the torment, he kneeled in his kitchen floor, keened and wailed, cursed his God and held his .44 pistol in his hand. He felt the weight of it, cold and unrelenting in the palm of his hand. He knew the scene someone would walk in on after he pulled the trigger. He knew the metallic smell that would hit whoever it was that opened his door, hours or days after the final moment. He put the gun in his mouth, let it rest against his tongue, and closed his eyes. And that's when he felt it. It was so subtle, so gentle, he almost missed it. But it was there, around him, in him, a presence of someone else. It wasn't like the heavy cloak of judgment and condemnation he'd wrapped himself in. It was airy and ethereal, the barest glimmer of something better that got larger and brighter the more he focused his awareness toward it. The gun on his tongue tasted bitter and when he laid it on the floor, the gentle feeling of someone present with him that was good and real overwhelmed him with hope that he could crawl out of his Hell and live again, live differently, live better. With the decision to live came the long sought peace John had craved through every battle in the desert and every solitary stroll through the neatly trimmed grasses of the local cemetery. When it finally came it wasn't peace like a gentle rain. It was all-consuming, a monsoon that soaked in past skin and bones, deep down into tissues, cells, DNA strands. In those moments of surrender, John had been snatched out of the bowels of Hell, reborn as a man determined to dream again.

Chapter Seven

After watching Jonas leave with Brisa, Amy turned to Harbor. She expected the light-heartedness of the last few minutes to still reside in a smile on the angel's face. But the mood between Harbor and the warriors she stood with had shifted. They were more serious, and while Amy would not have called them anxious, she felt they were ready for something to happen, something she realized included her.

Quill stepped forward from the line once more and bowed his head toward Amy. "Princess, would you please follow us to the Stone Table?"

"Of course."

Quill led the group forward with Harbor at Amy's side, where she had always been, Amy was learning. The other five angels flanked them as they wound through the streets of Heaven. Amy's eyes roamed the wonders surrounding her. The buildings, all large castles and manors, stood immortal and pristine in a white stone that glistened in the light emanating from the sanctuary of the Throne Room. She ran her fingers over their rough surfaces and thought of the dried sand dollars she'd bought from beachside stores. Each castle was carved with intricate details of lion heads, eagles soaring from the tops of turrets, dolphins meeting in air over entrance gateways. Running swiftly at the edge of the gold path they walked was a stream of water. It gurgled and splashed beside her feet, running toward the fountain behind her. She followed it toward its source with her eyes and her gaze landed once again on The Throne Room.

As she passed their castles and manors, people came out of their gates and began to line the golden streets. Some splashed in the small stream of water flowing from the Throne Room, dancing and singing like children. Others smiled and waved at her, calling out greetings to the angels. She realized they were people, just like her, who had passed from their temporal bodies and now lived eternally. They were beautiful. Each one was young and strong, healthy and vibrant in a way that mortal human bodies could never achieve.

They all seemed happy to see her, smiling and talking amongst themselves in excited voices. She did not recognize any of them, but felt warmly welcomed, treasured even, by those coming out to see her. Harbor placed a hand on her shoulder. "Remember when I said you are our honored guest? They are delighted for you and excited that you have the opportunity to see things they didn't get to see during their lives of blind faith."

"Will I get to see anyone I know that has passed?" Amy thought about her grandparents and several friends who had died in accidents over the years.

"Not today. It is not your Judgment Day, nor is it your true Homecoming. When that happens, things won't be so low key and quiet. When you come Home for your forever, the festivities will be unlike anything you've ever seen. It's better if you don't experience those things yet. You still have to go back. And we need you to want to go back."

"I see." Amy considered Harbor's words. She found that it was already difficult to think about returning home to her quiet house, to the bills that were stacked up on the table, to the reality of Katey's disappearance. Life was ugly sometimes. It was hard and bitter to continually fight for steady finances, for good health, for peace of mind and spirit. Here there was nothing ugly or difficult, no reason to feel bitter or tired. Here there was a constant flow of joy and peace, allowing freedom to love and be loved in ways Amy had never known were possible. Here Amy felt whole and beautiful, perfected by the light that had consumed her from her bedroom all the way to the Throne Room. Who would ever want to leave?

Harbor pointed up to a tall staircase in front of them. Amy's breath caught in her chest at its splendor. It was carved from smooth, glossy marble. Gold and pink threads of color wove in and out of its smooth ivory surface, which rose in elegance to an ornate archway. Stretching to the left and right of the archway was a bridge. To the right was another large building, made of the same pristine marble. To the left, just beyond Amy's eyesight, was the Throne Room of God. As Amy climbed the stairs, she marveled that there was no seam in the stone. It seemed as if the entire staircase, even the archway and bridge, were all carved from the same massive stone. She let her hand rest lightly on the bannister, her fingers following ribbons of gold and hues of pink as she trailed the angels up the staircase. Any fool on earth could tell you Heaven was supposed to be a beautiful place. But the reality of it, the immense depth of true beauty and perfection, was overwhelming. She could think of nowhere on earth where she'd ever been so at peace with her surroundings and so in awe of their majesty.

They walked beneath the archway and Amy turned left, curious and drawn to where she knew Jesus would be. King Jesus, Jonas had said. She had sung about and to him all her life. She'd read about him and believed, mostly, that he was who he said was. But to be able to see him with her own eyes, touch just the tips of his fingers, would forever cast aside all doubt. She found that she hungered for that moment, for the ability to touch him, to see him, to hear his voice saying her name. It was a lover's yearning, a longing of one created to reunite with her Creator. But Harbor again placed her hand on Amy's shoulder. "Not yet, dear one. It isn't time. We have much to discuss."

Amy looked at Harbor's face, still magnificent and ethereal, but serious and somewhat sad. She nodded and followed the line of angel warriors to the right instead, entering a place she had never imagined. Inside the doorway of the next building, they again turned right and Amy found herself in Heaven's War Room. It was a long, rectangular space with open archways along both side walls, so that on one side was a view of all of New Jerusalem, the Throne Room visible and audible, and on the other side were the fields of flowers and trees Amy had come through just a short while ago. The air flowing was thick and sweet, cool against her neck. But the angels in front of her did not seem to notice the view or the fragrant air.

Quill, Harbor, Baum, Thistle, Shake, Fuente and Ruckus joined a room full of warrior angels, all dressed in the same red and gold armor, all crowding around the largest stone table Amy had ever seen. It seemed impossibly long, perhaps fifty yards, and fifteen in width. The warriors here moved like a machine, scrutinizing what they saw on the table, issuing commands to other angels, who obeyed without question, coming and going with grim determination. Amy inched closer to the table to get a better view of what held their attention so intensely.

Her jaw dropped at the scene before her. Spread out from end to end of the mammoth table was a map of the world. But it was not a static picture. Instead, it was interactive, like a holographic computer screen. Everything on it was moving at once; humans, angels, and dark shadows Amy knew immediately were demonic beings. When an angel wanted to see more closely what was happening in a particular place, he would simply hover a hand over the area on the map and it would spring into a larger image, clear and vivid. When the angel removed his hand, the image returned to normal, rejoining the billions of moving images on the table. Amy was mesmerized by the sight. They could see everything. Everything. Nothing seen or unseen to humanity escaped the eyes of these angels. When an angel saw a problem, he immediately turned to another angel standing in line behind him, gave an order, and that angel, splendid in armor, hand on his or her sword, quickly moved to the far end of the room. There, forming an alcove created from the same stone of the room and the table, was a massive lion's face. Into its mouth each angel flew at great speed and instantly disappeared, only to immediately emerge on the map, intervening for humans and fighting demons.

Amy was floored. She could not understand the words being said between the angels, but she saw clearly what was happening. Their words were another delight altogether. It was unlike any other language she had ever heard. Like Harbor's voice, there were traces of other sounds in these angelic voices. Amy heard wind roaring through pine trees, scattering their needles on forest floors. She heard rocks crumbling from the sides of mountains, hawks screeching in high flight, and the still quiet between waves reaching shorelines. The brilliance and beauty of this angelic language mystified Amy and delighted her at the same time. She wanted to smile, to revel in the sounds echoing off the stone walls around her. But the looks on their faces were not joyful. They were not here to delight her. They were working feverishly, fully aware that life and death hung in the balance for six billion humans, all waking and sleeping, working and playing beneath their fingertips.

Amy focused on the scene developing to her left. The commanding angel at the table held his hand over an area on the map. It sprang into a three-dimensional image so that Amy could see two vehicles headed toward the same intersection. In one car, a mother with two children in the backseat sang along with the radio. The light was green for her side. On a perpendicular street, a young girl was behind the wheel, her music turned up, and her attention focused on her cell phone. She had no idea the light had turned red. Amy could see the coming collision. The space needed for the young girl to be able to stop her car had already passed and she was sailing over the white lines at the intersection already, mere feet from a side-impact collision where one of the children was strapped into his car seat. Amy gasped, horrified at what was about to take place. But the angel had already issued a command to the one behind him. That angel disappeared into the mouth of the lion and reappeared in the scene Amy watched. The angel stood, resolute, in front of the car with the children in it and held out his hands to the oncoming, inattentive teen. Riveted, Amy watched the angel bend space and time in tiny intervals, slowing down the mother's vehicle and swinging the oncoming car around the front end, the two bumpers a hair's breadth apart. The teen driver dropped her phone, drove through the intersection and pulled over a safe distance past. The mother with the two children screamed, watching the oncoming vehicle careen past, then continued on her way, glancing back nervously in her rear view mirror. His job accomplished, the angel returned through the mouth of the lion and his commanding officer released the image, moving on to the next one.

Amy was rattled by how close everyone involved had come to serious injury or death and how easily the whole situation had been resolved. The closest thing Amy could think to compare it to was something out of

The Matrix movies or an ability a Jedi would have in a *Star Wars* thriller. But this was moment-by-moment life for them, she realized, as the entire world was spread out before her in constant battles of angels against natural and demonic forces.

She looked up to see Harbor and Quill returning, having spoken with the largest angel in the room, head and shoulders above everyone else. He was stern and beautiful, his skin the color of night without stars, his eyes the bright yellow of a canary's feather.

"We have spoken with High Commander Rapa," Harbor said. "Come with us to his private chambers."

Amy nodded and fell in step behind Harbor and Quill. She walked past the Stone Table and the other angels, still going and coming according to their orders, perfectly orchestrated and succinct in their movements.

At the far end of the room there was a door to the left of the lion's mouth. Amy followed Harbor and Quill through its high arch. She entered a smaller room, draped in rich velvet the color of rain clouds after a storm. The glow of Heaven still flowed through its glassless windows, lighting it and filling it with fragrant air. Amy thought the smells changed from place to place. One moment the aroma of roses and tulips filled her lungs. The next, pine trees and earthy moss.

In the High Commander's private chamber, Amy saw that the rest of her angels were already there seated around another, smaller stone table. Rapa, mammoth and magnificent in strength and authority, sat at the head. Harbor pointed to the bench-like seat directly opposite Rapa and Amy sat down, small and delicate next to the eight warrior angels surrounding her.

Amy was intimidated by Rapa, who easily reached eight feet in height even seated. But when she looked into the soft yellow of his eyes, he smiled and the love of God poured out of him, filling her with peace and tranquility. "Princess Amy." His voice was impossibly deep and rumbled like thunder. "I am honored you have come to help us."

Chapter Eight

John Yates awoke with a start when his cell phone buzzed against the glass top of his night stand and rang shrill and loud six inches from his head. The first thought that came to him was not words, but instead Amy McEwan's face. In that instant he hoped it was her. Hoped that the first voice he heard today was hers.

One glance at the screen crushed that hope. It was Chuck, his partner working on Katey's case. John swiped the screen and cleared his throat.

"Hey. What's going on?"

"Wake up, Sleeping Beauty. We have a lead."

"Tell me." John was already out of bed, pulling out clean jeans from the bottom drawer of his dresser.

"It came from the neighbor across the street from the Johnsons. June Silberry, who just came around from anesthesia after a scheduled knee replacement. It seems she saw the news and called the hotline."

"What does she know?"

"She says she saw Katey get into the maroon SUV."

"Great! I want to interview her this morning."

"That isn't the best part."

"What's the best part?"

"She says Katey smiled and waved at the driver, then ran over excited, climbing right in like she knew the person."

John paused an extra second, letting that sink in. "I want to look at all relatives and close family friends. Again. Deeper. I want to talk to everyone."

"I thought you might say that."

"But I'm starting with June Silberry. What hospital is she at?"

"Centennial. I'll meet you there in twenty minutes."

"Perfect."

"You're buying breakfast."

"Deal."

Chapter Nine

Around the small stone table, staring at eight angel warriors, Amy reminded herself several times that it was not a dream. But she wasn't at all sure she should believe herself. Rapa, the mighty commander of the Stone Table, faced her.

"Princess Amy, you are very much aware of Katey Johnson's disappearance."

Amy nodded, realizing Rapa must know, from looking at the map, where Katey was being held.

"She is in great danger and Father God would like you and Prince Jonas to remove her from her enemies."

"Wow. Okay. How do we do that?"

"That's the complicated part," Harbor said. "Katey's life is not any more or less precious than any other child's. But she has been targeted by Satan because he knows she is special."

"Why is Katey special?"

"She is marked by Light. She is a Torchbearer."

"What does that mean?"

Quill interjected, "All believers carry the Light of Jesus within them. It's part of their identity in him. But some are born carrying that Light before they ever make an outward confession. They carry some of him into the world and never fully leave his presence. Because of that, they have special assignments during their lifetimes on earth. They become evangelists, healers, intercessors who operate on a high plane. They move Heaven to Earth, light to darkness. They abolish the works of the enemy."

Rapa nodded. "Satan has targeted Katey because of her position in the Kingdom of God. Katey doesn't realize her place in it yet. She is young still. But there will come a day when Holy Spirit will collide with her maturity and she will come into her full identity as a Torchbearer. Satan is determined to stop that time from coming."

"Are there many Torchbearers?" Amy asked.

Harbor nodded. "Some. More that we are now in the Last Days. He always targets them. Many times we can intercede and protect them. But we were prevented from helping Katey yesterday."

"Why?"

All the angels looked to Rapa. He splayed his hands, palms down, on the table. Amy judged each of his hands to be roughly the size of basketballs. His canary yellow eyes looked past her shoulders to the Throne Room. He nodded once, then settled his attention back to Amy.

"The spiritual dimension is much like the world you live in, Princess," Rapa began. "But the systems of your world are counterfeit, cheap imitations of the basic laws and principles that operate here in Heaven."

Amy nodded, feeling like she should be taking notes.

Rapa continued, "In your world, there are laws people must obey. If those laws are broken, there are consequences. Do you understand?"

"So far."

"We have spiritual laws that work the same way. Ours became complicated when Lucifer committed treason and a third of our forces fell with him to Earth. When that happened, and he received dominion for a time on Earth, our ability to operate with ease and full authority from God on the physical planes was impeded and hampered. He, in essence, has legal authority over the things of your world."

"I'm not quite sure I follow you. God is still greater than him, right?"

Rapa cracked a smile. "That, Princess, is something you never have to worry about."

Amy caught her bottom lip in her teeth. "Then I guess I still don't understand what you're saying. What does his authority on Earth have to do with Katey? Why can't you just send one of those angels out there to whisk her away? I watched one of them change the laws of physics like it was nothing. Getting Katey back should be a cinch."

"Right now, Satan has a legal authority over Katey that we cannot supercede. We must operate through physical means in order to get her back safely and in time. But because of where she is and who has her, we want to include you and Prince Jonas in the rescue. If you succeed, more than just Katey will be saved. And more than just one will be brought to legal justice in both worlds."

Amy let that sink in. "How does he have legal authority over Katey that you can't override if she is a Torchbearer?"

"That's an excellent question," Rapa said. He turned his head to look at the row of angels to Amy's right. "Thistle?"

Thistle nodded, regarding Amy calmly. She was roughly the same height as Harbor, but her skin was much darker, the color of sand soaked by a salty, cold ocean. Her eyes were the color of dark steel, but her hair was a breathtaking, shimmering emerald green, styled in short spikes across her head. "I am Katey's angel," she said. "It is my job to cover her with the light of Heaven and keep her from the clutches of the dark forces that seek her."

Amy nodded, mentally checking off each angel's identity and role in their adventure. Harbor was her angel and Shake belonged to Jonas. Quill was in charge of intelligence and Thistle belonged to Katey, which left Ruckus, Baum and Fuente's identities open.

"I was stopped from preventing Katey's kidnapping because she went willingly to her captor."

Amy felt like she'd been slapped. "I don't understand. Why would Katey go willingly? That's insane."

Thistle shook her head, the different hues of green in her hair shone in the light streaming through the windows. "She went willingly because her captor is known to her."

Thistle looked across the table to the angel directly to Amy's left. "Baum?"

Amy swiveled her head left, knowing her shock must be clearly registered all over her face. She'd never been good at hiding her emotions and wouldn't even begin to try in this place. Baum seemed to be the most serious of the bunch, his dark brown eyes hooded by knitted eyebrows.

He spoke to Amy. "I am her captor's guardian angel, Princess. His choices have grieved me for a long while and I am in constant intercession for him with the Father. His soul hangs in the balance and the balance is dangerously tipped toward Hell."

Amy tried to focus on all the facts. "Who is her captor?"

Baum sighed. "Andrew Dodson, her blood relative."

"Uncle D.D.?" Amy was shocked.

"Yes. He is her mother's brother. You met him at her birthday party in early December, correct?"

"Yes, um, were you there?"

At this Baum smiled, displaying a row of perfect teeth. "Of course, Princess."

Her comment seemed to strike everyone in the room funny and the tension lessened a degree or two. Amy tried to wrap her mind around the news of Katey's uncle having kidnapped her. Angela, Katey's mom, had tried to set her up with Drew at the party. He was Amy's age and worked as a manager at a *Best Buy* in Murfreesboro. She said he'd made some bad choices in his early twenties and served some time, but that he'd cleaned up and was doing well for himself. Amy had heard the concern in Angela's voice for her brother and from other conversations, had pieced together that she had tried to help him off and on over the years with deposits into his bank account and rides to various rehab facilities. But Angela had believed him to be good underneath all the rough edges, and cleaned up after years of fighting addictions. Clearly her faith had been misplaced. Amy had considered going out with him, but Jonas had come down with strep throat and had given her an easy out.

"Drew kidnapped Katey?" Amy repeated, still looking at Baum.

"Yes. We must act quickly, but we must do it through the means provided by your world."

Amy's thoughts were scrambled. "I need you to spell that out for me, I'm afraid."

Quill, a braid of white hair flowing down the front of his crimson armor, held up his hand toward the center of the round stone table. "We have the beginning of a plan, Princess Amy."

With his words appeared a three-dimensional image in the middle of the table. Amy's breath caught in her chest as her eyes rested on the smiling face of John Yates.

Katey – Part Three

I woke up again and this time I hurt all over. This cage is too small and I want out. I want to leave. I want to find D.D. and tell him to call momma. She'll help him again. I know she will. She always helps.

But D.D. isn't here. There are two people I don't know. The man is tall and has a long ponytail that is even more blonde than my hair. He carries a TV and sets it on a table and the woman turns around and stares at us, all of us, in our cages. She has silver bangle bracelets all up and down her arms and her black hair is pulled up pretty. But her face is mean and she looks at us like we are bad. I want to tell her I didn't do anything wrong and I shouldn't be in a dog cage, but I'm afraid. I'm afraid to make any sounds at all.

She tells us she's going to let us out so we can use the toilet in the corner of the room. She says it in English and something else. I think it's Spanish. One by one, she unlocks our cages and leads us to the toilet. It's dirty and I'm embarrassed to pee in front of all of these people. I don't like them and I don't want to, but I need to go. So I stare at my feet while I go. I have on my *Minnie Mouse* shoes. They have red sparkles on them and they're my favorite because they match my backpack. I don't know what D.D. did with my backpack and I don't know how to feel about him.

But right now I have to concentrate. Because the woman says she is our new teacher. She is going to show us a video about the things we have to learn to do and if we are good girls and we don't say a word, she'll give us food.

We stand by our cages and we watch the video. I know I should not be seeing this. There are people on this video doing things I've never seen before. I've seen my momma and daddy kiss each other on the mouth, but I've never seen them do these things to each other. I don't want to watch this and I look down to stare at my *Minnie Mouse* shoes again.

But this angers the woman. She walks right up to me and yanks my head back by both of my pig tails. She slaps me so hard my teeth rattle against each other and I can't breathe. She slaps me again and again. My head hurts still and now my face hurts and I can't stop the tears and she screams at me in words I can't understand and then she grabs my chin hard and points my face at the TV. She says, *Watch it and learn it so you can please your owner.* And now I can't look away.

Chapter Ten

The hour John spent questioning June Silberry at the hospital had been relatively helpful. In his line of work, nosy neighbors were a Godsend. Ms. Silberry, waiting for her sister to give her a ride to the hospital for her surgery, had been standing at the window. She saw the maroon SUV parked right outside her house. She watched the man in the driver's seat sit and observe the neighborhood, a ball cap and the hood of his coat covering his face. Once the McEwans left their driveway, he stepped out and waved to Katey. She smiled and waved back, running right up to the vehicle and climbing in the side door on the driver's side. Ms. Silberry thinks he caught her looking because he barely got the door latched before the SUV was in drive and rolling, the backpack still in the street. She did not notice a license plate number or any further distinguishing characteristics of the SUV other than it was old and not in great condition.

But she had provided him with some much needed ammunition for his day. Katey knew her kidnapper. That was huge. He had his two best people, Riley and Dana, working over family and friends again.

"Our net just got smaller," Chuck said, tossing his coffee cup in the garbage and heading toward his Honda.

John nodded, mentally ticking through his list of known possibilities. "Riley and Dana should have something by now. Why don't you head back and pull everything they've got. Work from the nuclear family out. I'm going to the Johnson's. Time to double check the neighborhood."

"I'll call you when I have something."

John stood by Chuck's car, arms crossed over his chest. He stared at the cityscape of downtown Nashville, turning over the facts he knew. Based on initial reports Riley and Dana had pulled yesterday, there were two main suspects he needed to zero in on. One was a family member and one was a family friend, both with records. Inexplicably, he felt peace settle over him and a burning knowledge of two things: they were close and they had to hurry. "Let's get this guy today, Chuck. I want him in handcuffs by tonight."

Chuck slipped behind the wheel and gunned the engine. "Alright, Superman. Let's get on with it then."

John jogged back to his car, his mind plotting next steps. The problem with his planned thought process was the vision of a certain redhead that kept popping into his mind, wrecking his concentration. He wondered if Amy McEwan had slept much after her dinner of ice cream and fries with Jonas. He wondered if she was trying to remember more and would call him. No matter. He had a good reason to talk with her again, he told himself. A real reason. Bona fide. He wasn't inventing an excuse to see her again. He was just conducting a thorough investigation.

John sighed and got on I-440 to cut across town. The last thing he needed was a beautiful distraction like Amy McEwan.

Chapter Eleven

Amy stared at the image of John's face hovering like a holograph over the small stone table. He really was a handsome man, she thought. Kind, smart, considerate, and too great a temptation for her to consider. She hadn't gone on more than a handful of dates since Jonas' birth and she wasn't about to allow herself romantic interest in John Yates. She'd decided after Jonas' dad had wished her luck with their son and walked out the door that she needed distance between herself and all men. That was the only way to protect herself and Jonas from more pain than either of them could continue to live with.

With that reminder, Amy snapped her thoughts back into the present and zeroed back in on the conversation at hand.

All the angels looked from the image of John's face back to Rapa, who looked past Amy's shoulders one more time toward the Throne Room, before speaking again. "John Yates is one of the detectives working Katey's case. He is strong in his faith and works well within the guidance Holy Spirit offers him. More than once he has followed that guidance and solved a case that would not have been solved without that supernatural intervention. He is, even now, on the right track to finding Katey. But we must expedite the process for Katey's sake as well as the other children with her."

"How?" Amy asked.

"You're going to help him." Rapa waved his hand and the image of John's face disappeared.

Amy's heartbeat began to race. "Me? I don't think that's such a great idea. I mean, I'm happy to help Katey, but I know nothing about police work, you know. I'm a teacher. Surely John can handle this without me poking around, getting in the way."

She would have gone on excusing herself had she not felt the weight of eight angels staring at her. Emotions roiled within Amy, casting shadows of fear and doubt on her confidence. John seemed to be triggering all her deepest fears and insecurities, forcing up all her defense mechanisms. Backing out of potential relationships and uncomfortable situations had become one of Amy's specialties. She could excuse herself out of dates, parties, holiday gatherings and any ordeal in which she might get too close to someone or feel emotions she didn't want to feel. But this was different. And deep down, Amy knew it. It wasn't just her heart at stake. It was Katey's life and the lives of other children involved.

Amy looked at Harbor, who undoubtedly knew the internal struggle she was experiencing. But instead of disappointment in the angel's eyes, Amy saw love. Then she felt it. Love emanated from Harbor toward the core of Amy's spirit. She felt those defense mechanisms shake from within and forced herself to push past them. She took a deep breath and gave Harbor a small smile of gratitude. Then she looked back at Rapa, who seemed able to wait patiently for an eternity.

"I'm sorry," Amy said. "I understand this situation is bigger than me. I will help any way I can."

Rapa smiled and stood up, as did the other seven angels around the table. They all focused their eyes behind Amy and bowed their heads before bending down on one knee. Amy had no idea what to think or do, so quick was their response. Then she felt a hand on her shoulder.

The touch was warm and gentle, but it seemed to radiate through her whole body in a cascade of joy and peace so complete that in the space of one breath, she felt whole and connected in body, mind and spirit in a way that she had never known she'd been missing. She knew immediately whose hand touched her and her breath caught in her throat. Tears sprang to her eyes as she focused on the hand resting lightly on her shoulder. The hole in it was larger than she imagined, but its presence did not scare her. Instead she tilted her face up and looked at King Jesus.

Love. He was the embodiment of love. But it wasn't the warm fuzzy feeling characters in books and movies discussed. It wasn't even the shape and breadth of the love she felt for Jonas. His existence was love altogether powerful, electric, and monstrous in its enormity and weight. It was love that was courageous and brave, having fought battles against giants both physical and spiritual and won. He was love that was a weapon, battle-tested and undefeated. He was love that conquered all opposition. And all of him was focused on her.

His smile stretched across his face in startling beauty as his eyes focused on hers. His face was angular, his skin olive-toned. His black hair was shorter than she thought it would be. The crown on his head stood about half a foot high, its polished gold shining brightly, only outmatched by the rubies, sapphires and diamonds glistening in their prawns. His eyes, though, held her rapt attention. They were deep and dark, brown like coffee, and yet reflecting other colors as well; first the gold of the sun on lake water, next the green of moss on trees. Amy held her breath as he knelt down beside her, still seated in the chair, and moved his hand to her cheek. "Amy," he said, "I couldn't wait for you to be here with us. I've anticipated this moment your whole life."

She listened to the sound of his voice, noting that it didn't carry the sound of the wind and waves in it like the voices of the angels. It carried something else. His voice was a song that held within its timbre benevolence, the beauty of the first dawn, and absolute, unquestionable authority. She knew this voice. She knew him. She'd always known this voice, even though she didn't remember hearing it until now. It was familiar to her, like air to her lungs, and hearing it somehow brought her more fully into her own sense of herself, allowing her to relax and marvel at the God-Man before her.

Instead of behaving in high royal fashion, King Jesus surprised Amy by laughing. He put his other hand on her face and leaned forward to kiss the top of her head. Then he pulled back and squatted in front of her. "What do you think?" he asked.

Amy blinked.

Again he laughed. It was brief and beautiful and put her more at ease. He nodded at the angels in the room who sat back down. "Only a handful have seen Heaven with mortal eyes, Amy. It's truly a gift. I've been excited about you coming here your whole life. It changes everything, don't you think?"

Amy nodded, still not able to find words. Her human brain tried to process him, his words, his whole being. But the spirit within her was light years ahead of her mind, fully aligned with his peaceful demeanor and relaxed delight.

He stood and pulled her to her feet as well. He continued to smile and look into her eyes in a way that made her feel as if he saw everything. Then she realized he did see everything. He knew it all. Every bad decision, every painful moment, all her insecurities. He'd dealt with them already when she first arrived and began worshipping him. And now, he stood before her, loving her so completely that any last vestiges of her defenses against love and intimacy were blown away like smoke in a storm. All that was left was her. And she suddenly realized that she was enough. He wasn't asking her to be anything more than who she already was.

"There are so many things I want to show you, Amy," he said. "Some will have to wait for your Homecoming. But some I can show you now."

He seemed excited and inexplicably pleased just to be with her. Amy realized, though, she'd still said nothing to him. She let out a breath she didn't know she'd been holding and without any forethought, she threw her arms around his neck and hugged the King of Kings. He hugged back, lifting her off her feet and swinging her around like she was a little girl. Laughter bubbled up from her chest and spilled over, mixing with his own. Love. Happiness. Never had Amy known either like she knew them now. And finally she found her voice.

"Jesus, you have changed everything by bringing me here. Everything. I feel completely different and I never want to leave you."

"You never will. I'm always with you." He set her back on her feet and held her hands. "Do you remember when you asked me to be a part of your life? To allow my spirit to reside in your body?"

Amy thought about that moment. It seemed so long ago. She'd been six years old at the time, too young, some said, to know what she was doing. She'd spent the night at her grandmother's house. Grandma Pearl had never made her feel anything less than wholly beautiful and accept- ed. After reading about Jesus' crucifixion and resurrection, Grandma Pearl had talked long about all the things Jesus had done for her over the years. She told her small granddaughter story after story of supernatural provision of money and food, protection and healing. And finally, when Amy said she wanted all of those things too, Grandma Pearl had led Amy in a prayer that allowed Jesus to merge with Amy's mind, spirit and body.

"I remember," Amy said. "Grandma Pearl led me to you."

"Yes, she did. And because you said yes to me, I've never left you. Not for one moment. Even when things were really bad, I was still right here." He laid his hand over her heart and once again his touch brought relief to places within Amy she hadn't known were hurting. Years of isola- tion and loneliness melted away and the exposed nerves steeped in pain flared for a brief second before he soothed them and brought about com- plete transformation. In the time it took for Amy to draw another breath, she knew he had yet again changed her for the better.

He lifted his hand and looked at Rapa. "You've done well explaining the situation, old friend. Thank you."

Rapa bowed his head. "My King."

King Jesus looked at the rest of the angels, who waited on him with reverence and adoration in their eyes. "Our time is short with Amy. There are a few places I want her to see. Then we'll discuss a few more details before you all begin the mission."

Chapter Twelve

John Yates turned the corner onto Iroquois Drive and parked on the street between the Johnson's and Amy McEwan's house. He wanted and needed to talk to both families. But truth be told, he wanted to see Amy first. Before he even knew what he was doing, he stared back at his reflection in the rearview mirror, checking his teeth.

Come on, Yates, he thought. *It's an investigation, not a date.* Rolling his eyes at his own vanity, he stepped out of the car and walked to Amy's front door, wondering how likely it would be for her to say yes to a date with him. The fact that he even wanted to ask her surprised him. He hadn't been on a date since Candace died. Hadn't wanted to. His sister had tried a few times to set him up with some friends of hers, but he wasn't interested. His heart had been through enough and no one, in his estimation, could compare to Candace's beauty, kindness and sincerity. That might still be true, he reasoned. But Amy McEwan had sparked something in him that hadn't felt alive in several years.

John shook off thoughts of a date with Amy, reminding himself he had no business thinking of anything outside of his investigation. He rang the doorbell and waited. He could hear nothing in the house through the door. He glanced at the car still in the driveway and rang the doorbell again. Still no sounds of movement in the house.

A feeling of dread and unease immediately settled over John. Rolling his shoulders back, he cracked his neck and took out his cell phone. Knowing Amy most likely called a friend or family member to come pick them up, he looked up her number from an email Dana had sent compiling all relevant witnesses and their contact information. No answer. He left a voicemail, but could not shake the anxiety building within.

He started across the lawn to the Johnson's house, but turned back and circled Amy's house from the outside. There was no sign of any kind of disturbance. All the windows and doors appeared shut tight and no footprints stood out beneath the back windows. He went to the sliding glass doors in the back and peered into the eat-in kitchen. No sounds. No movement. No disturbance of any kind.

He called Amy's number again, walking back around the house. As he passed a window, however, he heard a cell phone ringing. It was probably plugged in and charging. Would she have gone off without it? Was she home and ignoring him? Or was she home and not all right?

John's anxiety increased exponentially as he called her number again and stood outside the window once more, verifying that it was indeed her phone ringing. He went back to the sliding glass doors and knocked loudly. He rapped on the glass and peered in, checking for any signs of someone being home. There was nothing.

He considered his options and the possibilities. It was possible they were out with friends and she had left her cell phone deliberately. It was also possible that whoever had taken Katey had come back and taken Jonas or Amy or both. After all, Katey had known her kidnapper, according to the neighbor. Perhaps Amy knew the person as well and had let him in unaware. With that sobering thought, John pulled out his grandfather's Swiss Army knife and jimmied the lock loose on Amy's back door. Before sliding it open, he pulled out his police-issued *Glock 40* from its holster, gripping it firmly.

Slowly, making as little noise as possible, John eased the door open, sweeping the kitchen with his eyes, noting the stack of dishes still in the sink from their ice cream and fries last night. The front door was locked from the inside, the chain still over the door. They hadn't left that way. Were they still inside and unable to answer?

He hesitated, then called her name. "Amy? Are you here? It's John Yates from the Nashville Metro Police Department. We spoke yesterday."

As he spoke, he made his way through the house, taking in Jonas' empty bedroom, the superhero sheets still disheveled and toys strewn across the floor. "Jonas? You here, buddy?"

John kept his gun trained, his senses heightened for any sounds or movement in the house. There was nothing.

He opened the door to the master bedroom, noting the unmade bed and the pile of Kleenex on the bedside table. He checked the bathroom and every closet. There was no sign of Amy and Jonas. John reholstered his gun and picked up the cell phone beside her bed, right next to the small window he had been standing beside. In addition to his three phone calls, there were two text messages from Amy's coworkers checking on her and one from Angela Johnson, asking Amy to come next door as soon as possible. The first text message had come in at seven in the morning. Surely she hadn't gotten Jonas up and out of the house before then voluntarily. Something wasn't right. It was time to call for back up. John pulled out his cell phone and started to open up his contact list to search for Chuck's name when something launched toward him from the doorway.

Chapter Thirteen

The King of Kings had his arm securely tucked around Amy's shoulders as they walked out of the building housing the War Room with its behemoth Stone Table and lion's mouth portal. They went back down the pink and gold-hued staircase, the seven warrior angels striding behind. As they walked, King Jesus and Amy talked. She marveled at the ease of conversation between them. He was relaxed and seemed to be enjoying having her with him. He pointed out different buildings and spoke to people as they passed by. He brought up different things he loved about Amy, like the fact that her favorite pizza came from a small hole-in-the-wall pizzeria she'd found on the west side of Nashville. It was owned by an immigrant family who poured their heart and soul into the restaurant. Amy noted how proud he seemed of that family and their dedication to their dream, even when things were tough.

Amy listened and watched the Lord of All interact with everyone he came into contact with in Heaven. His ease and readiness to love was matched equally by the benevolent but firm authority he exuded. Everyone loved him unequivocally. But they also seemed to acknowledge the reality of Jesus as King and Ruler, the final authority for all things. She could see their respect in the soft bowing of their heads, the quiet awe as they said his name. Jesus himself did not ask for any of it. In fact, he seemed to wear the crown on his head, so regal and gleaming in the light of Heaven, much like a worn baseball cap. His carried the identity of King of Kings as easily as he carried his identity as a man. Fully God and fully human. Amy thought she was beginning to understand how those two things could exist together within him.

They passed mansion after mansion, all elegant and gleaming white in the light emanating from the Throne Room. Her eyes kept floating to that space, so holy and pulsating with life. Jesus smiled, "Amy," he said, "I'll take you there soon."

"Really? I don't know why, but I'm drawn there. I feel it deep within."

"That's because you *are* drawn there. Naturally. *'Deep calls unto deep at the noise of your waterfalls; all your waves and billows have gone over me.'* That's in the forty-second Psalm. Do you remember that verse?"

"It's familiar to me."

He nodded. "Your spirit is connected with all of this. Even when you're in the middle of the craziest day of your physical life, your spirit is still tied with me, with Papa God, with the other saints in worship. I pray for you and think of you constantly. Holy Spirit living in you allows that connection."

Amy tried to wrap her mind around his words, still taking in the majestic sights of architecture and natural beauty. "So the deepest part of me, my spirit, communicates with the deepest part of you, even when I'm not aware?"

He squeezed her shoulders. "Exactly. You and I can't be separated, Amy. It would be like separating dawn and morning. We are combined."

"And that happened because I invited you?"

"Yes. It is this way for everyone who gives me that invitation."

"I think I've got it."

Jesus laughed again and pointed up, toward the tallest structure around. "This is it, Amy. One of my most favorite places."

Amy followed his pointing finger and took in the soaring height of the castle before her, so expansive and on such a grandiose scale, she was at a loss to think of any other castle on Earth or in fact, in Heaven, that could equal its size and beauty. Great sculpted arches, coming to tall points at the apex of windows rising to twenty feet, graced the entire bottom half of the structure, which ran at least four football field lengths' wide. An ornate balcony crested over the arches, its rail displaying a series of familiar carvings: whales, elephants, palm trees, mountain ranges, monkeys, baseball bats and soccer balls, trains, planes, dolls and more fantastical elements of childhood ran the length of the balcony. Three more stories climbed above the rail housing rows of stained glass windows sparkling in every color, the whole marvel topped off by flying buttresses and towers on each end.

"Wow," Amy said. "That's impressive."

Jesus smiled. "I like it, too."

"What is it?"

He slipped his arm from her shoulders and grabbed her hand, leading her up a steep incline to the front doors of the castle. "Come and see."

Amy's head inched further and further back the closer they got to the massive front doors. Made entirely out of gold, they appeared to have been hammered into a series of mosaics, standing two stories tall. Each panel pictured a different childhood game or moment: two girls jumping rope, their pigtails and skirts flying up as their ankles kicked above the swinging rope, a group of boys, barefoot and running hard after a ball, a knot of kids waiting for the splash of the one just about to let go of a rope swinging out over a pond, a mother rocking a child. They were images of fun, happy moments shared by kids of all eras around the globe.

As they neared the golden doors, one side opened and an angel bowed low, her soft violet hair pinned in braids on top of her head. "My King," she said, lifting her face to him and smiling, "they'll be so excited to see you."

"Fiolett, you know I can't resist."

"Will it be soccer today? Baseball? Or maybe tug-o-war?"

Jesus pulled Amy to his side and introduced her. "Actually, Fiolett, my play time today will be short. This is Prince Jonas' mother."

Fiolett bowed once more, then gave Amy a quick embrace. "We have so enjoyed him today. What a gift he is! So full of laughter. It's contagious."

"Jonas is here?" Amy tried to peer past the angel's shoulders. "Can I see him?"

Fiolett moved to the side, opening the doors up wider. "Of course, Princess. You may see them all."

His hand still on her back, Jesus led Amy through doors that opened up into a giant courtyard, complete with a waterfall and pool, an expanse of green grass, swings, teeter-totters, large twirling slides. Covering all of it, in constant motion, were children. Hundreds and hundreds of smiling, laughing, running, jumping children. Angels mingled among them, swinging them high, twirling them around, hugging them, racing them, playing every game a child could want to play. Far back on the grassy hills, she could see children riding elephants and petting lions, all tame and completely at ease.

Amy blinked. Twice. Three times. It was all still there. "Where are we?"

"The Children's Palace," Jesus said. "Some are waiting for their families because they died too soon of illness, injury, or miscarriages. Many are here because they were aborted."

Amy's eyes filled with tears. So many children taken too soon because of a broken world, because of broken bodies that couldn't support such vibrant life. So many unwanted children, killed brutally in abortion clinics and back alleys across the world. Each of them, no matter the circumstances of their physical lives and deaths, were very much wanted in this place. Here they were adored, loved, and treasured.

Off to the right she saw a side door open and an angel escorting in a beautiful Asian woman. Her long black hair swayed as she walked and she wrung her hands, as if in nervous anticipation. Amy knew she was not an angel, but a human like herself who was experiencing her Homecoming. The angel stood to the side while two more held hands with a group of five children. They walked with the children to the mother, who began to weep. Amy watched, tears sliding down her face, as the mother knelt down and opened wide her arms. The five children nearly knocked her over with the force of their exuberant hugs, touching her face, her hair, kissing her eyelids and hands and shoulders, anything they could find. They loved her, showering her with affection, and she them.

Jesus watched, then said quietly, emotion also filling his voice, "Her name is Yeeun. Those are her five children. Two she aborted. It was a terrible time for her. She was young and things were done to her because of the schemes of Hell. But she came to me not long after. I got rid of the Hell in her life. Unfortunately, her body was scarred because of the abortions. It could not sustain the next three pregnancies. Her heart was still full of love and joy, though. And because she remained open, she became a mother to ten children through adoption and fostering. Hers is a beautiful story. And now you see the ending, when her heart is able to fully heal and she can kiss the faces of those she lost."

Amy watched as the children waved to their friends behind them, and then skipped out the side door with their mother, delighted to be with her in a long overdue reunion. As they left, another woman came in and more children were brought forward. She wanted to continue to watch, but at that moment, she heard a loud whoop and squeal and someone yelled, "It's King Jesus! He's come to play again!"

Amy turned back to the courtyard where fifty to a hundred children came running toward them in a miniature mob of giggles and smiles and squeals of delight. The warrior angels behind her quickly took off their weapons and armor, stripping down to the same leather pants and white tunic that Jesus wore.

She watched, happiness washing through her as Jesus lifted up a child in each arm and hoisted them to his shoulders. Two more attached themselves to his legs, each sitting on a foot. He took off then, high-stepping toward the grassy area, the children so excited they could hardly contain themselves. Shake soon followed, tossing up the nearest child in the air, a small boy with dark skin, eyes and hair, who squealed as he sailed through the air, caught again by Shake who put him down and began racing him toward a big group of boys waiting for the angel. The rest of the warriors followed suit, Harbor quickly joining in a game of double-dutch, Thistle heading straight for the swings, and the others disappearing into the crowd of children to play and dance with as many as they could.

Amy watched them play, overwhelmed at the sheer number of children taken too soon from her world. Jesus said they'd died too soon. Some of them had probably fought long battles with cancer or been victims of domestic violence. No doubt, she mused, their stories would each be unique, painful, perhaps even beautiful. And Jesus knew each one. Knew their histories, their families, their dreams, and desires. Lord of All, even the smallest.

She stood along the edge, taking it all in, marveling at the beauty of the courtyard, the soaring columns around it that held up three levels of the palace, all made of caramel-colored marble with darker streaks of coffee and chocolate running through the columns, the floors, and the balconies, which overflowed in green ferns and fragrant flowers of every kind and scent. As she watched, she caught her breath as four angels stood atop the edge of the balconies high above the courtyard and, spreading their wings wide, they tipped and dipped toward the floor. They soared low, each grabbing a child who stood with arms upstretched, and shot up again, looping and twirling in mid-air, all four children smiling and squealing their delight. The angels, each male and as tall and broad as the warriors Amy had come to know, landed gently, placing the children who had just flown with them into the green pastures in the back of the courtyard near the lions and elephants. A crowd of children soon surrounded them, begging for rides. In unison they each picked up another, leaped straight up into the air, and began twirling the children in airborne dips, dives and corkscrews, each safely tucked in their arms. Amy watched, unable to stop smiling at their happiness. She marveled at the angels' strength and speed, thinking of how fearsome it would be to see that same strength and speed not in fun playtime, but in a battle, broadswords drawn.

She looked up and down, side to side, trying to find Jonas. Fiolett had said he was here and she had no doubt that he was having the time of his life. She was just about to find an angel to ask where he might be when she heard his voice. "Mom!"

Coming from the center of a group of children was Jonas, riding high above the rest on King Jesus' shoulders, who was jogging back to her. Jonas bounced up and down, his arms stretched up as tall as he could reach, as if he were on his own private rollercoaster ride through Heaven.

King Jesus came closer, grabbed Jonas under his arms and flipped him off his shoulders. Amy wondered how he kept the crown on his head while pulling such antics, but Jesus didn't seem to pay much attention to it. Instead he knelt down and grabbed Jonas up tightly, hugging her son. She knew what Jonas was feeling. She knew King Jesus was quietly, unobtrusively erasing every hurt her son had ever felt, replacing every negative, fatherless moment of his young life with the overwhelming certainty of himself and his all-consuming love for Jonas. Soon he whispered to Jonas, who nodded, turned, and leaped into Amy's arms.

"Mom! This is the coolest place ever!"

Amy laughed, hugging him tightly and kissing his blonde hair, now unruly and sticking up in every direction. He placed his hands on either side of her face, squishing her cheeks before planting a big kiss on her forehead. Then all his words spilled out in a rush of excitement. "Mom, you'll never believe all the awesome kids in this place. Did you know they get to pick their age while they wait? And while they're waiting they play all the time 'cause there's so much stuff to do! I rode a lion today, Mom. A lion! And an elephant and something else I'd never even seen before. And I rode down that waterfall back there, and I raced two angels and won! And I played this new game with some kids I met, only they said the game was actually very old, and I saw dolphins, Mom. Dolphins! Because there's an ocean right behind us."

Amy saw King Jesus watching them, a sparkle of sheer fun and amusement in his brown eyes. But then the seven warrior angels disengaged themselves from tangles of children and began making their way back to where they stood, promising to come back for more play time as soon as they could. The reality of what lay ahead came crashing back to her conscious thoughts. It was not Katey's time to come to this place. She knew it in her heart. Katey would be as happy here as all the other children were. But she needed to live. She was a Torchbearer. And Amy needed to save her life.

No doubt reading her thoughts, King Jesus nodded, locking her gaze in his own. "Just one more thing before we go to your last destination in Heaven."

He turned and held out his hand to a small boy. King Jesus squatted down on his haunches and held the boy in the circle of his arms. Amy smiled at the child, who had dark hair and gray eyes. It was his eyes that startled her recollection.

King Jesus did not wait for her to wonder. "This is Sam. Sam Yates. He is John's son."

Amy sucked in her breath. She had no idea that John Yates had lost a son. No idea that when he protected them from the reporters, watched her son settling into the couch for cartoons, that he might have been thinking of this child now standing before her. She knelt down, too, but could find no words.

In the end, it was Jonas who spoke, sticking out his hand to give Sam a handshake. "Hi. I'm Jonas."

Sam smiled. He was not sad. He was not sick. He was not hurt in any way. He was beautiful and whole.

Sam shook Jonas' hand. "Hey, Jonas. I'm really happy to meet you."

Jonas smiled back. "Me, too."

"Will you do me a favor when you go back to your other life?"

"Sure."

"I want you to tell my dad something."

"All right. What is it?"

"Tell him I'm okay. Tell him it didn't hurt when the crash came. I was asleep and when mom came here to Heaven, she brought me with her. We're both fine now and really happy. But we miss him. I miss the sound of his voice."

Sam briefly cocked his head to the side, as if remembering the deep tones of John's voice. "But he doesn't need to stay sad anymore. And you need to tell him that. He has to keep living in every way."

Sam looked at Amy and smiled again, then looked back to Jonas. "Tell him we'll wait for him here. But it needs to be a long time before he comes. Tell him to live fully, Jonas. No more sadness. Just lots of the stuff that makes life fun."

Jonas moved forward and threw an arm around Sam's shoulders. Jesus enveloped them in a bear hug, lifting both boys off their feet when he stood and swung them around together. Then he set them on their feet again and Sam turned, walking back toward a woman standing off to the side. She was beautiful, with dark hair twisted up in an ornate braid, a small smile lifting the corners of her mouth as she held up a hand to Sam. She gave Amy a long look, widened her smile, and inclined her head in a bow. Then she took Sam and walked down a long corridor away from Amy, Jonas, and their heavenly entourage armed and ready for battle.

Katey – Part Four

The woman with the silver bracelets calls herself Maestra. She made us watch the video two times. She talked to us about what the people were doing to each other and explained that everything the woman does, we will do. Because that is our new job. We are *man pleasers* and our bodies will work for us.

We were good girls, but she didn't feed us. Instead she gave us sleepy juice and told us to rest in our cages. Because later, we have to watch and learn more.

I slept. I dreamed about my momma and daddy, about D.D., and about my room at home. I kept seeing a face in my dreams. It's a beautiful face. The face belongs to a woman with spiky green hair. She tells me in the dream that I am going to be alright. I don't have to worry or be afraid. And I want to believe her.

But I am awake and Maestra is back. There is no light in the windows anymore and she turns on bulbs hanging from the ceiling. It is time to learn again. She is here with the man with the long ponytail. There are three more men in the room, too. They stand along the wall and they watch while Maestra takes off her clothes and lays on the bed with Ponytail Man. He is naked also and I don't want to watch what they do. I don't want to watch but I am afraid one of them will come over and hit me again. She talks to us while she does the things to him we saw on the video. She is a good teacher, she says, and the men laugh and laugh and touch themselves. So I pretend to watch. My eyes are open, but my sight is focused on my dream.

Chapter Fourteen

John rocked to the side, avoiding the blur coming straight for him from behind the bedroom door. His heartbeat frantic, it took him two full seconds to realize there was no danger. Instead, Dog purred loudly at him, twitching the tip of his black and white tail, pleased with his sneak attack. He batted John's gun with his paw, oblivious to the ridiculous scene he'd just caused.

John released his breath in a big huff, briefly sitting on the side of Amy's bed. "Cat, I mean Dog, you and I are going to have a long talk." He looked again around Amy's bedroom, everything in its place except the pile of tissues on her night table. "But not yet."

Before calling Chuck, John decided to check the house one more time, looking in every closet, under the beds, in every cabinet even, to make sure no one was there. The front door was still locked from the inside with the chain drawn, nothing was disturbed, no windows were open or even unlocked. He paused in the doorway of Jonas' bedroom, his gut clenching at the thought of Jonas also being kidnapped right out from under his nose, on his watch. Jonas was the same age Sam would have been and he absolutely would not lose another child.

Pulling up his contact list, he dialed Chuck's number and left a voicemail. He updated his partner on what he'd found at Amy's house and dictated the next steps he wanted accomplished. He wanted everyone called they could identify as family members or friends of Amy's. If they couldn't find them that way, he wanted forensics in the house immediately to finger-print everything.

Ending the call, John stood still in the bedroom, listening. At first he listened to the house itself, hearing the heat kick on as Dog stretched and kneaded Amy's pillow. And then he was submerged in prayer, without even realizing he meant to begin. He reholstered his gun and slipped his phone in his pocket, then lifted up his hands and poured out his heart to God. He prayed for Katey and her captor, but surprised himself at the strength of his emotions as his words poured out on behalf of Amy and Jonas, pleading for their protection, fearing the worst.

With his eyes closed and his voice raised in urgent petition, he did not notice the atmosphere around him become charged with an electricity that sent goosebumps down his spine. He continued to pray, stopping only when he heard a loud crack in the air to his right. Dropping to one knee and pulling his gun in an automatic gesture of defense, his mouth fell open as he stared into a vast expanse of the most beautiful, all-encompassing light he'd ever seen.

Chapter Fifteen

King Jesus walked between Amy and Jonas, pointing out more sites, including the market square hosting large wooden tables and barrels filled with pomegranates, figs, carrots, squash, oranges and other fruits and vegetables as well as an array of spices in every color and aroma imaginable. Amy breathed deep the scents of cinnamon, rosemary, sage and mint. She found herself in a throng of saints who walked along the cobbled gold streets, laughing at each other's jokes and going about the business of living. Really living, without any threat or fear of any kind. No one sat around on clouds here. It was life, joyful and full, beautiful and precious, entirely grounded and centered around the God-Man at Amy's side. He stopped beside a barrel of yellow corn, the sweet, fresh scent of harvest still wafting from the corn husks, and breathed deep, sticking his nose into a tuft of corn silk. He stood and complimented the brown-eyed, smiling saint who'd grown the corn before motioning Amy forward.

They ascended a set of rose quartz stairs inlaid with rock crystal that gleamed beneath her feet. Amy could feel her pulse quicken. She knew they were almost there. Even if she hadn't felt her spirit leaning toward that special place of holy worship, she would have known it by the sound alone. It was loud, pulsing, vibrating in a steady rhythm of music played by hundreds and hundreds of every instrument imaginable. She heard guitars and violins, tympanis, tubas, castanets, and cymbals. She heard pianos and electric guitars, the high pierce of a trumpet line and the staccato of snares. It should have been a tumultuous cacophony, a barrage of too much equating to nothing but noise. Instead, the instruments combined into a roar of harmony, blending in an ebb and flow of worship that, as she neared, quieted so that only voices could be heard.

Amy, Jonas and King Jesus climbed three final stairs to stand under a large arch, one of many along the outer perimeter of the massive structure. As she peered in, her heart raced at the site. Below her in a bowl twice as large as any stadium she'd seen pictured on Earth, was the Throne Room. Amy's breath left her in one swollen whoosh, and she buckled to her knees, her hands coming to rest on the sandaled feet of the King.

The soaring columns were made of opals that glinted gold, pink, blue and green in the light of the Holy of Holies. The floor was made from lapis lazuli, highly polished and gleaming blue, running straight into stairs of dark sapphire in the middle of the bowl that rose to the Tree of Life. Its roots rested in a river of water that seemed to have its source in and through the tree as the crystalline water flowed down and out around the sapphire stairs and entered the golden streets of Heaven. The trunk of the tree rose two stories and held up branches full and weighed down with green, healthy leaves. The tree itself was alive and aflame in an eternal fire that blazed with the presence of the Father. The fire did not burn the tree. Instead it purified life itself, birthing it into the healing waters that flowed freely into trickling streams of pure elixir.

Twenty-four golden thrones housed the twenty-four elders, twelve on each side of the tree. Their white robes caught the reflection of the flames from the Tree of Life, casting a ballet of light and shadows between them. Their arms were raised in worship and ribbons of light in every color shot up and around them like small fireworks displays. The rainbowed lights were their prayers, their intercessions on behalf of humanity, and their acknowledgment of the holiness that filled them within and without.

Surrounding the tree and the thrones of the elders like a wall mosaic of worshippers were the saints. The redeemed. Thousands and thousands of humans who had lived their lives and come Home, becoming more upon their return to the Father than they'd ever been able to achieve in their brief humanity. They sang of his holiness, of his love, of his faithfulness to each one of them. They broke apart, each lifting voices to worship in their own languages, lifting up their hands, swaying, jumping, spinning, dancing before him in wholeness. Then their voices blended together again in one tongue. Amy could not place the language she heard, but she understood the words with her spirit. The words were his. The words were him. And Amy lifted her eyes from the worshippers to the One they worshipped.

Suspended above the Tree of Life, the throne of God rose high, higher than Amy's eyes could truly grasp. The Father was seated there, in body and yet still in spirit form. He was light, color, sound, energy, and solid form all at once. His likeness was human, but more in every way. He was impossible to grasp and yet impossible to miss, and Amy stopped trying to understand. Instead, she just worshipped, pouring out her love in a jumble of words and sounds that came in awed whispers and snippets of song bursting forth from a dammed up place of love never before opened within her spirit. She lavished her love on the Father much as the woman in the book of Matthew had lavished Jesus with expensive perfume. Amy gave her love freely, holding nothing back. She could not remember ever doing so and didn't want it to end, for as much as she poured out, she was filled in greater measure.

Slowly she became aware of Jesus kneeling with her. He did not attempt to pull her from her place of worship. Now she knew he never would for in that place they were connected as one. Creator and created, Lover and beloved, harmonized in the way the chords and words being sung around them came together in a river of song that washed away everything except the overwhelming presence of the One seated on the Throne. Jesus pulled aside the curls of red hair hiding her face and leaning close, he breathed on her. She felt the soft breeze of his breath on her neck throughout her whole body, feeling heat and light vibrate through her in shock waves. The spot his breath had touched on her neck felt hot as her hand skimmed over her skin.

She raised her eyes to his and saw in their depths the intensity of a warrior. "I have marked you with a seal that connects your body and spirit in a new way. No longer will there be a veil for you between the physical and the spiritual. You will see dimly because you will still be in your flesh.

But you will see more, know more, and bring more to the world around you because this place, this moment will stay with you as present tense. You will never fully leave this moment and one day, you will stand here again by my side, fully joining the voices of the redeemed."

The strength in his eyes and his voice drew Amy from her knees to her feet. She heard the music shift as she turned to face her King. The voices quieted as drums began, first softly, then picking up pace in rhythm and intensity.

"You marked me?" she asked. "Like a tattoo?"

He smiled. "Yes," he said. "Like a tattoo, only more and different. Others won't see it. But you will be able to feel it when you enter into worship and when I need to remind you that *I am* with you."

"What does it look like?"

"It looks like me, only in the persona of the Lion of Judah. It is the insignia of one of my warriors."

Amy nodded, still transfixed by the worship within and around her. She turned to find Jonas, realizing she'd completely lost track of her son upon entering the Holy of Holies. Her brief moment of worry dissipated when her eyes landed on her son, dancing with all his might, eyes closed, arms stretched toward the Father, head thrown back as he called out his love to his Creator without inhibition. He twirled and jumped and he wasn't alone. Shake was dancing with him, his massive arms stretched out beneath his wings, now unfurled and relaxed in a shimmering white display of strength and ethereal beauty. Amy watched Jonas worship alongside his guardian angel, both fully surrendered to the moment, even as Shake hovered over her son in protection and covering.

Soon Amy's attention was drawn back to the music. The drum beats had grown in their intensity and now pounded out a steady rhythm that vibrated Amy's sternum within her chest. No marching band drum line could compete with the precision and intricate pulse woven into a complex pattern of hammered cadences that excited and propelled each soul into a new plane of worship.

"It's time," King Jesus stated.

"What do you mean?" Amy asked.

"They are waiting for us." He motioned for her to walk forward and as she did, she realized Shake was now holding Jonas' hand, who looked like he'd never been more refreshed, rested, and ready for the moment at hand. Their entourage of angel warriors stood wing to wing in a row of might and splendor, pointing them to a balcony on the other side of the great room.

As Amy moved forward, she smelled first the salty sea breeze as it blew in from the row of open arches. Nearing the balcony Jesus led her toward, she saw in the distance, perched on high cliffs of dark rocks, more mansions. Every bit as large as the ones surrounding the Holy of Holies, these were not made from luminescent white stone. Instead the homes she viewed now were created from a dark honeyed color of wood and large gray stones. Even from a distance, the craftsmanship and attention to detail among the giant beams, naturally laid rocks, and sparkling walls of glass was noticeable.

Outside their homes and gathered near the edge of the cliffs were more saints closely watching as Amy neared the white balustrade beside King Jesus. As she did, her breath caught in her throat at the great expanse of water laid out before her, white capped waves rolling gently toward the shoreline. The water was a gorgeous, clear turquoise blue that reflected the light emanating from the Throne Room like diamonds. Finally coming outside to stand on the marbled surface of the white balcony, Amy's jaw dropped. Before her stood the Army of the Lord.

All along the beach in tight formation, stood angels and saints, armed with swords of every kind. Some carried large bows, their backs supporting quivers full of arrows. They stood at attention, pride rippling off them in an energy wave that Amy felt like the heat of the sun. There was nothing that could defeat them, she realized. Death held no power for them. Darkness could not touch them. Hell could not keep them. Victory belonged to this army of angels and saints, and they stood before their King, ready to be sent.

Amy was robbed of all words as the entire army knelt. Angels and saints, side by side, bowed their heads to their Commander and King, who began blessing them with words of encouragement. He introduced Amy and then Jonas, who was lifted up on top of Shake's shoulders to get a better view. She doubted neither of them would ever forget this moment, with the pounding of the drums behind them like a heartbeat that connected the two of them to an undefeatable army, ready to join them. Amy followed Jonas' eyes to the far left where she had to blink a few times to be sure her vision was clear. Behind the rows of eight to ten foot tall angels kneeling next to saints of varying heights, were more angels. Massive angels. Angels that towered stories higher than anyone else. They were the size of buildings. And while they were utterly still at the moment, Amy sensed how massive their destruction could be when loosed with the authority to annihilate whatever lay in their path. Not just because of their size. But because of their solid strength and the power of God literally flowing in life and vigor within them.

King Jesus turned to her. "Amy, this is my army. They serve me and are in a state of constant action to take back what is mine. We take part in small missions and battles night and day in every part of the world. Each one brings us closer to the final battle when I will return and rule."

His return. People sang songs about the second coming of Christ and she'd heard a few sermons about it. But it had never hit her with urgent force as it did now. Heaven wasn't just a far off place. It was a coming reality. A full-blown physical and spiritual place that would settle itself like a blanket over the brokenness of Earth. Everything about King Jesus was real and powerful, like the army before her. How could she have gone so many years without knowing this? Without living inside the intensity of how close the second coming actually was?

Quill stepped forward, his onyx skin gleaming in the light of the Holy of Holies. He gazed out over the Army of the Lord, then, as if sensing a new presence, looked up above them to the apex of the Holy of Holies. Amy followed his eyes and gasped. Towering over them all stood another angel, every inch of him sinewy muscle and hardened warrior. The sword he wore attached at his waist measured as long as a man was tall and gleamed silver in the light of the Holy of Holies emanating below his booted feet. His face shown with the brilliant light and his golden hair was pulled back away from his strong features. He was unyielding and yet looked toward the army with intense pride and ownership. She heard Rapa whisper his name as he bowed his head and knelt to one knee in respect. "Michael, Archangel and my Prince Regent."

Amy watched Michael draw his sword and touch it to his forehead, slightly bowing his head to Rapa. With one last glance at the Army, he knelt and bowed toward King Jesus before standing and retreating out of Amy's sight. She was jolted once again by the supreme power and unfathomable authority of Heaven. No force in the universe, however dark and evil, could claim victory over the Army of the Lord. And here she stood, side by side with their King, joining them.

Rapa stood once more and motioned for the army to stand as well. As they did, one particular unit stepped forward. Amy tried to count the number of angels and saints who now stood directly in front and below them. As best she could tell, there were about two hundred warriors looking directly at her, Jonas, Quill and King Jesus. Resplendent in their red and gold armor, swords and bows gleaming in the light, they awed her yet again.

Quill spoke. "Princess Amy, these are the warriors assigned to our mission to get Katey back from her captors. I will meet with them shortly to explain the details. What you need to know is that when you return and begin working with Prince John, these warriors will be awaiting commands from you and Prince Jonas."

Amy didn't even try to hide her surprise. "I'm supposed to command them to do things?"

Quill smiled. "All you have to do is ask for help. I'll take care of the details of their response." He turned to Jonas. "You, too, young prince. When you call, we'll be there."

Jonas, still perched on Shake's tall shoulders, waved at the warriors staring up at him and gave Quill a thumbs-up. "Got it."

The commanding angel grinned at Jonas, then turned back to the unit of soldiers and motioned to one particular saint. The man stepped forward and ran up the stairs leading from the beach below to the balcony. When he approached Amy, he bent on one knee before his King, then stood and bowed to Amy.

"This is R.P.," Quill said. "He will remain close to you in battle and will be the one you see. We are allowing him to cross the boundaries between the physical and the spiritual to make your communication with us easier. You will speak to him and he will speak to me."

Amy extended her hand and R.P. shook it. A full foot taller than Amy, she noted his strong physique, dark buzz cut and chocolate brown eyes. With a lopsided, relaxed grin he winked at her and Jonas. A thought suddenly occurred to Amy. "Were you a soldier in your time on Earth?"

R.P. nodded. "Yes, ma'am. I was a United States Army Ranger."

"I see. Were you killed in the line of duty?"

"Yes. But only my body. I carry on the fight with my brothers and sisters here, under the leadership of our King."

Amy returned his smile. "I'm glad you'll be at my side, R.P."

"It's my pleasure."

R.P. stepped back as Shake set Jonas down by Amy's side and rejoined the line of warriors behind them. Jesus put his hands on their shoulders and kissed each of them on their foreheads. "I am so proud of you both," he said, his gaze magnetic and intense. "The places you are going will be dark. You will be sent directly into the heart of the camps of the enemy. You will be tempted to be afraid. But don't let fear control you. It's a tactic Lucifer will use to chain you into submission and inaction. Know your place as children of the King of Kings. Know the authority I have given you to command and control. Say my name and *I am* there."

As King Jesus spoke, Amy felt his presence fill her. He was love, joy, peace, and an immense bank of power that strengthened not only her spirit, but her body as well. She felt stronger, more certain of who she was in him, and more able to do anything that was asked of her. Not because she was different, but because he was different. Because he was more. And because he was hers. Her King. Her Savior.

Amy's eyes involuntarily closed as she let herself float in the reality of his person, his authority, and his undying presence within and around her. She lost focus on the army below her and the Throne Room beside her. The pounding precision of the drum cadences began to fade as the light of the Father became brighter, warmer, and all-consuming. Soon she was lost in the light.

Katey – Part Five

I don't know if I'm awake or asleep. It is dark and cold and the sleepy juice Maestra gives us makes my head hurt and my throat dry and scratchy. Creepy-crawly things bite and scamper across my skin and I need to go to the bathroom. But I can't get out of my locked dog cage.

One of the other girls cries. She cries all the time. And I want so much to cry, too. But I am scared to cry. I am scared to move. I pretend to sleep so the man in the room will leave me alone. He is big and hairy like a bear and he unlocks the cage of the girl with the big brown eyes. He pulls her out by her feet and yanks her up to her knees by her hair. Then he makes her do something Maestra did to Ponytail Man. And I squeeze my eyes shut tight and try not to listen to her cries and her choking sounds.

Please, God, I pray, *please get me out of here. Please help me. You're good at miracles,* I tell him. *You'll be good at this, too. Please, God. Help me.*

Chapter Sixteen

His gun trained steadily in the center of the light that had ripped open the air in Amy's bedroom, John gasped as two figures emerged from it. He lined up his sights and held steady, waiting for provocation to fire.

But just as suddenly as the light appeared, it was gone, leaving the room in a play of dim shadows and streaks of light from the windows. After his eyes readjusted he blinked twice. Amy and Jonas stood before him, hand in hand, smiling like they'd been there the whole time watching his charade with Dog the cat, who meowed from his perch on the pillow. Not knowing what to think of their sudden appearance, John didn't move or speak.

It was Jonas who broke the silence, completely oblivious to John's tension. "Mom! That was the coolest thing ever! I've got to go see if my room is still there."

He broke into a run and sped out the door to his adjacent doorway. Still John did not move. He tried and failed to make sense of what he was seeing. People didn't appear out of thin air. And while he liked Amy immensely, he found himself completely at an impasse to trust her at all. His gun stayed trained on the center of her chest while his thoughts ran wildly trying to decipher her presence.

"John? I know this is weird. Really, you have no idea how weird this is." Amy kept glancing at the gun and back at his face. She waved her hands when she talked.

"Keep your hands where I can see them." He hadn't meant for his voice to be so rough with her, but he had no idea what her intentions were.

"Okay," she said, putting them up at shoulder height. "I'll do whatever you say. I promise. I know you're really freaked out right now, but I can explain."

"I'd love to hear it."

"Yeah. I bet you would." She swallowed and sighed. "Only the explanation is a lot crazier than you think. And I wasn't really expecting to see you so soon." Her eyebrows furrowed. "Wait a second. What are you doing in my bedroom? With a gun?"

"I was looking for you."

"You were? Why?"

John sighed. "Because you weren't here. And the door was locked and chained from the inside. And you left your cell phone plugged in. And I was worried. There have been some developments in the case."

Amy nodded. "That's really nice of you, John. Thanks for checking on us."

John felt more confused than ever. She hadn't been here before. He knew she hadn't. He'd even checked the kitchen cabinets for crying out loud. And what was with the light show?

"Do you think you could put the gun down?"

"Not yet. I need you to tell me how you suddenly appeared in your bedroom in a flash of light. And where you were before that."

"I will," she said. "But I need you to believe what I tell you. With your heart, not with your head. Because it's not something you've ever heard before."

The cynicism spiked in his voice. "Try me."

He watched her take a deep breath, glancing at his gun again. "An angel came to us last night. She came just like we did. Suddenly. Like a window opened in the room."

"An angel."

Amy nodded. "Yes. She came and she took us to Heaven."

Inwardly John groaned. Just his luck. He finally found a woman who piqued his interest after six years of celibacy and she was certifiably nuts. All the same, he lowered the gun and reholstered it. Trying not to roll his eyes, he said, "Go on."

Visibly relieved, Amy dropped her hands back to her sides. "I can tell you don't believe me. But hear me out. You're a pastor, after all."

He clenched his teeth. Being a pastor did not make him a gullible doormat. "I'm listening," he said.

"She took us to Heaven." At this Amy's whole countenance changed. Her smile lit up the whole room and her eyes brightened with unreserved joy. John was taken aback by the change. The green of her shirt brought out the green of her eyes and even though he was determined to squash her story like a bug, he couldn't help noticing how pretty she was.

"John, you wouldn't believe how beautiful it is! The songs, the scriptures, the books people have written don't nearly do it justice. It's a city so perfect and picturesque, I don't even know how to describe it to you in words. I saw things I never dreamed of. Mansions and grand homes, markets and fountains, staircases made of marble and oh, the outer walls of New Jerusalem…John, they're magnificent!"

He felt his mouth dropping open as her explanation spilled out. Either she was an actress giving the best performance of her life or she really believed what she was telling him. Maybe both. But she wasn't done.

"Then the angels took us to the War Room and that's where we met Rapa, the Commanding angel. He's huge, but so kind. And he told me all about Katey, John. I know who took her."

That got his attention. "You know who the kidnapper is?"

"Yes. It's her Uncle Drew. Angela's brother. Andrew Dodson."

"How do you know?"

"He told me."

"Who told you? Dodson? You've been in contact with the kidnapper?"

Amy's eyes widened. "No! The angel told me."

John pulled out his cell phone and called Chuck again. It went to voicemail, which ticked John off even further. Dodson had been one of the two primary suspects the neighbor had helped narrow their list to. He quickly explained in a message he'd had a tip. The investigation should center in on Dodson. And that Amy and Jonas had been located. For now, he left it at that, never taking his eyes off the woman in front of him, still beautiful and smiling at him with a warmth and joy that should have comforted him. Instead, it further irritated him.

He ended the call and crossed his arms, staring her down. "When was the last time you spoke with Mr. Dodson?"

"At Katey's birthday party in December."

"Not since then? Have you seen him recently?"

"No and you're not listening to me. I need you to hear me out, John. I know you think I'm crazy right now, but I promise you I am telling you nothing but truth. It's a wild, unexpected, life-changing truth. But I need you to believe me. I need you to trust me. And Katey needs it, too."

He stared into her eyes. They didn't waver and her pupils didn't change. Her breathing didn't quicken. She wasn't licking her lips or wringing her hands. For a moment he just stood there watching her and in the silence he heard the still, small voice of Holy Spirit deep within his conscious thoughts. *Believe her.*

He visibly shook his head, completely against the voice. All logic, all reason told him to call protective services and have Jonas removed immediately for his safety and to have Amy McEwan brought in for questioning and a psychiatric evaluation. But the urging inside him was insistent, burning in his spirit like a blistering flame. *Believe her.*

He didn't relax his stance, but he relaxed his mind. "Keep talking."

He listened as Amy recounted her time in Heaven. She described angels and castles in extraordinary detail. He watched as tears streamed down her face when she talked about King Jesus, about his authority and his love, and the ways he healed her. She kept going and when she described the mansion full of children, John sat down heavily on the edge of her bed. He found himself wanting to ask if she'd met a boy there who could have been his son, but stopped himself. If he asked that question, it would mean he believed her. And he wasn't at all ready to accept her wild tale as any sort of truth. And yet, he paused, what if it were true? She wouldn't be the first to have a supremely supernatural experience.

Amy continued talking, her arms flailing around her in excited gestures as she described the Throne Room of God and the orchestrated freedom of worship from the redeemed. John thought of Candace, of her sweet voice raised in song every Sunday morning in the front row of the church they pastored. She would have been one of them, he thought.

She would want to sing to the King. He felt his walls of defense against Amy's story crumbling, but still he would not believe. Could not let go of the thought that she was lying. That she was covering up some kind of involvement in Katey's disappearance.

He wanted to interrupt her and tell her that was enough. But it wasn't enough. And she wasn't finished. She told him next about the Army of the Lord, going into great detail about the force amassed on Katey's behalf. She finished by imploring him to help her and the angels find Katey. In the silence that followed John was left wondering what on earth to say next.

He was saved from deciding by Jonas, who bounded back in the room and tackled John in a hug. It surprised him and caught him off guard. "Are you okay, little man?"

Jonas leaned back and blew blonde curls out of his eyes. "Are you kidding? I'm having the best day of my whole life! I went to Heaven and met Jesus and a bunch of angels and all kinds of kids that live in the coolest place ever. Did you tell him, Mom?"

John's chest tightened. The kid believed the story. Fully. He opened his mouth to suggest a ride to the police station when the stubborn voice in his conscience said, *Wait. Listen. Believe.*

John sighed. *Fine,* he responded in his spirit. *I'll play this game for one more minute.*

Jonas looked from Amy back to him. "Did she tell you about the kids in the really cool mansion? The one with the waterfall and the animals and the angels that swoop down and take you for rides?"

"She told me a little bit about it. But why don't you tell me in your own words?"

I'll get her now, he thought. I can catch the discrepancies in their stories and have no qualms about ending this charade.

Jonas launched into his story and much to John's chagrin, he could not find anything different from Amy's story. Jonas threw in more descriptive details, but nothing that conflicted with what Amy had said. "What a cool story, Jonas. Thanks for sharing that with me."

Out of the corner of his eye, he saw Amy's shoulders droop. Clearly she'd hoped he would buy this fantastical story of theirs. He started to rise from the bed but Jonas put his finger in the center of his chest and held him down with a piercing gaze and three little words. "I'm not done."

John opened his mouth to explain the ride they were about to take when Jonas rocked his world with a simple announcement. "I met Sam."

John felt the blood drain from his face and the air rush from his lungs. "How do you know about Sam?"

"I met him. In the castle with all the children. He wanted me to tell you some stuff."

John tried to focus on breathing in and out. "There's no way you could know Sam. He died before he was born."

Jonas nodded. "I know. He was in an accident with his mom. But he said to tell you that he's okay. It didn't hurt. He was asleep when it happened and he woke up with her in Heaven. He didn't feel a thing."

John's vision blurred. "Jonas, you don't know what you're saying."

"Yes, I do. I know what he told me. And you need to listen because it was really important to him and to King Jesus that you know these things."

"What things?"

"That he misses you. He misses the sound of your voice. But he doesn't like that you're sad all the time."

Jonas tilted his head to the side and studied John's face. "I didn't think he was right at first. Because you didn't seem sad last night when you helped us inside and made the news people leave us alone. But I think Sam was right. You are sad. But you hide your sadness way down deep where other people can't see it."

Suddenly the dam broke. The walls of defense against their story crumbled into dust and a tidal wave of emotion took hold of John. His belief in God cemented the reality of an afterlife for his late wife and child. But Jonas' words built up the thin line of belief into a structure of substance made up of his son's voice and a life that he still lived. Sam had never drawn breath with his body, but he was alive in the spirit realm, in Heaven, where he played in waterfalls and danced with angels.

Jonas used both hands to smear John's tears across his cheeks. "He's really okay. Sam's more than okay. But he's worried about you. He says you need to live life more fully. And have fun. Lots of fun. No more sadness."

John smiled despite his tears. It sounded like something he would have said as a boy. He'd been all about having fun at Jonas and Sam's age. No doubt his son would be the same. "Thanks, Jonas," he managed to get out. "I needed to hear that."

He'd needed to hear it not just to release the last vestiges of grief he'd held on to since the accident, but also because, he realized, he believed them now. There's no way Jonas could have known about Sam. No way Amy could have known. The quiet insistence of Holy Spirit inside of him had led him to this moment of deeper belief. His son was okay.

"John," Amy said.

He turned to her and saw that tears glistened on her cheeks as well. He felt like a prize fool. He hadn't believed a word she'd told him. Hadn't it just been two weeks ago he'd been working on a sermon about living in blind faith? He owed her an apology.

Before he could open his mouth Amy spoke again. "She's okay, too."

"Who?"

"Your wife. I saw her. At least I think it was her. We didn't actually get introduced."

He squeezed his eyes shut as the waterworks started up again. But Amy kept talking. "She was beautiful, John. Such a treasure. She had long dark hair that was braided and pinned on the top of her head."

He bowed his head, the image clear in his mind. "That's how she looked on our wedding day."

Amy swallowed and finally came forward, resting her hand on John's shoulder. "She's okay, too. Just like Sam. She was whole and perfect. There was nothing at all wrong with her. No injuries. No pain. The accident killed her body, but not her. She's living a new life in Heaven. And she'll be there when you go Home."

Jonas chimed in. "Yeah, but Sam said you can't come yet. Not for a long time. You're supposed to live here." He shoved his finger back in to John's chest. "And have more fun."

Chapter Seventeen

Amy's relief when John finally accepted the wild truth of her experience in Heaven was short-lived as the reality of their next steps hit her with a frenzy of urgency. Her mind started to race with questions but she stopped her thoughts and centered herself in an internal quiet place. Closing her eyes, she simply asked, *What next, Lord?*

Within her mind she could see a vision playing out like scenes from a movie. As if she were still in the War Room staring at the global montage over the Stone Table, she saw a compound in a tropical place. There were palm trees and the air was humid and sticky. Men with guns patrolled the perimeter walls, made of a chain link fence topped with razor wire. The scene in Amy's mind zeroed in on a particular room where she knew more men sat around tables. They spoke in a language that sounded like Spanish and seemed to be planning something. They stared at a map of the United States while scrolling through internet sites with photos of young girls. They placed pins on the map and began planning routes, pick-ups and drop-offs, and placing prices on the children's lives.

Amy's stomach revolted at what she saw. Opening her eyes again, she realized John and Jonas were staring at her. Not sure if she was going to be sick or not, she turned around and took several deep breaths.

She felt John's hands resting lightly on her shoulders. "Amy, I'm sorry I didn't believe you."

She hugged her stomach, still overcome with nausea. "It's okay. That's not why I'm upset."

"What is it then?"

"I asked King Jesus to show me what to do next."

Her pause caused John to gently turn her around to face him. "And?" he asked.

"He showed me. It was like a movie playing in my mind."

John nodded. "Okay. That's usually called a vision. Lots of people had them in the Bible. Lots of people still have them. What did you see?"

Explaining every detail she could recall, she watched his face drain of color. "That's the lion's den, Amy. We know about those places, but police forces can't take them down. Especially not American forces. We don't have the jurisdiction."

"Why? Where do you think it is?"

"South of the border. Mexico maybe. Honduras, Guatemala, they're all hot spots."

"That makes sense."

"Amy, we don't have the time or the resources to deal with something like that. I believe it's real. I believe in your vision. But our problem is here and now with Katey. We can't traipse thousands of miles away across the border and rattle that cage on a wing and a prayer. No way. We've got to take one step at a time, carefully planned and executed."

Amy nodded her head, seeing his reasoning. With her acquiescence, Jonas popped his head between them. "You're both wrong."

Amy and John looked down at Jonas. "What do you mean?" Amy asked.

"You're thinking with regular thoughts. That won't work right now. You have to think with God thoughts."

John cocked his head to the side and sat back down on the bed, lowering himself to Jonas' height. He was quiet for a moment, then seemed to come to a decision. "I'm all ears, little man."

Jonas closed his eyes for a few seconds, just like Amy had done. She knew he was listening to further instructions. "We think small," he said. "God thinks big. We think in little boxes, but he doesn't have boxes. He thinks likes the ocean moves."

Amy squatted down beside Jonas, not touching him so as not to distract him from the flow of God within him. "Keep going, sweetheart. We're listening."

"We have to go there. To the hot place you saw where the bad men are. We have to stop them from getting in their trucks and coming for more kids. We won't be able to save Katey unless we stop them."

"How, Jonas?" John asked. "How does God say we should go there and stop them?"

Jonas kept his eyes closed and stayed silent for another minute. Then he opened his eyes and grinned. "We ask him to take us."

John crossed his arms over his chest and half a smile hiked up his face. "We just ask him, huh."

"No. You ask him."

"Why me?"

"Because he needs you to believe him just a little bit more. He said close your eyes and walk forward."

Amy watched John's chin drop to his chest as he heaved a huge sigh. She heard him mumble, "Figures. I hate blind faith." With that he stood up and grabbed Jonas' outstretched hand, then held his other out to her.

That one small gesture stopped her in her tracks. It shouldn't have, but how long had it been since she'd held a man's hand? Since she'd dated Jonas' father? Resistance began to crawl its way forward through her conscious thoughts and she hesitated touching him, aware of her growing attraction to John Yates and her long-time desire to save herself and Jonas from attachment to any man. And then she remembered more. His face, his voice, his breath on her neck. King Jesus had healed her heart, had taken away those doubts and fears. He had made her a warrior, equipped to fight for Katey. She would not back down now. She would not wear those fears again like spikes of armor against the rest of the world. And definitely, she decided, not against John Yates. Instead, she placed her hand in his, watching as his fingers closed around her palm. She released a deep breath and looked into his eyes, gray like a bank of storm clouds over the blue of the ocean. His gaze didn't waver. He just gently squeezed her hand and began to pray.

Amy didn't concentrate on the words he said because as soon as he began to speak, the atmosphere in her bedroom peaked and the air ripped apart to reveal the light of Heaven once more. Behind her she heard Dog meow several times before Jonas said, "Come on!"

He led them both forward into the spiritual dimension. But instead of walking toward the massive pearl gates she'd seen the first time, she walked into the light and immediately felt a wave of oppressive heat. It smacked her in the face and settled around her like a blanket. As the light dissipated, she found that the three of them had passed through the doorway she thought would lead them back to Heaven and instead had led them to the lion's den, as John had called it.

All around them was jungle, the vegetation too close for comfort. It was dark among the trees and the sound of thousands of insects and nearby animals stalking their lunch caused Amy's nervousness to escalate into a tsunami of near panic. *We're really here, she thought. God has sent us into Hell on Earth. What now?*

Chapter Eighteen

If John thought the last half hour was an emotional roller coaster, with the violent disbelief of Amy's crazy story turning on its edge to a shocking proof that required belief, followed by the moment when Amy had chosen to trust him, placing her hand in his and sending sparks through his whole body with her touch, the present moment was enough to make his jaw drop to his shoes. Blind faith indeed. His prayer for help had literally transported them thousands of miles in less than a second straight to the heart of a jungle full of ruthless, violent men intent on destroying lives. Of all the prayers God had answered for John, he suddenly wished this one wasn't one of them.

Amy had his hand in a death grip at this point, which told him she wasn't any more comfortable with their current situation than he was. Thick green foliage grew up and around them in a tangled mess of waxy or softly furled leaves, some seeming like overgrown cousins of the familiar trees from home. Only Jonas seemed to be completely relaxed, taking in the surrounding jungle with a smile and one single word: "Cool!"

Out of the corner of his eye, John saw movement just to their left. Without thinking he stepped in front of Amy and Jonas, shoving them behind with his left hand while his right drew his gun. A man stepped out. He was dressed in black fatigues and an easy smile that reached his brown eyes and made his imposing height less threatening. John didn't move his gun from its position trained on the middle of the man's chest.

"R.P.!"

Amy's body relaxed when she said his name and she pushed John's arm aside, walking toward the soldier. "Thank God you're here!"

The soldier's smile didn't falter. "I told you I would be."

She smiled back and John felt a growing irritation at their familiarity. He reholstered his gun and stuck out his hand. "John Yates."

The soldier shook his hand. "I know who you are."

"Really? Because I have no idea who you are."

The man Amy called R.P. looked back at her. "Didn't you tell him about us?"

John's imagination flew into overdrive with those words. Before he could stop the words, they flew out of his mouth in accusation. "Us? You mean the two of you? As in...?"

"John!" Amy said. "Oh my goodness. No!"

He watched her turn five shades redder than her hair, from the neckline of her shirt all the way to the curls that fell lightly on her forehead. R.P.'s laughter seemed to rumble up from his toes.

Amy's hands flew over her face and she peeked between her fingers. "He's an angel, John."

John felt his face becoming every bit as red as hers was. "Oh." He looked at R.P. who was still laughing. "Sorry. I'm a little new to this whole thing."

R.P. slapped him on the back, an amused, rakish smile hitched up on the right side of his face. "It's okay, brother. If I were still part of this world, you better believe I would have my eye on her. They don't come along as good as this one every day."

Amy groaned and covered her face again and John smiled. "Agreed."

"But she's wrong about one thing. I'm not an angel. Just a saint. A guy who's already lived on Earth and passed through to my eternal life. Now I serve in King Jesus' army. And today, I'm fighting with you."

Amy peeked back through her fingers and John breathed a sigh of relief. Help had come directly from Heaven. He sure hoped R.P. had a plan. But instead of sharing that plan with an organized strategy that would have put John's mind at ease, R.P. knelt down in front of Jonas, who had remained quiet during the strange exchange between the adults.

"Prince Jonas. Good to see you again." R.P. gave him a fist bump.

"Hey," Jonas said, grinning. "Where's everybody else?"

"They're here. You just can't see them."

"Why not?"

"Because you're not in Heaven anymore. It's harder here in the physical world. You have to know Heaven is with you and really believe it inside yourself because you can't see it with your eyes. Can you do that?" R.P. asked. "Can you believe in what your eyes can't see?"

Jonas studied him and looked past his shoulders, clearly wanting to see the massive army he'd witnessed on the shores of the turquoise waters outside the Throne Room. Then he sighed and looked back at R.P., jutting his chin up in the air. "I wish I didn't have to, but I can do it. I believe."

"What do you believe?"

"I believe King Jesus is real. I believe the big army he showed us is here. And I believe we'll be okay even though there are some really bad men we have to fight today."

R.P. bumped his fist with Jonas' again. "That's exactly right."

John thought about the examples God used over and over in scriptures to show how pure a child's faith was and how much easier it is to follow him when you believe with the power of that purity instead of mucking it up with doubts and fears. Doubt was easy. Faith was hard. But not for Jonas, John realized. He just chose to believe. So instead of giving in to the hundreds of thoughts flitting through John's mind about the danger they were all in, the insurmountable odds stacked against them, and the unbelievable reality that he was standing in a jungle somewhere in Latin America outside a compound filled with armed and dangerous thugs when minutes before he'd been in Amy's house in Nashville, he chose to believe Jonas' words. They were going to be okay. If God could bend space and time and bring them here in the blink of an eye, he would see them through the rest of this crazy situation.

"Welcome to Honduras," R.P. said, then turned and walked back in the direction he'd come from.

John hurried to catch up. "So what's the plan?"

"The compound is just up ahead. You're going to sneak in through a hole in the eastern section of the fence. They don't know about it yet because I just put it there."

John tried and failed to keep his heart rate from beating in triple time. "Then what?"

"Dead center of the compound is their HQ. You're going to go in there and get the intel we need. International authorities are already on their way to pick up these guys."

"Interpol?"

"Yep. But you need to get in there and look at the maps before the cavalry arrives. Take pictures with your phone, then get out of there. You'll need to disappear before everyone else shows up. If not, it'll just complicate things."

"Yeah, I can see that. But I'm not sure I get what you're saying. You want me to just walk in there and take pictures of the intel? Somehow I don't think they're going to be cooperative."

"They will be."

"How do you know?"

"Because Amy's going to make them."

John looked at Amy, who had been keeping up and listening in. If he hadn't been in the same state of shock, he would have laughed at the open-mouthed look of horror and disbelief on her face.

"R.P., you can't be serious. I don't know a thing about combat! I'm an elementary school teacher, for crying out loud!"

"True. But you're also a warrior in the army of the King of Kings. And we are all under your command." He stopped and turned an intense gaze her way. " *Look, I have given you authority over all the power of the enemy, and you can walk among snakes and scorpions and crush them. Nothing will injure you.* That's in Luke, chapter ten, verse nineteen. Do you believe it or not?"

John swallowed. Now was the moment to either believe who Jesus said he is, or walk away from the whole thing. It was no easy task either way. But he watched Amy take a deep breath and nod her head. "Yes," she said. "I believe him. I know him. He would not lie."

R.P. smiled. "Princess, you make me proud." He turned to John. "Do you believe it?"

"Yes."

R.P. clapped him on the back, then knelt down and began drawing out a rough map of the compound in the dirt of the Honduran jungle. Once he'd explained the planned route for John and Amy to follow, Amy laid a hand on his arm. "What about Jonas? They can't see him, R.P. They'll take him."

"Don't worry about Jonas. He's just going to watch this time. He's with me."

Amy nodded, pulling her son close in a tight hug and kissing his cheek. Jonas squeezed her back. "It's all good, Mom. Really. I feel it way down deep inside."

"You amaze me, sweetheart."

He squished her cheeks together and pressed her nose to his. "I love you, Mom."

John had to stand up and look way. These were the moments he'd missed out on with Candace and Sam that hurt the most. Holidays were awful, but remembering the little stuff was worse. No goodnight hugs and kisses, no tickling matches on the couch, no sweet whispers of love. Six years had helped him grow accustomed to the absence of those moments, but he had never become numb to them.

A small hand squeezing his brought his attention back to Jonas. "I'll be watching out for you, too. Me and R.P." His grin was so wide it made John smile. For Jonas, the whole thing must have been like his biggest hero stepping off the television screen and becoming larger than life in the blink of an eye.

"Thanks, little man. Your mom and I will be back soon. Stick right with R.P., okay?"

"I will. But hurry up. We've got to get Katey."

Chapter Nineteen

In all her life Amy was certain she'd never been more ill-prepared for anything. Even becoming a single mother hadn't been as scary as this. But she followed John closer to the chain link fence surrounding the compound, crouching low and stepping only where his feet had been. R.P. had said she should subdue the men in the HQ. But he wouldn't tell her how. Perhaps he didn't know.

John slowed and stopped as they approached the edge of the tree line. Two more steps and they would be out in the open, crawling through the hole in the fence and quickly moving to the center of the compound. Logically, there was no way they would live through the next ten minutes. But logic wouldn't have allowed their presence anyway, and the oppressive heat and humidity hung like a second set of clothes on her body, assuring Amy they were physically in that spot. It wasn't a vision this time.

Bending on one knee, John turned and took her hand. He brought it to his lips and brushed a light kiss across her knuckles. More than a little surprised, Amy blurted out the words before she could think them through. "What was that for?"

John smiled. "It has occurred to me that my faith is not as strong as I thought it was and I'm a little nervous right now."

Still feeling the warmth of his hand, Amy let out a big breath. "Me, too."

"So here's what I'm thinking. If we get out of this and get back to Nashville in one piece, I'd like to take you out to dinner."

Amy blinked. "Like a date?"

"Yes. A date. As in man meets woman, man likes woman, and man takes woman out on a real date. A romantic date. A date nowhere near a building of murderous outlaws. How does that sound?"

Amy looked down at his hand and ran her index finger softly over the black Celtic cross above his thumb joint. Then she looked back into his gray eyes and let herself feel the happiness his words brought instead of the fear they would have carried before their adventure had begun. "It sounds great, John."

He let out a nervous breath and squeezed her hand. "I was hoping you'd say that. If not, it would have made the next few minutes even more awkward."

Amy looked over his shoulders to the small concrete block buildings inside the chain link fence. They weren't large, maybe twelve by twelve square. Probably bunkhouses, she thought. The razor wire she'd seen in her vision looped across the top of the fence in front of them. "You know I have no idea what I'm doing, right?"

"Me, either," he said.

"So before we go in, I'm just going talk to King Jesus for a second, okay?"

"That's an even better idea than the romantic date."

Despite the stress level squeezing her lungs, she smiled at his sense of humor. Then she closed her eyes and let her thoughts drift inward toward the face that was forever burned in her mind. She whispered his name and with his name came a flood of words she wasn't fully aware of, but they locked her focus into him. She remembered the sound of his voice and the touch of his hand. She remembered the way the light shone through the nail holes and the unbending timbre of authority in his voice. She remembered Jonas' words about not thinking in boxes, but instead thinking God thoughts. *God thinks like the ocean moves.* In her mind she saw the ocean waves lapping quietly on a shoreline, then crashing against rocks, and finally rising up in a terrifying tsunami of destruction. No boxes. No limits. *What is possible is*, she heard him say. *Go!*

She opened her eyes and saw that John was staring at her with a troubled look on his face. "He told me I'm supposed to let you go first."

She nodded, knowing more than she could tell him with words. She would have to show him.

"I don't like it, but I'm going to do it. Let's switch places."

As soon as they were situated, Amy grabbed his hand and keeping her eyes fully open and trained on the hole ahead of them, she prayed once more. "King Jesus, make us invisible to human eyes."

She felt a wave like warm water pour over her body and at John's gasp, knew he'd felt it, too. Not looking left or right, Amy walked straight ahead to the hole and crawled through. John crawled through right behind her. With Amy still leading, they quickly ran right to the first concrete bunker and squatted down.

Her heart drumming in her ears, Amy tried to slow her breathing and remain calm. She looked at John, who nodded once. Together they ran from the first hut to the second, then the second to the third, closing in on the center concrete block structure, a bit larger than the others. Amy studied it, noting the bars over the glassless windows and the wooden shutters propped open with sticks to let in the humid breeze blowing through the jungle.

She tensed her body, ready to move forward when John grabbed her arm and pulled her back flush with the wall they crouched against. Then she heard the footsteps. They were coming around the right side of the building. *Invisible*, she prayed silently. *Keep us invisible, Lord!*

The guard came around the corner of the building. Amy didn't know anything about guns, but the one he carried looked like it could do serious damage. He carried it like a shield in front of his chest, which was scarred and marked with burns visible beneath his black muscle shirt. He didn't spare them a glance, but stopped where he was and studied the ground right in front of them.

There was no way he couldn't know they were there unless God was answering her prayer. Thirty-six inches, she calculated. That's all that lay between her and certain death.

The guard squatted down in the dirt in front of her and John, whose grip on her arm was quickly making it numb. She watched the guard's eyes study the footprints she and John had left in the dirt. He traced the size eight outline of her blue *Sketchers*, then glanced back at the trail they'd made from the previous hut to the one they were at now.

Desperately trying to keep her breathing under control and not make a sound, she watched the guard reached his hand out to touch the last footprint, which sat solidly beneath her foot. *What will happen*, she thought, *if he touches my foot? Will he be able to see me then? What do I do? R.P.!* Her spirit screamed his name. *R.P., do something!*

Sweat glistened under the thin black hair on the man's scalp. He looked confused, but determined as he reached forward, an inch away from her shoe. Suddenly his fingers fisted up and his head jerked around toward the back of the compound. After one loud crack, a massive tree crashed with a thunderous jolt and the crunch of buckling metal. The ground beneath them shook as the massive tree hit, falling squarely across the southwestern side of the fence and smashing two trucks beneath its bulk. Men yelled out commands in Spanish and all ran toward the tree and the crumpled vehicles. Jumping to his feet, the guard took off after his companions.

Still undiscovered, Amy let go of the breath she'd been holding and looked at John. Despite the beads of sweat tracing his jawline, a smile lit up his whole face. "That was so cool!" he whispered.

She gave him half a smile and rolled her eyes. "Adrenaline junkie," she teased.

Peeking around the side of the building, she saw the door to the HQ standing wide open. Evidently everyone had left to check out the damage from the tree. *Maybe we can sneak in and back out with the pictures before anyone even notices we're there*, Amy thought.

Signaling to John with a tilt of her head, they again crouched low and ran toward the open door to the HQ. John stepped in front of her then, drawing his gun and slowly sticking his head around the door frame. He looked back at her. "Empty. Let's get this done."

Katey – Part Six

Morning. Sunlight shines through the windows in the top of the wall. But it's not bright. Too much dirt on the glass makes it muddy sunlight and that's how I feel. Muddy. Nasty. Sick. I want to be hungry but I feel too bad. I want to go back to sleep but my body hurts from being curled up on these cold metal bars all night.

Maestra comes down and one by one, unlocks our cages and lets us use the toilet in front of everyone again. This time I don't care who watches. I'm just glad to go in the toilet and not on myself. She says we get to eat now and hands us a baggie of cereal and more sleepy juice. When we wake up, she says, we will learn to be touched and we will practice some things we learned yesterday on the men who watch us. Ponytail Man smiles right at me.

Chapter Twenty

Holding tightly to Amy's hand, John slipped around the edge of the door and into the HQ. The stench of body odor, cigarette smoke and sweat hit him full force causing his breath to catch in his throat. Beside him Amy gagged. A lightbulb hung in the center of the room, illuminating what the sunlight coming in from the partially shuttered windows didn't. Two card tables stood together in the center of the room with six metal chairs around them. Spread out and layered on the tables were maps, held down by a laptop computer.

John slid the gun back into its holster, leaving it unfastened. He let go of Amy's hand and pulled out his cell phone. Amy peeked over his shoulder and gasped. "It's just like in my vision, John. The maps, the markers, the routes drawn out. It's all here."

John's blood was humming through his veins at top velocity as sweat trickled down his back. He'd been fighting images from his past since the oppressive heat had hit him upon arrival. *This isn't Iraq*, he told himself. *No one is dying today*. Breathing deeply and slowly to calm himself down, he moved the laptop and started photographing each map. One was of the whole United States with red circles drawn around every major city and many smaller, more rural ones as well. New York, Miami, Atlanta, Dallas, Albuquerque, Phoenix, Las Vegas, Los Angeles, and Nashville. To the right of this map was another one. It was only of Nashville and had several areas and neighborhoods squared off. Finding this map was like striking gold. Metro Police would benefit a hundred ways from this info. As long as he could figure out how to tell them where and how he'd come across it in a believable way. Because who in their right mind would believe the truth? Certainly not his by-the-book, stoic chief.

"Shift the maps," he whispered. "I need to photograph everything."

Amy quickly pulled out the bottom layer and spread them out. Asia, Africa, Eastern and Western Europe, all covered in red circles and blue squares, with routes in between in black sharpie. John tried to keep his excitement under control. They could take down entire factions of the human trafficking ring with intel like this. Snapping the last picture of a map of Germany, John was about to pocket his phone and head back to the hole in the fence with Amy when a series of clicks and crunches sounded behind them. He knew those sounds well and briefly wondered how many guns had just been cocked and pointed at them. Evidently the whole invisibility covering hadn't lasted quite as long as they'd needed it to.

"Bienvenidos, gringos," a man said from the doorway. John could hear the sneer on his face in the tone of his voice. "Americanos o europeos?"

Still assessing the number of men surrounding them, John quietly replied. "Americanos."

The man barked a laugh. "We did not know you were coming. We would have had a bigger welcome party for you."

The words were smooth but the threat in his voice was real, confident, and close. John cast his eyes toward Amy. He expected to see fear, which would have mirrored his own emotions perfectly. But there was no fear on Amy's face. There was no sense of anxiety or even worry in its smooth lines as she stood with eyes closed and her lips turned up, as if she were listening to her favorite song.

"Have a seat, gringos," said the man. "We should talk first."

John swallowed, allowing the cold calm of his training to kick in. *Make him talk*, he thought. *Stall him. Keep him busy long enough for the international forces R.P. mentioned to get here. Got to keep Amy safe. I'll figure out something to tell Interpol once we're out of danger.*

"Nice place," John said, keeping his tone light. "We were thinking of buying a vacation home here. Know of any for sale?"

"Shut up and sit!" The man shoved the barrel of his revolver into John's back, clearly out of patience.

John began to move forward toward a chair, determined to appear cooperative, when the quiet sound of Amy's voice made his heart stop.

"No," she said.

It seemed every eye and ear surrounding the HQ bunker tuned in to her small, firm refusal.

"Perdón?" the man said, his eyes on Amy and his gun now pointed at the back of her head.

"I said no. I will not sit."

John felt the color drain from his face as he turned to see what the man would do to her. Hit her? Shoot her? Bind her? He wanted to be ready to stop all of it. But how could he with so many guns loaded, cocked and pointed at both of them?

The man allowed him to turn around fully and face him. He was short and stocky with an unkempt beard that grew in patches over his dark face. John was struck by the large tattoo covering the left side of his neck. A large scorpion, pincers and stinger raised, was encircled by a snake, its fangs bared, primed and ready to strike. The scripture R.P. had quoted came back to John in a flash: *You can walk among snakes and scorpions and crush them.*

John had no time to ponder crushing the man before him, however, because without warning he lowered the gun to John's left foot and fired. Pain shot up his leg in a blinding wave that caused him to scream and fall to the ground before he could process what had happened. He knew without even looking that bone was splintered in pieces and blood was pouring out of his body. In the haze of pain he heard Amy's gasp and looked up in time to see the man bring his arm back for a forceful blow to the side of her head with the butt of the gun he'd just fired. Amy did not give him the chance. Instead she spoke. Her words were loud and clear enough that everyone around her fell under the sound of her voice. "You are paralyzed in Jesus' name!"

Gasping for breath and control, John watched the man's hand stop suddenly in its downward thrust toward Amy's head. A few inches away from the red, bouncy curls John loved was the butt of the gun, hovering in midair in the man's frozen hand. Glancing back at the man's face, John saw a look of surprise captured. The only thing he seemed capable of doing was moving his eyes back and forth between John and Amy.

She knelt down beside him. "John! I'm so sorry! I didn't say it when I should have. I hesitated and he shot you. I'm sorry!"

"Not your fault," he said through gritted teeth. The sweat that had beaded on his skin from the humidity of the air began rolling down his neck and back in rivulets of shock and pain.

"We've got to get you out of here. We need help." Her breath caught in her throat. "There's so much blood, John."

Starting to shake, John kept his teeth locked together. "S'okay. Be fine."

"You're not fine," Amy said, putting his arm around her shoulder and using her weight to balance his as she tried to pull him up from the dirt floor of the HQ. They were completely surrounded. A dozen different guns, some semi-automatic and very impressive, were all pointed at them and ready to be fired. Only no one could move. Not one of them made a sound. Their eyeballs moved frantically back and forth in their skulls, trying to make sense of their paralyzed states. John and Amy ignored them.

Using every bit of self-restraint and control he could pull together, John allowed Amy to place her hand around his hip and lead him forward toward the door with her as a makeshift crutch. Every hop he took fired searing pain from the gaping hole in his foot all the way up into his chest. He was leaving a trail of blood. Interpol Forensics would have a field day. His first problem, though, was getting out of the HQ. Three more men stood behind the lead man in the doorway, including the guard that had almost discovered them. Still paralyzed, his eyes remained trained on Amy and John as they scooted around and between all the frozen bodies surrounding the HQ. Out in the bright sunlight, John noticed every single man in the compound in the same shape, some paralyzed in mid-stride as they hurried toward the scene John and Amy had caused.

Realizing Amy was near tears, John tried to make light of the situation. Between huffs of breath he said, "Some party trick, Amy."

She glanced up at his face and he could see the tears spill out and make tracks down her pale cheeks. Even so, she gave him a small smile as she continued to hold his weight up and take him toward the hole in the fence. "I'm full of tricks, John Yates."

"Can't wait." In the distance he could hear the rumble of trucks and a helicopter closing in. He didn't know whether to be relieved that someone was nearby who could wrap up his bleeding foot or panicked that he was going to have to explain their presence in this compound. With Jonas right outside of it. And a dead guy sent from Heaven helping them out. *Perfect*, he thought. *I'll get shot, lose my job and get put in a nut house all in the same day.*

Amy stopped moving. "How about I see if I can pull off another trick?"

Starting to get dizzy, John whispered. "Go for it."

She closed her eyes once more and without any fancy words prayed simply and to the point. "King Jesus, we need a way out. Open the door?"

John felt it before he saw it. The atmosphere sizzled and broke apart in blinding light right in front of them. Without hesitation they stepped through the portal.

Chapter Twenty-One

She knew he was trying hard to stay strong and calm for her benefit. But he was weakening, leaning more on her as blood and adrenaline drained from his body. Once the light dimmed, she held him against her still, her left hand tight against his hip, her right locked onto the forearm draped over her shoulder.

As she became fully aware of their new surroundings, the first thing she noticed was the sudden and severe drop in temperature. Her skin, having grown used to the damp heat where they'd been, prickled in goosebumps as cold air and an icy wind hit her full force. The second thing she realized was that as the extreme brightness of the portal dimmed, the natural daylight she had been in wasn't there. Instead, wherever they were was darkening. Twilight deepened from dark purple to navy blue through the forest of snow-laden oaks and maples around them. As her eyes adjusted, she became aware of a third thing.

R.P. was coming toward them like a shadow emerging from the trees. Swiftly and silently he came forward and took John from her arms, laying him down in the snow at her feet. She crouched down beside him and looked at R.P.'s face. It was not grim and worried as hers was. He glanced behind him and nodded once.

Jonas emerged, running into her outstretched arms first and allowing her to cover his face in kisses. "You're alright, Mommy?"

"I'm fine, sweetie."

"But John's not, right?"

She couldn't help the sob that escaped with her words. "No. He's not alright."

Jonas broke out of her embrace and looked down at John. He took in his pale face, his grip on R.P.'s hand, and scanned down his body to the left foot where his boot had been blown apart and blood pooled in the snow beneath it. Before she realized what he was doing, Jonas walked around her and knelt beside John's injured foot. He reached out a small hand. "Jonas, no. Don't touch him, honey. He's hurt."

She felt R.P. snap his attention to her before his words could come out. "Do not stop him."

It dawned her then, that the supernatural abilities King Jesus had given her in the compound – invisibility and the ability to paralyze – were not unique to her. They were gifts of power available to all God's children. Jonas included. How narrow-minded she was to assume that because Jonas was a child he was inept at receiving and acting out commands from his King. So instead of stopping him, she watched him, praying for King Jesus to act through her son.

John's free hand reached up to hold hers and she grasped it with both hands as they watched Jonas. He closed his eyes and began to whisper. He invoked the name of Jesus over John's body and over his injury. He placed his small hands over the bloody, gaping hole in John's boot and tilted his head back toward the darkening sky. Praise for Father God poured from his mouth in simple, pure words of unshakeable faith and joy. He invited Holy Spirit to flow through him and into John's body. He continued to praise and petition for healing of John's foot and as he prayed, she felt John's grip on her hands relax. She tore her gaze away from Jonas to watch John's face. He was smiling and his eyes were closed. He didn't appear to be in any pain at all. Instead he too was praising King Jesus, thanking him for his healing.

Jonas' hands lifted off John's boot and he sat back, slowly ending his prayer and smiling first at John, then at her. She bent down to see John's injury better and gasped. There wasn't even a hole left in his boot. Quickly, she untied the laces and carefully removed the hiking boot and the white sock beneath.

There was no injury. No gunshot wound. No gaping hole. No blood. God had heard Jonas' prayer and healed John completely. She felt John sitting up beside her and just to prove the point, wiggled his toes.

She couldn't stop the tears from falling. She'd been berating herself since the gun had gone off. In that secret, intimate place with King Jesus, she had heard his voice and known his command. But it seemed so preposterous at the time. Paralyze someone? Was that even possible? And even though his specific words to her *'What is possible is'* had been reverberating in her mind, she'd hesitated. She'd paused, allowing her disbelief to become greater than her belief. And in that pause, the gun had gone off. She'd been angry with herself and scared for John, not knowing how to proceed, how to fix it, how to help him in their crazy, upside-down adventure. But God had taken care of it. In the most unexpected, sacred moment she had been witness to another miracle. This time through the unshakeable faith of her son.

She pulled him into her lap and hugged him tight. "I thank God for you, Jonas." He squeezed her back and she felt two more arms wrap around both of them. John's forehead rested on hers and he gently laid a kiss on the top of Jonas' head.

"Thank you, Jonas," he said. "That was an amazing gift you just gave me."

"It wasn't me," Jonas said. "It was him. King Jesus. He filled me up with power like a cup of water and poured it all out into your foot. He even fixed your boot!"

"I know," John pulled away and winked at him. "Coolest thing ever, little man."

Jonas held up his hand for a high five from John, then jumped up to stand by R.P. again. Amy stood also, allowing John to pull his sock and boot back on, and wrapped her arms tightly around herself. The cold temperature they'd arrived in was starting to sink into her bones, causing her to shiver. John stood, pulling out a napkin from his pocket and wiping the last traces of tears from her face. He leaned close. "No more tears for me, okay? I'm better than I've ever been."

She let him wipe her cheeks with the rough napkin. "How many of those napkins do you have stashed away, detective?"

"It's my last one. That's why you can't cry anymore. Got to hit another drive-thru tomorrow." He winked.

She dropped her eyes to the snow as a blush crept to her cheeks. She rubbed her hands together to keep the cold at bay and glanced at R.P., who was looking past the trees to a distant point. "Where are we?" she asked.

"Germany."

"Germany?" John asked. "We're really getting around. I could get used to world travel this way."

R.P. smiled the crooked, rakish smile she'd come to associate with her friend and soldier saint.

"I guess that explains why it was still mid-morning in Honduras and the sun is already setting here," Amy said.

R.P. nodded. "Congrats to both of you, by the way. That was nice work. Especially you, Princess Amy. Way to put that faith to work."

She smiled at his praise and knocked her elbow against John's. "He helped."

"Yes, he did." Setting his hand on John's shoulder his gaze became more intense. "Now it's time to engage phase two. Pull up the photos, John. Send everything to your partner. Let him know you'll call him in a couple of hours with a rendezvous time and location. Tell him you're still narrowing the leads in the field."

She could see the mask of professionalism slip over John's face as he pulled out his phone and began sending photos and relaying information. Surely the marked locations and routes on the maps they'd found would help ratchet the investigation up into high gear. She couldn't bear to think of the sweet little girl she'd come to love, her blonde pigtails dancing as she ran with Jonas across the yard, in the hands of anyone like the monsters she'd met that morning. The thought terrified her. She thought of Thistle and her shimmering emerald green hair and prayed fervently that she was by Katey's side, protecting her as much as possible.

As she waited for John to wrap up the emails and texts with his partner and the other officers working the case, Amy surveyed the area around them. The forest was dense, but didn't look incredibly dissimilar from one she would have seen at home. The trees were taller and the snow much deeper than anything around Nashville, but it wasn't as foreign to her as the jungle of Honduras had been. R.P.'s gaze settled back in the direction she'd been facing when they had first arrived through the portal. Distantly through the trees she could see the twinkle of lights coming on as darkness fell.

"Where are those lights coming from?" she asked.

John stopped typing on his phone and turned to see what she was talking about as R.P. tilted his head in that direction. "That's your next target."

Quietly he led them closer to the edge of the trees, stopping before they would become visible. Amy gasped at the monstrosity before her. It was a castle, complete with guard towers on each of the four corners of brick walls that stood ten or twelve feet in height and two feet in width. Armed men were stationed in each tower while more stood guard in front of two huge front doors barred with iron. Instead of emanating beauty and opulence like the castles in Heaven, it instead spoke of dominance and intimidation, as if even the ground it sat on was oppressed by its weight rather than holding it up as an example of grandeur.

John pulled his phone back out and flipped through the pictures until he came to a map of Germany. He enlarged it with a thumb and forefinger and studied it until he said, "Got it. I know where we're at. This place has a blue square around it and a black route coming from it toward Hamburg, then more routes leading out on freight lines and waterways. What does that mean?"

"It means this is a drop-off and pick-up."

John was quiet for the space of two breaths. "There are kids in that place? Being held?"

R.P. nodded. "Held and tortured."

John dropped his chin to his chest. When he raised his eyes level with the target again, Amy's eyes widened at the look on his face. The fierce determination and outright fury she saw there told her exactly what they would be doing next.

Katey – Part Seven

I miss my momma and daddy. And I miss Jonas. He's my best friend and I know he was worried when I didn't go over to play yesterday. I want to make it up to him. But I'm afraid I might not get out of here. I'm afraid they will keep me here and I won't see my family again. Will I be okay? Will I still be me without them?

Every time I sleep I see the beautiful face of the woman with the green spiky hair. She is so nice to me in my dreams. She rubs her hands smooth over my hair and tells me over and over again that everything is going to be all right.

But that's not what Maestra says. Maestra says men want to buy us. They want to make us pretty and take care of us. She says they will buy us nice things and all we have to do is make them happy. She says our bodies will do that for us.

We watch another video. This time I really do watch because I'm afraid not to know what it is I'm supposed to do. But watching makes my stomach sick. Maestra explains everything that happens on the screen and then she calls for the men to come down so we can practice.

I know Ponytail Man is coming for me. He's coming and I'm so scared I start to pee a little. Maybe if I wet my pants down there, he won't want to touch me.

But when she yells they do not come. She yells and curses and grabs a hammer off the wall and throws it up the stairs. It lands with a big thud and one of the men comes down. He is the quiet one in the Coca Cola shirt and he speaks in an upset voice with her. Something has happened, he says, to the boys in Honduras. And now Maestra is upset. She screams for us to crawl back in our cages and we do so the Coca Cola man can lock us up again. I am glad. So glad. And I try to sleep and get back to my dream as fast as I can.

Chapter Twenty-Two

Anger pulsed through John's veins like a living thing, bringing into sharp focus the opulent house before him illuminated in bright security lights. It should have been beautiful. Even from the hillside above and through the trees protecting them from the sight of the guards he could see massive chandeliers hung from a high ceiling in a large, open foyer. They sparkled through the window panes and shouted of wealth and privilege. But they did not project a welcome. Instead the lights seemed cold and cast moving shadows on the snow-covered lawn, a macabre ballet of light and darkness.

Jonas scooted between his side and Amy's, shyly reaching up to grasp John's hand. The innocent, sweet gesture of trust made John's breath catch in his throat. Softly Jonas whispered, "Is Katey in there?"

R.P. shook his head. "No, she's not. But the man who wants to buy her is. He was contacted by her handlers and is in negotiations for her price."

Beside him Amy gasped and closed her eyes. John reached out with his free hand and squeezed hers. "We're not going to let that happen, Amy," he said. "We're here to stop him. And we will."

"Yes," R.P. said, motioning them back into the shadows of the trees. "And I'm going to help you."

"How?" Amy asked.

Coming back to where they had been, R.P. quickly kicked snow over the pool of blood on the ground where John's newly healed foot had been. Then he squatted on the ground, focused his eyes and waved his hand. As he did a holographic image appeared in the air. John couldn't help the surprise in his voice. "Whoa. How'd you do that?"

He saw a big smile on Amy's face. "Just like in the War Room, R.P. You can do that, too?"

A teasing grin hiked up the side of R.P.'s face and his brown eyes winked at her. John reminded himself the guy was dead and unavailable to calm down the spike of jealousy at R.P.'s harmless flirting. As if he could read John's thoughts, R.P. looked at him and laughed. "Come on, brother. Let me show you what to do."

John knelt in the snow beside Amy, intentionally letting his leg touch hers. Jonas sat beside her, his expression one of surprise and excitement as he tuned into the cinematic images. Back to business, R.P. began.

"The children are held in individual cells on the bottom floor. It's below ground level, reachable by only one staircase to the right of the kitchen." His finger pointed at a closed door the holographic image zeroed in on after taking them though a blueprint of the house. "There are three boys and nine girls, all ranging in age from four to fourteen."

Nausea swept through John and he clamped down hard on his roiling emotions, using all his training to separate a natural human response to R.P.'s words from the professional, calculated response he needed to depend on. He gritted his teeth and watched images of each child flash on the screen. They were handcuffed to metal cots in various stages of undress.

"They've been drugged," R.P. said, "to ensure they stay cooperative and quiet." He looked at Amy and touched her hand. John tore his gaze away from the images to see that tears ran unchecked down her cheeks.

"Princess Amy," R.P. said gently, "you'll be responsible for getting them dressed and pulling them out of their drugged states."

John watched her struggle for control. She took several deep breaths and wiped her face with her palms, removing the tears and replacing them with a steady, determined gaze. "Okay," she said. "I can do that."

R.P. pulled his hand back and nodded. "Well done, Princess." Turning his attention to John he said, "You have a bigger job to do."

At those words John's stomach clenched and he could feel hot acid churning in his gut. He nodded once to acknowledge R.P.'s words, ready to do what he had to in order to free the children he'd just seen in images suspended over the snow. R.P. wasn't done, however. The air to their left split open in the blinding light of Heaven John knew signified an open door to the spiritual realm. He held his arm up over his eyes and squinted into the brightness, barely catching the rest of R.P.'s words. "You won't have to do it alone, though. You're going to have a lot of help."

The light dissipated into the darkness that had fallen in inky pools of softness among the trees they hid in. Before him stood three giant figures dressed in red and gold armor with a figure of a lion striking on the breast-plates, huge swords at least half his own size strapped to their sides, and translucent wings sticking up two feet further above their heads. Glad he was already kneeling, John made a conscious effort to snap his mouth closed again. He tried to think of something to say, but no words would form in his mind. Instead he just stared, taking in their beauty. One, who seemed to be smiling directly at Amy and reaching out to her had bright, sunny yellow hair and dark purple eyes. Seeing their warm greeting, John assumed she was the guardian angel that had come to take Amy and Jonas to Heaven originally. The second angel met Jonas, throwing him up in the air and setting him back down with a huge grin on his face. This angel's eyes struck John as so turquoise and clear and filled with light, it was like seeing the reflection of a noonday sun off the waters near a Caribbean beach. The third angel stood still, taking in John's appraisal and making one of his own. He was solemn at first, then a slow smile spread across his face. That smile relaxed John, relieving the coil of tension that had mounted in his gut from the first sight of their new target to the arrival of angels in their midst. John felt himself smiling back, taking note of the angel's height and breadth, his black hair pulled back and running down the corded muscles of his tan neck, and his eyes, a molten gold that sparkled as he extended his hand to John.

John hesitated briefly, then placed his hand in the angel's. With that first touch, knowledge of who the angel was jolted through John's aware-ness with scenes from his own life flashing like a movie on high speed in his mind's eye. He saw himself as a child jumping off his top bunk and climbing the trees in his grandma's back yard, this angel standing by his side, smiling and watchful. He saw himself in his first car the day it stalled at a railroad crossing with an oncoming train barreling forward, the engineer laying on the train whistle. He watched himself fumble with the seatbelt as the angel pushed his car off the tracks with ten feet to spare between the train and the driver's side door. He'd been in such a crazed panic, he thought the car had started in the nick of time, allowing him to escape with his foot pressed against the gas pedal. But it had been this angel's strength and assistance that had saved his life. The sands of Iraq came into focus and he watched some of his worst days flash before his eyes, this angel's large wings shielding him from incoming fire and pushing him away from hidden triggers in the ground. He watched more scenes play out, including the night he'd almost taken his life after Candace and Sam had died, the gun in his mouth, his life in the balance. He now saw the angel clearly behind him, one hand resting on John's shoulder, the other raised toward Heaven as the angel prayed and interceded on John's behalf. It was him, this angel, whose presence he had felt, bringing into focus the light and love of Heaven, ultimately saving his life and his soul. This angel, his guardian angel, had been by his side through his best and worst moments, not condemning or interfering, but loving in every way possible.

John found himself locked in a strong embrace, his cheek resting on the breastplate of the angel's armor. "You're my angel," John mumbled, trying to stop the tears that were leaking from his eyes. "You've been with me my whole life," he said, "helping me every time I needed it."

The angel stepped back from him, still smiling. "Yes," he said, "and it has always been my honor, Prince John. I am so happy to be able to reveal myself to you before your Homecoming. Because today," he paused, glancing at R.P., "we get to fight together, side by side."

"Please tell me your name," John said.

"Ruckus."

John smiled and stepped back, going for humor to break the emotion of the moment. "You guys win the prize for the most outrageous series of events to ever surprise me. It's been one continual shock after another."

Ruckus patted him on the shoulder and leaned down to his ear. "We're not done yet." He pointed out Shake and Harbor to John before the six of them settled their full attention on R.P., who stood in the center of the group with his arms crossed over his chest and a grin on his face that made him seem to John like the cat that ate the canary.

"You sly ghost," John said. "You enjoy throwing me off like this, don't you?"

"What can I say? I'm a sucker for surprises," R.P. said.

"What else have you got up your sleeve?"

R.P.'s elation nearly lifted him off the ground. "Come and see."

The six of them followed R.P. back to the edge of the treeline where the walled, guarded castle stood tall and intimidating in the valley below the forest floor. John heard Jonas and Amy gasp. He turned to see Amy's eyes widen and practically bug out of her head. Shake clapped his hand over Jonas' mouth just in time to muffle a squeal of delight. John looked back at the castle and the grounds surrounding it. He couldn't see a thing different from what they'd already seen and he glanced back at Amy and Jonas, now smiling with an infectious excitement he desperately wanted to experience.

Turning back to R.P., he shrugged his shoulders. "What am I missing?"

R.P. never took his eyes off the castle and grounds before them. Instead he said, "Jonas, help John see."

Wiggling out of Shake's arms, Jonas hopped down and pulled John's hand until he squatted in the snow eye to eye with him. Jonas' smile evaporated as he closed his eyes and concentrated. John knew he was zeroing in on Holy Spirit's words and direction. John waited, watching Jonas' facial expression smooth into peace and confidence. Then he took his two small hands and placed his fingers over John's eyes. He blew one quick breath on John's forehead and then leaned close and whispered, "Be opened."

Pulling back his hands and stepping away, Jonas said, "Now look. See them!"

Still kneeling John turned his head back to the castle and felt the air knocked out of his chest in an explosion of shock. Heavenly warriors were everywhere! Taking up nearly every available square foot of space around the castle walls were angels and saints, armed to the teeth with broadswords, bows and arrows. Two rows of angels knelt in the snow just in front of him halfway down the hill, flames already burning on the tips of their arrows which were focused on the four towers at the corners of the wall. On the opposite side, five hundred yards off, a monstrous angel stood silent and grim, towering over the wall, his head easily reaching the highest turrets atop the apex of the castle roof. He was a giant force of destruction awaiting the moment of release. John estimated the fighting force to be at least two hundred angels and saints, appearing battle-experienced, ready, and waiting. All of their attention rested on R.P., who, John realized, stood as commander of this battle.

John's breaths had been coming in gasps as he tried to process the scene before him. He tried to slow his breathing down and stand back up. Amy moved away from Harbor and came to his side, reaching out and intertwining her fingers with his. "It's all real, John. Just like I told you."

John looked down at her, tears blurring his vision. "I believed you. I did. But now I think I believe everything a bit more."

He cupped her cheek with his palm and pulled her forward to brush a light kiss along her hairline. Tentatively, she wrapped an arm around his waist and held him close. "We can do this," she said. "All of us together."

John agreed, still holding her close to his side. He felt the large presence of Ruckus on his other side and looked back at R.P., who had turned his attention away from the Army of the Lord and focused back on the six of them. "What now?" John asked him.

R.P. looked directly at Amy. "The first thing we need to do is release Jonas and Shake to leave us."

"What do you mean?" Amy asked.

"They will not be a part of this battle," R.P. explained. "King Jesus has a different, no less important job for Prince Jonas to do while we are here. Shake is to accompany him and we will meet up with him when we're done here."

"Aw, man. I want to fight the bad guys," Jonas put his hands on his hips and glared at R.P.

"You will," R.P. responded. "But you have to begin Phase Three while we complete Phase Two. There are multiple battlefields going on at once, Prince Jonas. You and Shake have to go on to the next one while we take care of business here."

John watched Amy's face pale with every word coming from R.P.'s mouth. "You want to send him somewhere just as dangerous without me there?"

R.P. took her hand. "Yes, with my promise that he will be better than okay."

Amy closed her eyes and chewed on her upper lip. John could not imagine the inner turmoil she had to wade through to come to a place of trust in order to send her son along with Shake. After a moment, she opened her eyes and knelt in front of Jonas, pulling him into a tight bear hug. "King Jesus told me he'll be there with you and you'll be fine, just like R.P. says. So I'm going to let you go with Shake and try not worry about you."

Jonas hugged her back. "Okay, Mommy. Kick a lot of bad guy butt."

She laughed and kissed his cheek. "I will."

Her gaze traveled up and locked onto John's. A spark ignited between them, a recognition born from the intensity of the circumstances that spoke of understanding, trust, and solidarity. John found he couldn't break away from the green eyes that held his own and desire for more things than he could name blossomed as he watched her lips form the words. "The three of us will be just fine."

Amy gripped his hand tightly as they both watched Shake and Jonas walk through an open portal in the trees behind them. He heard her let loose a shaky breath and pulled her into the circle of his arms for a hug. "I'm proud of you," he whispered, letting his lips rub softly against her hair.

"For what?" Amy's voice wavered with emotion.

"For letting him go. For trusting God so much." He paused. "And for staying by my side."

She leaned back and looked into his eyes. For a moment John wasn't sure if Amy was going to tear up again or lean in to kiss him. Then the corners of her mouth lifted in a half smile and she tossed her red curls over her shoulder. "Enough mushy stuff. Let's kick butt and take names."

Chapter Twenty-Three

Stepping out of the comfortable circle of John's arms, Amy surveyed the Army of the Lord. Each angel and saint, armed and focused, awaited R.P.'s signal. She knew her role: release the children, get them dressed, and get them out. Acknowledging she had absolutely no idea how to accomplish that goal, she turned to the battle commander.

"How do we begin?" she asked.

R.P. pointed at the four towers standing taller than the rest of the walls surrounding the castle. "We're going to cause a distraction for the guards by lighting those guard towers on fire."

"How?" John asked.

R.P. leveled his gaze just behind Amy's left shoulder. She turned and watched four angels, resplendent in their crimson and gold armor, walk forward from the trees and stand before R.P. with large golden bowls in their hands. Inside sloshed an iridescent liquid that looked oily and carried a pungent, acrid odor.

"They're going to pour a little liquid dynamite on the towers and they," he said, pointing to the archers kneeling in the snow, the flames on their arrows lit and ready for release, "will light the whole place up."

"Liquid dynamite, huh." John said.

Ruckus shrugged. "Well it's sort of like lighter fluid, or petroleum, or dynamite, or all of that rolled into one. The main thing is, it'll rain fire." He winked. "Boom."

Amy and John smiled alongside their angels, an easy camaraderie binding them in a focused drive, already accelerating toward their ultimate goal.

R.P. continued. "After the towers are on fire and the guards are focused on them, the four of you will enter through the back gate. I have someone stationed there to blow it open at the same time the towers go up in flames. Once you're inside the courtyard, enter through the kitchen door, ground floor and to the right. The door to the basement will be on your left."

"What do I do with the children once I dress them and free them? Where should I take them?" Amy asked.

"Bring them back out the same door you went in. There's a Christian organization of human rights crusaders that is active in this area. I sent an anonymous tip in. They'll be here shortly. I'll meet you and lead you to them."

"And what about me?" John asked.

R.P. glanced at Ruckus, then back at John. "You're going to have to fight, John. You've been trained."

"Yes, with guns and with my hands." John thought about his years in the military. He'd learned to box there and he'd been pretty good. Several of the special ops guys he'd gotten close with had taught him some MMA moves, but he hadn't used his skills on anything more than a punching bag and an occasional idiot from the streets of late night Nashville in quite a while. He pointedly looked at the angels carrying broadswords and bows. "I might be rusty with some of those skills and I don't know how to fight like those guys."

"You don't have to," R.P. said. "You fight your way, they'll fight their way. You'll all be providing distraction and cover for Harbor and Amy as they release the children to safety."

"That's it, then? Distract and cover?"

R.P. again shared a look with Ruckus. "Not exactly. There's one more thing, but it's not your job."

"What do you mean?"

R.P. waved his hand and a face appeared in the air, another holographic image. Amy watched the face rotate left and right between them. The man appeared to be middle-aged, balding, with a puckered scar running from his nose to his left ear. "Who's that?" she whispered.

"Boris Kohlhaas, organized crime boss, pedophile, rapist, murderer, and unrepentant atheist."

Amy let those words sink in through her mind like pebbles through the surface of water. Each one held its own weight and form, solid and cold as realization dawned. "He wants to buy Katey."

R.P. nodded. "And many others."

John's eyes widened. "He paid the uncle, didn't he? Andrew Dodson. He paid him to kidnap Katey Johnson."

Again R.P. nodded. "Keep going. Follow the trail."

Amy watched John's face as his mind worked, clicking through what they knew and what they'd seen. "This is ground zero. Boris Kohlhaas funnels money to bottomfeeders like we dealt with earlier. They're the movers and the shakers, kidnapping and distributing. But he's the one that funds it all, makes the decisions, reaps the money from the sales of children."

"That's right," R.P. nodded. "Tonight we cut off the head of the snake."

Amy watched Ruckus place his large hand on John's shoulder, turning him to face the warrior angel's molten gold eyes. "But that's not your job. And you need to remember that. King Jesus was very specific that his blood not be on your hands. His death is my responsibility. His lifetime has run out. He has spent it in pursuit of evil. And now it is evil that will pursue him. I will kill his body and hand his spirit off to another angel, who will take him before the Father for his judgment."

Ruckus spoke the words calmly and factually. But despite the horror she knew Boris Kohlhaas had committed, she found herself squeamish at the thought of his death and eternal judgment happening in the next few minutes. She hoped she would not have to see any of it.

"What about the others?" John asked. "There are guards. What if they get in the way?"

Ruckus and R.P. looked at one another one last time and R.P. responded. "King Jesus says to do what you have to do. The primary objective is to break apart this ring and move on to the final battle. We must secure Katey Johnson and as many other children as we can."

He glanced at John with a secretive smile playing at the corners of his mouth. "Besides, the word in the ranks is you were a great boxer. I'm sure it'll come back to you."

R.P. turned back to the castle. He took one deep breath and rolled his shoulders back. Before them the guards chattered in German to one another and looked out at the night, oblivious to the army surrounding them and the imminent attack about to be launched. She saw in the hard jaw line and the flash of raw anger in his eyes the human man R.P. had been. A Ranger. His job as a soldier had transcended from one life to the next and she saw in him an unyielding resolve that would see every aspect of this mission through to the end. His voice held a rough edge in it when he spoke again. "Whoever gets in your way, John, will meet the combined force of your training and Ruckus'. You fight together. Side by side. Understand?"

John nodded. "I do." He pulled the Glock out of his side holster and checked it. "I didn't really come prepared for a big show down. But I'll use what I've got."

"Don't worry. You'll have what you need the moment you need it."

John nodded as Ruckus and Harbor both stepped back from the group and unsheathed their swords. Already so much taller and broader than most humans she knew, the swords they held in their hands were nearly as long as she was tall. The blades shimmered silver and gold in the moonlight. Each blade shot upward out of a gold hilt that curved around each angel's hand. Amy noticed what looked like scrollwork or a flowery engraving that briefly glowed gold, then returned to the cold silver of the blade.

"Our names," Harbor said. She pointed to the curvy loops and lines that had caught Amy's attention. "That's my name in the language the Father gave to angels."

Amy reached out a finger and lightly ran her hand over the surface of the blade. As soon as her skin touched Harbor's name, her ears filled with the sound of water rushing violently forward in a creek bed swollen with spring rains, the sound of limbs breaking under the heavy thrust of the water, and then the peace and sudden quiet of the still, unbroken surface of water at dawn. At the same time her mind saw King Jesus. He gaze was intense and unsmiling. He saw straight through to her heart and soul and when he whispered her name, his strength and power flowed into her like the violent waters she'd heard in Harbor's name, girding her up in his authority and energizing her for the battle now moments away.

Amy gasped and leaped backward, holding her finger up in front of her like it had been burned. But it hadn't and Harbor just smiled. "You ready now?"

Amy felt the power and energy transferred to her from her vision of King Jesus rushing through her veins like an adrenaline high. "You bet I am."

Harbor stepped back up to her side. "Good. Watch this."

Amy and John stood between their angels and watched R.P. raise both arms in the air above his head. Amy could feel the tension in the air like the taut wire of a guitar string, tuned high and tight. Every eye in the Army of the Lord rested on the Ranger-turned-Saint Commander. For the space of two breaths they waited. Then he looked at the angels with the bowls in their hands and let his right hand drop, pointing forward.

Amy's breath caught in her throat as the four angels lifted their wings and sprung into the air. Their wings were gossamer and feathery, but so strong and powerful she imagined steel skyscrapers would buckle before their wings would give out. Each one flew silently and quickly to the four guard towers of the castle and they hovered in the air, their golden bowls filled with the explosive liquid ready to be tipped.

Quietly, R.P. said to the archers kneeling on the hillside below them, "At the ready."

A row of fourteen angels pulled back their flame-tipped arrows. Amy held her breath. John interlaced his fingers with hers and squeezed. On her other side, Harbor tensed.

Loudly, so that every member of the Army of the Lord heard, R.P. yelled, "Loose!"

At his command, the four angels hovering over the guard tower poured out the contents of their bowls in an iridescent fall that intercepted multiple arrows shot in at the same time. Explosions rocked the towers mid-air as fire rained down. Some of the guards were immediately engulfed in the flames. Everyone who wasn't ran toward the towers from all points of the courtyard and the front of the castle. Amy watched, fascinated and horrified, as even the stones burned, consumed by the angels' acrid oil and flaming arrows.

R.P. turned to the four of them. His brown eyes were energized and electric. "Go," he commanded.

As one they all moved down the hill running as quickly as possible to the wall between the back two towers, now infernos. Amy listened to harsh guttural German shouts. She knew they were now exposed and had no idea if any of those shouts included their knowledge of Amy and John, now closing in on the back gate.

As promised, a figure stepped out, dressed as another soldier saint in the same black fatigues as R.P., the insignia of the Lion of Judah sewn on his sleeve. His blonde hair, buzzed short, glowed red in the light of the fires above them. He grinned. "Fun night, eh?"

He pointed in through the gate. "Just over there and to the right." He winked. "Door's open."

"Thanks," John said.

"Don't mention it. Move fast now but don't worry. I've got your six."

Still holding John's hand Amy ran toward the door to the kitchen. All around them the guards shouted, the fire roared, and the smell of burning hair and skin settled down to the ground with the cinders, making Amy gag. She briefly noted that Harbor and Ruckus had spread their wings over the top of John and Amy as they ran to the door. No cinders touched them and she assumed no one saw them beneath the shelter of the warriors' wings.

John let go of her hand. "Stay with Harbor." Nearing the door he planted himself to the right and held the gun in a ready position. He placed his hand on the doorknob and began to turn it when Ruckus stopped him.

"I go first, John. Every time."

John nodded and allowed the angel to open the door and step in. His frame more than filled the doorway. "Stay right behind me," Ruckus said.

Staying right at the angel's back, Amy followed John into the kitchen. While everything else in the castle and grounds seemed to be in complete disorder, no one seemed to be paying attention to the kitchen. As Amy cleared the doorway, she saw that the kitchen was part of an open design, separated by the dining room and living room by a well-stocked bar and a half wall. To her left past the bar was a large fire place burning in the alcove of a curving staircase. Down the stairs came two guards carrying the largest guns Amy had ever seen. Behind them came one more figure. Amy new without even seeing the scar on his face that the head of the snake had just slithered down the stairs.

Katey – Part Eight

I wake up to see D.D. kneeling in front of my cage. He is crying.

"I'm so sorry, Katey. I made a big mistake. I shouldn't have done this to you."

"D.D.?" The sleepy juice makes things blurry and my tongue is still too big in my mouth. But I know this is not my dream. D.D. has come for me. "Get me out, D.D.," I say. "Take me home."

D.D. looks around the room and runs to the tools hanging on the wall. He comes back with a big thing that looks like giant scissors and starts to cut on my chain. He keeps looking over his shoulder at the stairs and I know he is sneaking me out. "Hurry, D.D.!" I whisper. "Get me out!"

D.D. presses on the giant scissor tool with all his strength. He is crying and sweating and keeps saying he is so sorry. So very sorry.

But D.D. is not strong or fast enough. Ponytail Man comes down the stairs and points a big gun at me and D.D.

"Drew," he says, "what do you think you're doing?"

D.D. turns around and faces Ponytail Man. He doesn't drop the scissor tool and he curls his fingers into the top bars of my cage. I rub the tips of them.

"I made a mistake," D.D. says. "I shouldn't have gone through with the deal. I'm taking her back."

"Sorry, Drew. That's not how this works. The deal was made. You got the money. She's ours now."

"I'll give the money back."

Ponytail Man laughs. "I know you, man. You've already spent the money on Oxy."

D.D. pulls his hand away. "Not all of it. And I'll get the rest by tomorrow. Her dad has come into money. He's richer by the day. I swear I'll get all of it from him. More even. Just let me have her back."

Ponytail Man looks hard at D.D. and smiles a big smile. He walks over and takes away the scissors D.D. was using to cut me loose. Then he puts his arm around D.D. and walks him toward the stairs. "You don't think I know that about her dad, Drew? I know everything. The boss lady has a special plan worked out for your little niece. She's had a slight delay, but she'll be here tonight. That sweet little blonde thing's gonna bring in a nice ransom and a nice sale price. Why don't we take a little drive and talk, okay? I'll explain the details. You have nothing to worry about."

"D.D.?" I call.

He climbs the stairs and says over his shoulder, "I'm sorry, Katey." And then the door locks behind him and I think that my heart is actually breaking, breaking into a hundred million pieces of Katey. And I all want, all I can pray, is that those pieces float up and away on a warm breeze like yellow butterflies that find Home, my home, and make all the pain go away.

Chapter Twenty-Four

Every muscle in John's body was tense and prepared. He heard them before he saw them, their heavy boots clunking down the curves of the wooden staircase in the open living room. The two guards flanking Kohlhaas carried lightweight MG3 machine guns. Fully loaded John knew they would each carry up to one hundred and twenty rounds. Suddenly the cold steel of the Glock in his right hand wasn't much comfort at all. There was nowhere to hide. They'd have to stand their ground.

Beside him Ruckus flared his nostrils and smiled at John. His eyes glittered gold in the darkness of the kitchen. "Battle," he whispered, and looked at John's gun. "Put that away for now. We won't need it."

John wanted to argue the merits of one clean shot to a forehead but didn't want to draw attention to their quartet just yet. Amy and Harbor still stood with them and at the very least, he wanted Amy out of the sight of these guards before the first shot was fired. Slipping the gun back in its holster, he jerked his head toward the steel door behind them. It was the only one in the kitchen, right where R.P. said the entrance to the lower level would be.

Amy followed his gaze and reached toward the handle. But before she could pull it, the sound of a match being struck drew John's gaze back over the bar. The two guards with the MG3s flanked Kohlhaas, who had the audacity to stand there and light a cigarette. John watched the play of flames across the man's disfigured features before he waved the match and tossed it onto the tile counter.

"Who are you two?"

John almost smiled. The fool couldn't see the angels with them and had no idea he was completely outmatched. It would have been funny if he'd had a bigger gun to use. "Oh, you know," he tried for his best note of non-chalance, "we were just in the neighborhood."

"Do you know how I knew you were Americans?" Kohlhaas asked, taking a deep drag and blowing the smoke toward John.

"Why don't you enlighten me?"

"I could smell your stench from upstairs."

John bore the sound of their laughter with the knowledge that he would soon be able to wipe the smiles off their faces.

"Besides," the man continued, clearly believing he had the upper hand, "no one else would be so stupid as to wreak havoc in my home." He stubbed out his cigarette on the tile and crossed his arms over his chest. Behind him, John knew Amy had tugged twice on the latch of the door. It hadn't budged.

"So tell me, American, how you came to light my house on fire and break into my kitchen."

"We just wanted a little excitement tonight. This seemed like a good spot for a barbecue."

"Don't screw with me. The only reason either of you are still breathing is because your information is useful to me. I will give you one more chance to tell me what I want to know. Then she will tell me. But I warn you. It will be difficult for her to speak with my cock down her throat."

John wanted to fly across the kitchen and slam his scarred face into the tile where the match still smoked. His threat against Amy caused rage to expand in John's gut like a mushroom cloud. But he didn't speak. He didn't move. Because unbeknownst to Kohlhaas and his goons, Ruckus had walked over, larger than life, until he stood behind the three of them. He met the angel's golden eyes and suddenly, like an instant download of strategy and training, John knew all of Ruckus' intentions. It hit him like a gale force wind and the knowledge of what he and Ruckus could do side by side, would do, left him breathless. But his awe was replaced immediately by the urgency of his next move.

"You know, Kohlhaas, we're not alone."

The man shrugged. "I assumed not. How many clowns did you bring for this circus of yours?"

John smiled. "No clowns. Angels."

Kohlhaas raised his eyebrows. "Angels?" Laughter bubbled up from his paunch and a twisted smile caused the scar to carve his face into a grotesque mask.

John stood still, listening to the underworld figure laugh for what might be the last time. As he did, he was aware of the soldier who'd blown the outside gate quietly making his way in. Without saying a word, he placed something on the steel door between the handle and the latch. John assumed it was an explosive device since Harbor made a motion to Amy to move away from the door as soon as she could.

Kohlhaas got his laughter under control. "Angels? Now that changes things." He chuckled again and tapped his forefinger to his temple. "I know what to do with sweet American angels. I do hope they are untouched and have large breasts. I get the best price for those."

John didn't bother answering. He saw righteous anger rise up in Ruckus, who spread his wings and his arms. When Ruckus stretched to his full height and width, the guards and their guns looked like plastic toy soldiers.

Ruckus blew softly on the three heads of the men he towered over. Then he leaned his head down to Kohlhaas' left ear and said, "Boo."

All three jumped and turned toward Ruckus, their frightened yells of alarm at first sight of the striking figure the warrior cut put a smile on John's face. Behind him he heard the soldier saint start a quick countdown. "Clearance in three, two, one."

John rolled forward and to the side, looking behind him to see Amy blocked entirely by Harbor's body, her wings unfurled like a shimmering armor of diamonds. The explosive the soldier saint had rigged went off and the door blew open, the rattling clang of metal against brick making the guards and Kohlhaas turn back around to see the door to their prisoners now blown open.

"Nein!" Kohlhaas snarled. "Tötet sie!"

John didn't have to speak German to know what the guards had just been commanded to do. They raised their massive guns, ready to spray the kitchen with bullets. But before they could do more than move them an inch, Ruckus' hands clamped down on the muzzles. He squeezed and the barrels collapsed like aluminum foil. Ripping the now useless machine guns from the guards' hands, he tossed them behind and looked at Harbor.

Not needing further instruction, she grasped Amy's hand and led her to the stairway. The power to the manor now completely shut down due to the fires, John caught Amy's eyes briefly as she hurried toward the darkened door. In her eyes he saw the promise of everything he wanted for the rest of his life and in his spirit he cried out to Jesus, fear suddenly stabbing him with an ache he hadn't felt since the two Indiana State Police Officers stood on his doorstep and apologized for the death of his wife and son. If he let Amy out of his sight now, would he get her back?

Like a rushing wildfire he heard the voice of his King. *Amy is mine*, King Jesus said. His voice was commanding and authoritative, but gentle enough to calm John's fearful thoughts. *She fights with me and is under my protection. Let her go.*

He did. He watched her enter the darkness of the stairwell. As he watched, Harbor spoke and a bright flame popped up in the palm of her left hand, illuminating not only herself and Amy, but something else that caught his eye. Painted in black against the red of the bricks in the stairwell was the symbol John had seen tattooed on the neck of the Honduran thug he'd left not more than an hour ago. Four feet in diameter was the scorpion, its stinger and pincers raised, encircled by the snake, ready to strike.

They'd crushed the scorpion already. It was time now to send the snake to Hell.

Chapter Twenty-Five

Amy followed close behind Harbor, watching the play of light and shadows bounce between the flame in her hand, the shimmer of her wings, and the darkness that seemed born into the bricks of the wall they followed down the curving staircase into Kohlhaas' cellar. After so much noise from the explosions and the fires blazing above, the oppressive silence below made the roar of blood in her ears seem deafening.

At the bottom of the stairs Amy couldn't see past the circle of light from Harbor's hand, but she could feel the space open up and hear the difference in the reverberations of their footfalls. Without being asked, Harbor lifted up her left hand and blew against the flame. Pieces of it, like individual candle flames, flew up and out, landing in the light bulbs hanging from a heavy brass chandelier in the ceiling. The greater circumference of light illuminated a bare room, brick and circular, with a metal table against the far wall. Set in neat rows and labeled containers were syringes and glass vials, bandages, restraints, and what looked like medical instruments. Amy swallowed against the bile that rose into her mouth, aware that she was seeing devices used for torture against children.

"Harbor, we have to get them out. Now." She glanced up at Harbor's face and jumped back a little. The angel's face was not serene and peaceful in the normally harmonic beauty she personified. Her face was contorted in a level of anger Amy couldn't estimate. She could see a pulse point on the warrior's temple popping up and down rapidly and wondered at the amount of destruction Harbor could cause if she lost even a shred of her control.

Resolute, she nodded once, then tore her gaze away from the table of instruments and syringes and led Amy to another door. This one had no handle. It was cold stainless steel, interrupted only by a large key hole.

"Should I go back up and grab that soldier who blew the door open in the kitchen? Maybe he has some more explosives."

Harbor stared straight ahead at the door. "There's no need. Stand back."

Amy heard the solid edge of all-encompassing anger in Harbor's voice and quickly scooted herself back and to the side closest to the staircase. She watched, mesmerized, as the gentle light of love that Harbor normally carried within her like a caress built up into a banked fire of wrath, making her skin and hair glow in a fierce, harsh light that continued to build in intensity until it shone forth from her eyes, nose, ears, and fingertips. She opened her mouth and took a breath. The sound that came from her mouth Amy knew in her spirit was the angelic word for *fire*. She knew because the sound of flames licking at dry wood, consuming it in a hungry whoosh, grew in strength and volume until the roar of an inferno came not just in sound from Harbor's mouth, but in existence. The word became presence, the sound became fire. And the weight of the word against the door caused it to melt away. The steel heated, changing from cold gray metal to molten red, orange and blue, then began to melt into dripping beads and curling fingers from the center to its edges, quickly disintegrating into black ashes that swirled around the room like fine eyelashes in the breath that left the warrior's mouth.

Harbor ended the word and let silence descend first into the heat of the charred doorway, then into the crackling air of the room, then into her own body. She breathed deep and relaxed her stance, then turned to Amy and held out her hand. "Now we can get to them. Let's hurry."

Amy closed her mouth when she realized she'd been standing there with it agape and her eyes bugged out watching Harbor's ability to quickly melt steel like cotton candy on a warm tongue. She joined the angel and followed her into a hallway that hosted a dozen doors, six on each side. A sliding door sat square near the top of each one. Tentatively, Amy walked up to the first one and slid back the metal. "It's too dark. Can you light it up?"

Harbor lifted her hand toward the lights in the chandelier and motioned her open palm forward down the length of the hallway. The light dispersed and sconces along the walls glinted to life. Inside the cell fluorescent light panels illuminated a sparse chamber with tile floors and walls and a drain in the center of the room. While the rest of the castle was meant to be decorative and comfortable, these rooms were meant for discomfort, pain, torture, and quick cleaning of blood and other body fluids.

Urgency gripped Amy. "Open the doors, Harbor. Please. We have to get them out of here."

Harbor nodded and stepped forward, but Amy jumped away. "Are you going to melt it again?"

Harbor smiled. "I can't do that without scaring the child inside. She's been through too much already. I thought I would just unlock it instead."

"Good idea."

Harbor touched the lock with one finger and spoke against the key hole. Amy didn't know the exact word she used but the sound was an instantaneous snap and loud crunch that echoed off the walls and down the hall, as the locks on each door sprang loose. The door swung open and Amy entered the cell.

The sight nauseated her with equal measures of disgust, fear and fury. The girl on the narrow cot lay completely naked, her hands manacled to the metal frame at her sides. Her feet also chained to the cot, she lay motionless. The room smelled of sweat and semen. Her high cheekbones were blackened with bruises and dried blood caked the side of her mouth and pooled on the sheet below her face. Burns marred the perfect, tawny skin of her small breasts and despite the chill of the room and her uncovered body, sweat dampened her thick, black hair.

Amy sucked in a breath and approached the bed. "Sweetheart?" Not knowing the girl's name or mother tongue, she tried for a gentle tone of voice that didn't require an understanding of English. "We're here to help you. We're going to get you out of here."

The girl's eyes opened, but stared past Amy without seeing her. Clearly the drugs she'd been given and the abuse she'd lived through had stripped her of full awareness. Amy looked at the handcuffs and chains on her wrists and feet. Even after they removed them, which Amy had no trouble believing Harbor could do, she would have to tackle the girl's unresponsive state. There were twelve children, R.P. had said. How could she get them all up and out of here at one time?

She was just about to pose the question to Harbor when she heard the angel hiss on an intake of breath. At the foot of the cot, Harbor stared at the soles of the girl's feet. Her fists were clenched as she stood straight and tall, unblinking, livid. Amy moved to stand beside her and cried out at the sight. Someone had taken a knife and carved the Star of David into the soles of the child's feet. The wounds were deep, bloody, and becoming infected.

Amy fell to her knees as an unexpected swirl of emotion took hold of her in a maelstrom. She could feel him within and around her, feel his fury, a holy, righteous anger that stood up within her and roared. Jesus, the Messiah, the King of the Jews and the Lord of All filled her whole being with the force of his fury on behalf of the sweet child before her. As his anger swelled in every cell, every muscle, the skin on her neck began to overheat and burn. She placed a trembling hand to the spot he had breathed on, marking her as his warrior. She heard the roar of the Lion of Judah reverberating in her ears and felt his anger ebb in her spirit into a solid core of purpose. She called out his name. "King Jesus! Do not hold back! Bring revenge on behalf of your people, on behalf of this child, and help me deliver her from Hell. Send me help, Lord. Show me what to do."

The spot on her neck continued to pulse as a portal opened in the room and three more angels entered, bringing peace and the sweet, clean scents of lavender, mint and eucalyptus. Their presence in the room immediately bled out the tension and anger of the previous moment and Amy knew instinctively they were not warriors. These angels carried no swords, but instead held vials of crystal in their hands. They were healers.

Harbor relaxed as well, bowing her head slightly toward the three healers. "Amy, this is Kapas, Vela, and Langis."

Amy felt the mark of the Lion ease from burning to tingling. The three angels stood within their own light, emanating the goodness and the favor of the Father. Instead of armor, their white robes extended all the way to their sandaled feet. A gold braided cord wrapped around their waists and their long hair, shining in various hues of white, hung loose around their shoulders. One stepped forward and lightly touched Amy's fingertips. As she did, Amy felt an overwhelming peace and strength flow into her veins.

The angel spoke. "I am Vela. We're here to help you revive these precious ones and get them to safety. But we must act quickly. The battle going on upstairs won't last much longer. It's time to move them out before this structure crumbles beneath the fists of the mighty one."

Amy recalled the huge angel waiting for his turn in battle, towering over the castle and the rest of the Army of the Lord amassed and waging warfare. No doubt one good swing from his fist would topple the bricks from their foundation.

Harbor began moving toward the door. "Amy, you and Vela work through this side of the hallway. Langis, Kapas and I will free the others."

Amy nodded and turned to watch Vela kneel at the girl's feet. "Amy," Vela said, "break off her chains."

Amy shook her head. "I can't. Harbor has taken care of all the locks. I'll call her back."

She turned toward the door when Vela's voice stopped her. "That's not what I told you to do, dear one. You are a co-heir with King Jesus, daughter of God the Father, who created the universe and set time in motion. Who or what can stand against the power that pumps through your veins?"

He thinks like the ocean moves. Jonas' words came back to her with Vela's pronouncement. She remembered what King Jesus had done through her in Honduras and knew the time to follow through was now. There wasn't time to overthink and analyze, only time to *do.*

Kneeling at the side of the bed, Amy stared at the metal restraint trapping the girl's left hand against the rung of the cot. She closed her eyes and centered her spirit and her thoughts on King Jesus, opening herself up to him, to his words, to the power of his being. She filled her lungs with the air of the room and as she did, awareness of his intentions filled her as well. Along with the awareness, came belief, greater faith, and then came the words wrapped in the flesh of the indwelling Word.

She leaned forward and spoke against the metal lock. "Break open."

So full of faith and knowledge and purpose, she didn't even blink when the metal cuff snapped into two pieces and the girl's wrist hung free. Leaning across her small body, Amy did the same thing to the other restraint, thrilling in the clink of metal as it broke in half and fell to the floor.

She joined Vela at the girl's scarred feet and released them from their restraints in the same way. The soles of her small feet had been soaked in the iridescent oil poured out from the angel's crystal vial. Gone were the streaks of blood and the swelling and redness of infection. The Star of David still scarred her feet, but the scars were healed over, an integrated part of her flesh.

Vela stood and walked to the girl's head. She still stared blankly past them at the far wall, in a stupor induced by trauma and drugs. Vela looked at her with kindness and love that radiated out in waves of warmth from her eyes. "Amy," the angel whispered, "call her by name as I cleanse her body and mind."

"But I don't know her name."

"Ask Holy Spirit."

Amy nodded, quieting her spirit and whispering to the spirit of the King that filled her in buoyant faith. Immediately she felt the name rise up within her, taking its shape and sound, appearing in her mind's eye in a flowery script. Gently, but with strength and perseverance in her voice, she spoke the girl's name, letting her breath move over strands of thick, black hair. "Katya. Katya, wake up."

There was no response. "Again," Vela encouraged. "Call her out of the mists of her Hell."

"Katya," Amy said, watching Vela tip the vial and pour across the girl's forehead an oil that looked clear in the vial, but turned gold and sparkly upon contact with Katya's face. It settled like glitter across her dusky skin, scattering gold through her black eyebrows and across the bridge of her nose like a splash of freckles. "Katya," Amy repeated, "awaken."

As if rising up out of a deep dream, Katya filled her lungs with air and stretched her whole body. Every muscle tightened and relaxed in feline grace, from her eyelids to her small, delicate toes. She opened her eyes and looked back and forth between Amy and Vela. Her brow creased and she opened her mouth to ask what Amy knew would be a long list of questions they probably didn't have time to answer before R.P. gave the green light to the mighty one's fists. But before Katya could speak, Vela bent low and whispered in her ear. Amy watched, mesmerized, as the words she spoke floated like vapor, white, lacy, and perfumed, alighting delicately on the shells of Katya's ear and entering her body and mind, releasing understanding and peace. Later, Amy thought, she'd like to soak in her tub with her favorite rose-scented candles perfuming the air and give some serious thought to The Living Word becoming living words. But for the moment, she stripped the sheet off the bed and wrapped it around Katya's naked body. Not only did she not have anything else to use, but the relief workers R.P. was bringing to the scene would have DNA evidence in the semen-soaked sheets.

In the hallway Kapas stood next to a young boy. He was a tiny, tow-headed child with round blue eyes that Amy knew had seen and experienced far too much. But beside the healing angel, he did not appear hurt or scared. He was anxious, but not afraid. Blood stained his sheets as well and Amy could see he had been marked like Katya. But instead of the Star of David, this toddler had a cross carved into his chest. Ornate and intricately detailed, it stretched from shoulder to shoulder and halved his small body from neck to waist. How Amy wanted to scoop him up in her arms and lavish kisses from his head to his toes. But she could not. Five more doorways stood open on her side of the hallway. Five more children waited for deliverance from Hell.

Katey – Part Nine

No one has come back. D.D is gone and it seems the rest have forgotten about us. Our sleepy juice has worn off and some of the girls whisper. I hear places they're from: Mexico, Florida, Alabama, New Jersey. No one wants to be here. We all got tricked in a bad way.

The girl with the big brown eyes looks at me and I smile. I hurt all over and I'm hungry and I need to use the toilet again. But our locks are closed tight and so we just sit together, alone in our cages.

"I'm Katey," I whisper to the brown-eyed girl. She is closest to me and stares a lot. But she shakes her head and smiles just a little. She doesn't talk back.

I can't move my arm much, but I point my thumb at myself and say again, "Katey."

This time she smiles a bit bigger. "Mariana," she whispers, and jabs her chest with her thumb.

I want to ask Mariana if the hairy bear-like man hurt her last night, but I don't know the words she uses in Spanish and I'm afraid to know what she will say. Will I have to do that to him tonight? I don't know if I can.

The other girls whisper more, but no one wants to be loud. Every minute Maestra is gone is good. Sometimes I hear shouting and things breaking upstairs and then it is silent again.

Through the window I see the sunlight has changed. It is weaker through the dirt and I know that night is coming. I decide I will stare at the light and the muddy smudges until there is no more light at all. But a face in the window staring back at me makes me jump and rattle my cage.

Suddenly the window pops and swings on a hinge so it is bent at an angle and the face I saw pops through.

"Jonas?" I say, forgetting to whisper.

He smiles so big and beautiful at me that I almost forget I'm locked in this dog cage. But I can't get out to help him through the window. Instead he seems to grab on to the thin air and dangle his feet before dropping to the ground. All the girls are holding their breath and staring. We all listen and my heart beats like a hammer in my ears. But no one upstairs seems to notice Jonas has arrived.

Chapter Twenty-Six

With Amy down the stairs and out of sight, John turned his full attention to Ruckus, Kohlhaas, and the two guards. Their machine guns now useless and thrown to the side, they closed in around their boss and got in ready stances to fight. John took a deep breath. It had been a while since he'd taken on opponents their size, but he was ready. Adrenaline pumped through his body like an elixir, warming his muscles and focusing his mind.

As he came around the counter to stand by Ruckus, a movement to the right caught his eye. Three separate bodies formed from the shadows edging the room. They became, birthed from darkness into solid masses that grew as tall as Ruckus. Whereas the angel emanated light, these creatures devoured it, existing as darkness and void at the same time. Once they were fully formed and walking with purposeful strides toward Ruckus and John, he could see that their features were twisted and marred, their skin gray and dull. Their wings, blacker than any night John had ever seen, were deformed with lumps, rips and ungrowth. Demons. They had once been beautiful, John thought. They had once stood in the Father's presence and loved him, served him. But evil had corrupted them, transformed them into hideous caricatures of the glorious creatures they had once been. They existed now as false versions of themselves, adrift in the universe their Creator had made without being united with their Creator. John almost felt moved to pity them. Almost. But one look in their eyes, glowing red like coals from the fires of Hell, and he knew that whoever they'd been before was no more and who they were now sought destruction and death. And his name was on their blistered lips.

Ruckus moved so quickly John didn't have a chance to think through their motions. In a fast swirl of light and darkness, John found himself back to back with his guardian angel. John faced Kohlhaas and his thugs. Ruckus faced the demons assigned to protect them. The eight of them eyed one another, perceiving strengths and weaknesses, guessing at abilities. Their enemies, all on the perimeter, began pacing a slow circle around John and Ruckus, who turned with them, remaining back to back.

Out of the corner of his eye John saw one of the demons give a mock bow to Ruckus. When he spoke, his voice was gritty, like glass underfoot in gravel. "Ruckus, my old friend, congratulations to you and the others for a splendid attack. Truly, it has been a pleasure to watch."

"Vier, I have not been your friend for many ages. But on behalf of our King, I do thank you for the compliment."

John heard the demon spit. When the spittle hit the floor, it sizzled. "The Christ is not my King. My allegiance is to Satan. He is the rightful King of this wretched planet. Man is his pawn. Leave them to us."

"Your ruler still has rights to Man for a little while longer. But not the ones that bear the mark of King Jesus. They are not your master's and they are not yours. Back off, Vier."

They all continued their slow circle. With each word coming from the demon's mouth, John could see the skin pallor of the guards becoming more and more pale, their eyes becoming wider from fear and sudden, terrible understanding of how wrong they'd really been. Kohlhass, on the other hand, seemed to be enjoying the exchange immensely, mollified and satisfied with the false pretense of power the demons projected.

"We don't need rights of ownership to manipulate and persuade them, Ruckus. We have our assignments. You can't stop us."

"I can stop you. And I will."

John realized Ruckus was finished talking when the metallic ring of his giant broadsword pulled from its scabbard cut the air in a dissonant chord. The guards shifted their eyes from John to the sword and he took advantage of their distraction. With his left leg he landed a kick square in the chest of one guard while his right elbow jammed into the throat of the other. John swiftly followed his elbow with the back of his fist, smashing the man's nose. Blood poured from his nostrils and ran in two streams down his chin, dripping onto his t-shirt like tye dye.

The first guard recovered from being thrown off-balance and came at John with his fists. Blood still poured from the second guard's nose, but he joined the two-on-one boxing match nonetheless. John parried and blocked, launching his own fists again and again into jaws and eye sockets, hard abdominal walls and forearms. He felt their fists pounding his temples, his stomach, and his arms, but he realized after a few blows, their efforts were half-hearted at best.

Behind him Ruckus moved like fluid power. He could hear the angel's mighty sword slicing through the air with a whoosh and ringing like a deathly bell against the demons' swords. He heard Ruckus breathe in deeply and then the sound of water freezing and cracking under pressure filled the room. In the same instant, he heard a demon screech in pain and lash out in a guttural language John had never heard. The sound sent chills up his spine. Ruckus fought not just with physical means, but with supernatural forces as well.

John blinked sweat from his eyes and judged his two opponents, still coming at him from both sides, but doing so with reluctance. They were still trading punches and bruises back and forth, but John's thoughts hung on his weapons of choice versus Ruckus'. Fear danced like a writhing creature in the eyes of these men. What more could John bring to this combat, when two men's souls hung in the balance?

"You don't have to do this," John said, huffing the words out between breaths and blocks.

The guards said nothing, but both landed two solid punches against his ribs. John gritted his teeth against the pain and tightened his elbows. "This man," he panted, "isn't your King. He's a boss man, like so many others. He doesn't care about you. Doesn't love you. Would kill you himself if it suited him."

With those last words the guards stepped back, breathing hard. The one bleeding from his nose wiped at the slowing stream. John knew he'd hit a nerve. Keeping his block in place, he tried again. "Look at him. He doesn't care if you live or die. He hasn't lifted a finger to protect you."

"Shut up!" Kohlhaas screamed from his position against the counter. He was enjoying the show and seemed to have no intentions of jumping in the fray. He motioned with two fingers. "Tötet ihn."

The two guards resumed their attack, forcing John into the offensive as well. They traded punches back and forth, sweat and blood beginning to fly out from their fists and hair. John grimaced as his right knuckle ripped open after catching on a tooth from the bleeding guard, who kept spitting blood out of his mouth. That guard's head snapped backward and he raised it slowly, shaking away the dizziness. John was conscious of the still swinging sword arcing down and back up, meeting demonic swords and scaly armor. He heard the sound of rocks sliding and fire crackling. It wasn't sorcery. It was the power of God unleashed, sound becoming matter.

Again, he tried to reach the guards. "Repent," he said. "God loves you. He will accept you still. You don't have to die for this scumbag. He won't lift a finger to help you. Would you risk eternal damnation for him?"

The guards breathed hard, sweat trickling down the sides of their faces, now blooming with swelling and bruises from John's fists. His left eye was swelling shut quickly, but he willed himself to focus on them. "Walk away. Say these words: 'Forgive me, Jesus, for my sins. I repent and turn away from evil. I will serve Satan no more and instead turn to you. Fill my heart, Jesus. I am yours.'"

The guards did not strike out at him, but Boris Kohlhaas did. Flying forward from the counter, he head-butted John with the force of a cement block, knocking John's skull backward into the equally hard armor of the angel warrior pressed against him. Ruckus' wings, tucked in close to his body, buffered the hit, but John still felt the room spin as a wave of nausea knocked into him with the same debilitating force as the pain in his head.

John went down on his knees, trying to get his bearings. He instinctively blocked his head with his forearms, waiting for the next hit. When it came, he would probably lose consciousness. He hoped Ruckus would be able to protect him from a fatal blow. But the hit didn't come. Instead, John heard a scuffle that turned into a different kind of fight as the two guards that had been saving face before their employer by fighting John switched their allegiance.

Bracing his hands on the polished wood floor, John looked up, allowing his eyes to come into focus. The two bloodied guards held Kohlhaas, their biceps bulging against his wicked twists and kicks. He cursed them to Hell in three languages, calling them every foul name he could think of. He swore to kill them in a number of different ways and swore to seek his vengeance on their families. The guards said nothing. Not one word.

Instead they held his arms behind his back and used their legs to sweep his feet out from under him, pinning him to the floor. One of them sat on his back and kept his wrists held taut while the other placed a heavy boot against Kohlhaas' face, bearing down with his body weight.

Behind him John heard the sound of battle between Ruckus and the three demons cease. Easing up on his haunches, John felt the whirl of the room begin to still. His head pounded and he still felt sick, but at least he could focus his vision. Behind him Ruckus moved to the side so that he could take in the whole scene at once. John heard the smile in his voice. "The tide of the battle has turned."

His gritty voice winded from fighting, the demon called Vier responded. "He is ours. You know his mark. Let us kill his body and take him off your hands."

John stood, looking from the demons' gray faces, grotesque and furious, to Ruckus' calm expression. "He is not yours until the Father's judgment is complete. And you know, as well as I, that the death of his body has been assigned to me."

Vier spat again, the liquid sizzling on contact with the floor. "Then finish it."

John watched Ruckus' expression change from a picture of serene calmness to one of horrible fury in less than a second. "You do not order me, Pawn of Satan. You will cease to speak in my presence!"

Clearly the angel's patience was wearing thin with the demons sent to fight him. Though outmatched in every way, they seemed intent on needling Ruckus. He wondered briefly at the history between the three demons and his guardian angel. How well had they known one another before the Fall? How many battles had they fought on the same side and then on opposite sides?

Before he could consider that thought further, Ruckus moved to kneel at Kohlhaas' head. The man, unable to move with the weight of his two guards bearing down on his head and back, squeezed his eyes shut, refusing to take in the splendor projected by the warrior angel. Ruckus ignored him as well and focused on the two guards.

"You have yet to speak the words. You will walk away from this tonight either way. But you must choose life with, or without. I implore you to confess the Christ as Savior and submit to his authority. If you repent of your iniquity and turn away from it all, things will get better for yourselves and your families." He paused, looking at each man. He focused on the one seated on top of Kohlhaas. "Nikolai, you were a believer once. You began your life in the presence of God. But you turned away from him that terrible night. You know the one of which I speak. And you need to hear this: It was not your fault. Her blood is not on your hands."

John watched, amazed, as the guard's eyes turned watery. He did not lessen his grip on his employer, but he lowered his head and nodded, blood still dripping from his nose and a cut above his eyebrow. "He loves you still, Nikolai," Ruckus said.

Kohlhaas erupted into screams of cursing and thrashed his body around, trying to get the upper hand and shut the mouth of the angel who continued to encourage his mercenaries to mutiny. Ruckus placed one large hand on the side of Kohlhaas' scarred face and swiped his thumb across the man's lips. It was a gentle caress, or seemed to be. But where the angel's thumb touched, flesh burned to flesh. Kohlhaas tried to scream, his agony great. But his lips melted together so quickly, so fully, his horror was muffled into sobs. This man's time was done.

John saw no remorse in Ruckus' eyes and it was in that moment that the judgment of the Father became a real and terrible truth. The words were spouted in sermons. The feelings evoked from the thought of judgment were even real. But the harsh reality of the final, terrible moment when God turns away from Man knocked the breath from John's lungs. Kohlhaas had been given life and free will. His choices had been made and his time was up. This small moment was nothing in comparison with the day coming for all men. John knew it with certainty in his gut. That Day of Judgment, that real and terrible day of fairness and just responses, would be a chasm of pain and agony that would blight the world's history like no other.

With that in mind, John stepped forward. He laid his hand on the one Ruckus had called Nikolai. "Brother, will you turn from this madness? Believe what you know in your heart. Not what this monster has led you to believe."

Nikolai turned his watery gaze to John's. "I have done things," he said, his voice breaking. "I have done things for this man I cannot even speak. God cannot love me beyond what I have done."

"Yes, he can. He hates what you've done. But he loved you even when you were doing those horrible things. He loves you still. Will you accept his love?"

The guard let out a trembling breath and nodded. He tightened his thighs so that Kohlhaas couldn't move and lifted his hands to Heaven. Words poured out of his mouth in his mother tongue of German and John prayed with him in English, lifting up his new brother and thanking God for an eleventh hour salvation.

Ruckus rested his gold eyes on the other guard. "What say you, Rutger?"

John turned his attention to the other man, who still stood with his boot propped up on Kohlhaas' blistered face. He had watched his friend's salvation silently as tears rolled down his cheeks. He took a shuddering breath. "I cannot."

"Why?" John asked.

"You don't know who I am."

"God knows."

"That's why I can't come to him. He knows. He knows everything."

"What have you done that you think God cannot forgive?"

Rutger did not shift his weight off his employer's face, but he lifted his hands in front of his own and turned them palms-up. He did not look at John, but stared at his hands. "Do you know what my job is? What I am called?"

"No," John said. He watched Ruckus look over his shoulders to the windows lining the walls of the ground level of the castle. He could hear it then. The battle had turned ferocious. The sharp clang of swords and the crackle of close fire split John's attention from Rutger. He could smell the smoke and hear more explosions rocking the castle walls.

"I am the Butcher."

His words sunk into John's flesh like the embers that fell outside. But Rutger wasn't finished. "Knives," he said, "are like extensions of my hands. I'm good. Too good. And when I met Boris, my tastes took on a particular flavor."

"What do you mean?"

"I carve the flesh of Jews and Christians. It is my gift."

John reeled from Rutger's words. He wanted to vomit on the man's resting boot or tackle him to the floor before snapping his neck. But the dead tone of sorrow and acceptance gave John pause.

"I hate what you've done," he said. "And Jesus hates it even more."

Rutger nodded, accepting the judgment. "Keep going," the German man said. "That's not enough."

Then John realized the twisted truth living in Rutger's mind. He could not fathom accepting the grace and love of God without first being punished. He could not allow himself love without first experiencing retribution.

John shook his head, aware that the sounds of battle outside the castle had grown louder and closer. "It doesn't work that way, Rutger. God will judge your actions. Of that you can't escape any more than I can. But accepting Jesus as King and Savior is your new gift. It's one he gives you freely. And if you accept it, it will cancel out the gift you were given by Satan. You will no longer have the gift of butchery. He will give you something different, something beautiful. Something that will honor him and bring you life."

Rutger continued to stare at his palms. "A different gift?" he asked. "I could cancel out the gift of death?"

"Yes."

"But I have persecuted his people. I have hurt them, killed them in despicable ways. So many children." His voice broke.

Ruckus interrupted. "We're out of time."

"Wait," John said. "Give him one more minute."

"We don't have a minute." Ruckus pushed Rutger aside and picked up Kohlhaas by his neck. The man, his mouth melted together like a figure out of a Dalí painting, looked terrified. John felt no pity.

Rutger, having been brushed aside, looked at John, his eyes wide. "You promise me? If I turn to God right now he will not kill me immediately?"

"I promise."

"And my family? Will they be safe?"

"Yes. But you must turn from this life and embrace a life with Jesus. And lead your family to him as well."

Rutger turned his back to Kohlhaas, who began his struggles again. Hitting his knees and raising his hands, the German man gave his life to Jesus.

Ruckus nodded, then turned to John, his voice soft. "That's good, John. I feel the joy of the Father in this. Those two," he nodded to Rutger and Nikolai, who had come over to embrace his friend, "can be like Saint Paul. I will pray it is so."

John looked at them, nodding. Of all the people he ever led to Christ, these two men would certainly be the most memorable. Narrowly missing a boot from the still struggling Kohlhaas, John sighed. "What about him?"

"His body will die and he will be taken before the Father." He nodded his head toward the three demons who had backed themselves up against the far wall during the salvations of Nikolai and Rutger. "They will receive him after."

The back door of the kitchen flew open and two more angels stepped into the castle. Their eyes, alight with the excitement of battle, zeroed in on the scene and took it in while walking quickly to Ruckus, who still held Kohlhaas suspended by the neck. One of them stood in front of the three demons, his sword drawn and ready. The other grabbed Kohlhaas by the shoulders, then laid him down on the countertop where Kohlhaas had laid the match and the stub of his last cigarette.

The man struggled, but the angel holding him laid one arm across his legs and one arm across his chest. His strength and size made Kohlhaas' struggle a waste of energy. Kohlhaas looked at the three demons, as if asking or demanding help from the ones he thought had been so powerful. They looked back, smiling in wicked enjoyment of bloodlust.

Ruckus turned to John. "You don't have to watch this."

John walked over to Nikolai and Rutger, placing his hands on their shoulders. "It's okay. I think we need to see the final outcome."

Ruckus nodded, then came to stand over Kohlhaas. His sword rested against his right thigh. "Boris Kohlhaas, son of Aldus, do you continue to deny King Jesus?"

John held his breath. Even this one, he thought, gets one last opportunity. Kohlaas stared hard at Ruckus, then closed his eyes and turned his face away. The angel nodded, lifting his sword and speaking one last time. "Be it as you say. Prepare to meet him."

In one mighty swing, Ruckus dropped the sword on the man's neck, severing his head from his body. The head flew across the room, spinning in bloody circles and coming to rest at the feet of the demons who had claimed him already. Their triumphant smile sent shivers down John's spine. He felt the men beside him shudder.

Still smiling, the demons retreated, melting into the shadows in the corners of the room until they had dissipated completely. Once their presence fully dissolved, John noticed the room brightened, even though there was still no power to the castle.

The angel who had positioned himself between the demons and the rest of the group sheathed his sword, then walked over to the severed head and picked it up. He strode straight to the front doors and as he neared them, the doors blew open as if forced by a tempest wind. Through the open doors John could see angels and demons in hand to hand combat, swords clashing, supernatural fire and ice sparking between them as their words became matter. The angel, resplendent in his crimson and gold armor and his ruby-colored hair, stood on the top step and held Kohlhaas' head high in the air. "Behold," he yelled, "the head of the snake!"

John heard cheers and hisses erupt from the warriors of Heaven and Hell. Each one stopped fighting. There was a momentary pause in all activity and then, just as the demons had dissipated into the shadows of the room, the ones on the grounds outside melted into the shadows of the grass and the woods surrounding the castle.

John turned to Ruckus, who had stepped away from the dead body on top of the counter. The angel who had been holding Kohlhaas down for his execution placed one hand on the man's chest, now soaked through with the emptied blood from his body. When he lifted his hand, an ethereal light came forward from the corpse and became the image of a man. Kohlhaas, in spirit form, stood beside the angel. Grasping him firmly by the arm, the angel led him into a portal that opened automatically. They stepped inside, and the portal closed. On the other side, John knew, Jesus would deny him as he had denied the King. The judgment of the head of the snake would be complete.

Chapter Twenty-Seven

Amy followed Harbor up the brick stairway that led to the kitchen. Above them she could hear men talking, then she jumped at the sound of a large sword crashing against ceramic tile. She felt Harbor's hand briefly touch hers before the sounds of battle got louder and one lone voice rose above the din: *Behold, the head of the snake!*

Amy felt her whole body sag against the wall. They'd done it. They'd killed Kohlhaas. The twelve children in line behind her were safe. Now she just had to get them to the relief workers R.P. said would be on the scene. On the heels of her relief, however, came a sudden fear. John. Her heartbeat tripped into a triple time staccato rhythm. Amy wanted to run the rest of the way up the stairs and see for herself that he was alive and well. Instead, she hung back as Harbor inched her way up to the doorway and silently filled it, taking in the scene before her and blocking Amy's view.

She tried to remain patient, but she was as anxious as the children behind her to get out of Kohlhaas' dungeon. A full minute ticked by before Harbor turned back to Amy, meeting her gaze. A small upward tilt to the angel's full mouth was all the emotion Harbor showed. Her words filled in the rest. "It is done."

The angel stepped aside as John's form filled the doorway. Before Amy could give herself a chance to rethink her immediate response, she took the last two steps in one leap and landed in his arms. He held her tight against him, showering the crown of her head in feathery kisses. He pulled back and ran his palm lightly down her cheek. "Are you okay?" he asked.

It was then Amy took in his battered face, his left eye swollen completely shut. Blood splattered his shirt and his knuckles were busted. "John! I'm fine but you're not okay at all."

"Sure I am," he said. "Just a few scrapes and bruises. Believe me it was all worth it."

He pulled her out of the doorway and wrapped his arm around her waist as he focused his attention on the children waiting quietly in the shadows of the stairwell. She felt his breath catch in his chest at the sight of them as Harbor, Vela, Kapas and Langis led them up and into the kitchen, their bloodied sheets dragging the floor behind them.

His voice shook as he spoke to them. "You're safe now," he said. "I swear on my life you are safe."

Ruckus came forward, sheathing his sword as he did. "We must move them now. The Hammer is about to be released."

Amy was about to ask what The Hammer was when, out of the wide open front doors, she saw and felt the monstrous feet of the mighty one move forward to the castle walls. The Hammer was probably aptly named, she decided, grabbing the hand of the nearest child and leading her out of the back door they had come in.

The battle now over, their path was lined on each side by mighty warrior angels. Their faces were marred with earth and some small cuts and wounds from battle. But pride gleamed in their eyes and love reverberated from their bodies even stronger than the word itself. As one, they all unsheathed their mighty swords and let their blades meet in the middle, forming an arc of safe passage to the back gate of the castle where R.P. stood, hands loose at his sides, a victorious smile on his face.

The children, each in their own language, greeted and smiled at the angels, who greeted them in return. One by one, an angel broke rank and fell into step beside each child and Amy realized that while each of them had been chained and tortured, their angels had not stopped fighting for their release. They'd never been abandoned and had never escaped the Father's gaze. He'd planned an elaborate scheme involving both physical and spiritual forces in order to get them back. Nothing could stand against the Once and Coming King.

On the other side of the gate the children suddenly halted. Some of them began walking back toward the castle or hiding behind the massive legs of the angels who stood by their sides. Amy rushed forward, ready to tackle whatever stood between the children and their freedom.

By her side, John grabbed her hand as she pushed her way forward and saw two men standing before the children, who looked visibly shaken and scared. Amy realized in horror that the two men were some of their captors. She tried to break out of John's grasp. "No!" she yelled. "We can't let them hurt these children anymore!"

"Amy," John said, "it's okay. They won't hurt them. They're with us now."

Instead of holding her back, he took her with him to stand in front of the two large men who spoke now in German to the children. Amy could not understand their words, but she saw the tears in their eyes and their hands raised in surrender as they both knelt on their knees before the children they had tortured. Over and over she heard the two men say, "Verzeiht mir, verzeiht mir."

Amy watched in awe as one by one, each child came forward and placed one hand on the top of each man's head. Some of them hesitated and had to close their eyes and consider forgiveness. But each one, grasping the hands of their guardian angels, released forgiveness, no doubt in varying measures, but released nonetheless. As they placed their small hands on the heads of the two men, they passed behind them into the darkness, their white sheets shining in the moonlight and the dying fires surrounding the castle.

But one remained. The smallest child, the young boy not even as old as Jonas, with the cross carved into his chest, stood still in front of his torturer. Amy recognized his angel as Fuente, part of her Heavenly entourage. Her long hair glistened in the moonlight like quicksilver as she stood still and silent beside the child she clearly had guardianship of. The boy did not extend his hand in forgiveness. Instead he held up his index finger and traced the intricate design of the cross halving his chest.

No one moved. The angels standing wingtip to wingtip seemed to be holding one collective breath. The man to the side of the boy began what sounded like a fervent prayer. The man before the child reached down into his boot and removed a knife.

Amy gasped and felt John immediately tense and jump forward to knock the knife from the man's hand. But he stopped when the man met his gaze. "I will not hurt him. I promise."

Amy watched as he ripped open his shirt, tearing it from top to bottom and letting the shreds hang at his sides. "I must do this," the man whispered.

"Rutger, no. You don't have to." John held out his hand but the man ignored him, plunging the knife into his skin. Amy's stomach turned as the knife began its slow course across and down his chest, blood pouring in a thick flow that soaked his jeans and pooled on the ground. The man made no sound save the gasps of air he pulled in with each sob. The boy watching made no sound at all. Neither angel, man, woman or child turned away as the man called Rutger marked himself with the sign of the cross, double lines around its outside edges, its corners sharp. In the center of the cross and over his breastbone he carved one more design. The Star of David. When he was satisfied, the knife dropped from his trembling hand and Rutger bowed his head down to the ground, kissing the feet of the boy before him.

Tears flowed down Amy's cheeks as well as John's, who came back to her side and held her hand in his. They watched as the boy bent over the top of Rutger's form and kissed the crown of his head. In English, he spoke the words over the man's head like a healing balm. "Now we are the same."

With that the boy walked into the shadows with the other children, R.P. leading them directly to a group of people who had emerged from the tree line. In their hands they held out blankets to the children as R.P. spoke with the relief workers.

Amy's attention was broken from the group as she saw Kapas and Langis reach out a hand and bring the two Germans to their feet. They both held their vials over the men's heads and let the crystal liquid pour over them, showering them in what turned to glittering gold oil that soaked their hair and skin as it ran in rivulets down their faces and chests. Before her eyes their bruises faded, their swollen knots dissipated, and the carved cross and star on Rutger's chest stopped bleeding. The deep grooves in his skin fused once more becoming a thick braided scar, raised and forever imprinting him as Christian.

Before she could ask, Amy saw Vela come up behind John and the same gold poured over his head and down his face, soaking his blood-stained t-shirt and relieving him of every bruise and cut. His left eye opened, no longer swollen shut, and he smiled at Amy, squeezing her hand and bringing it up to his lips for a kiss.

He released her hand, then went forward and hugged both German men in tight embraces before accepting two coils of rope from Ruckus and binding their hands. They did not ask for release, but instead voluntarily moved behind him toward the relief workers. They wanted to help the children in every way, including turning themselves into the German and international authorities, fully cooperative. Amy marveled at the details of King Jesus' battle plan. She remembered sitting with Rapa around the Stone Table and hearing him say that more than just Katey could be saved through this adventure she was on. He was right.

Harbor touched her right shoulder. "The Hammer has been given release. It's time to move."

Amy glanced up at the massive warrior who stood above the towering peaks of the castle. His fists, which looked to be roughly the size of *Volkswagens*, rose. Amy took off at a run toward the tree line as the rest of the Army of the Lord, this battle complete, dissipated like mist into the moonlight.

Chapter Twenty-Eight

R.P. moved the group further into the trees. It was clear the relief workers could see him and every human present, but were not given sight to perceive the angels in their midst. John glanced back through the trees and was treated to the sight of The Hammer beginning his work. Timber, roofing, bricks, stones, and glass shattered and went flying in every direction. The sound of the destruction was great and shook the ground beneath their feet. The relief workers began to panic, but R.P. kept them moving, stating it was most likely a little seismic activity.

Realizing his pocket was buzzing, John pulled out his cell phone and caught R.P.'s eye. The saint nodded and John answered. "Yates here."

"I've been calling you for forty-five minutes. Where are you, man?"

"It's good to talk to you, too, Chuck. I missed the sultry sounds of your voice."

"Cut the crap. Seriously, where are you?"

John glanced around. His partner wouldn't believe him even if he told him. "Doing some field work. What have you got for me?"

"A body."

John felt the blood drain from his face. *Please, Jesus. Not Katey. Not when we're so close.* "Who?"

"Andrew Dodson."

John let out a breath. "Tell me."

"We found the maroon van. Forensics has dusted it down. Katey's prints are in it as well as his."

"Where was it?"

"Off the beaten path between Hendersonville and Gallatin. A hunter came across it and called it in based on the Amber Alert we issued for Katey."

"How did he die?"

"Gunshot through the forehead. Looks like it was done about noon today. "

Well that's one way to get rid of evidence, John thought. "I want to know everything the coroner can give me. I want to know what he ate for breakfast this morning. Everything."

"We're already on it." He hesitated. "Listen, I don't know what's going on with you today, but seriously, you need to reengage. The chief is breathing down my neck about you. I don't know what he suspects, but you need to get here."

No doubt the chief had gotten some interesting news from Interpol. "Trust me. I've been engaged all day. Just off the grid."

"Get on the grid."

"Hang on." John put his palm over the phone and watched the relief workers take the children on through the trees with Nikolai and Rutger following obediently behind, seemingly content with their situation. Two more angels had joined their entourage, one beside each reborn man. After one last wave, Amy turned back to John and she and R.P. made their way to him. He briefly updated them and R.P. nodded.

"Tell Chuck you'll meet him at 11997 Tin Penny Road in twenty minutes. He's going to need some back up."

John blinked. "Is that where Katey is?"

"Yes."

John's mind clicked into high gear. "Chuck," he said into the phone, "I have reliable information on Katey Johnson's current location. I need you to come in hot and quiet." He relayed the rest of the information to Chuck and disconnected before his partner could ask any more questions. He rolled his shoulders backwards and forwards, the adrenaline already surging through his body once again.

He made the mistake of looking down at Amy, who was as pale as the snow under her feet. No doubt she was thinking about Jonas, who had been taken to the third battle site without her. John didn't hesitate. He pulled her tightly to his chest and hugged her, closing his eyes to enjoy the feel of her body curled against his in a perfect fit. He whispered against her ear. "Let's go, sweetheart. Let's end this thing."

R.P. laid one hand on each shoulder and John gasped as electricity surged through his body and made the whole world topsy-turvy for the space of two seconds. Instead of walking through the portal, this time the light enveloped them in a dizzying, mind-bending squeeze that pulsed through John's body in a powerful energy burst. Then just as suddenly as it had happened, everything was still and R.P. removed his hands from their shoulders.

John let go of Amy and looked around. He knew without asking where they were. It was cool north of Nashville, but not nearly as cold as Germany had been. The sun was just beginning its downward descent. Hidden behind the rusted shell of an old tractor, John looked around. A large farmhouse, old and in disrepair with a sagging roof and peeling white siding sat squat between four gnarled oaks. The remains of a barn sat behind it and an unmarked eighteen-wheeler was parked between. John wanted to slash every tire to insure no child would be leaving in it anytime soon. He glanced at R.P. who was focused on a lone figure walking across the field between the house and their hiding spot amid the junked farm machinery and cars dotting the land.

Amy's eyes narrowed. "That's not Shake. Where is he? R.P., where's my son?"

"Everything is going to be okay, Amy," R.P. said. "Let's get caught up on what's going on here."

Amy chewed on her upper lip and wrapped her arms around herself. John watched the figure approach, his quick strides eating up the distance across the field, scattering a flock of birds into the cold evening breeze. His buzzed blonde hair finally pinged John's memory as the same saint that had blown apart the back gate and the door to the basement at Kohlhaas' castle.

R.P. held out his hand to the saint warrior and they clasped forearms. "Shalom, brother," R.P. said.

"Shalom," he replied, nodding at Ruckus and Harbor, who had materialized beside them before locking his eyes on John and Amy. "I'm Seamus, by the way. Didn't have a chance to introduce myself before. Some fun we're having, eh?"

John shook his hand and smiled. "Some fun."

Amy could not hold it in any longer. "Where is Jonas?"

Seamus held her gaze. "He is waiting with Princess Katey."

"He's with Katey? You already rescued her?"

"Not exactly."

"Then what do you mean? How is Jonas with her if she's still being held?"

"He voluntarily gave up his freedom to be with her until her rescue."

Amy's already pale complexion whitened so dramatically John reached out and pulled her up against his side in case she lost consciousness. "But Shake said he would take care of him. He promised!"

R.P. stepped forward to get Amy's attention. "He's keeping his promise, Amy. Jonas will be fine. I give you my word."

Seamus, every inch the soldier saint R.P. was, put a steady hand on her arm. "We have everything under control. Jonas is fine. In fact," his eyes danced, "he's running the show quite impressively."

It was John's turn to be surprised. "Jonas is running the show?"

Seamus nodded, "And doing so very well."

"I don't understand," Amy said. "Why is Jonas in charge? He's six years old."

R.P. and Seamus exchanged a look. "True," Seamus said, "but then he's not like most other six year olds, is he?"

John watched Amy's mouth fall open. "A Torchbearer," she whispered. "Jonas is a Torchbearer, too."

She said it as a statement to R.P., who nodded and smiled at her. "Now you're with us."

John looked back and forth between the soldier saints and Amy. "I'm lost. What's a Torchbearer?"

Amy wiped away a tear. "A Torchbearer carries the Light of God into the world more so than the rest of us do. They bring Heaven to Earth, light to darkness. Katey is a Torchbearer and that's why we were sent to save her. I just didn't realize Jonas was one as well. I feel foolish. It all makes so much sense now."

"Don't feel foolish," R.P. said. "Feel proud."

"I agree," Seamus said. "If you could see him in there now, you'd be amazed."

"What is he doing?" John asked.

R.P. and Seamus glanced back at the farmhouse. "Let's get into position," R.P. said. "Then you can see for yourselves."

"What about Chuck? He's bringing in SWAT, the Chief, TSP, everyone. The whole world is about to descend on this place."

Seamus winked. "I guess we better hurry then."

Katey – Part Ten

Jonas has snuggled himself up around my cage and is holding my fingers through the bars. "Are you okay?" he asks.

"I'm better now," I say, squeezing his fingers. Mariana looks at him with wide eyes and I know she wants what I want. "Do you think you can get me out? And the other girls, too?"

Jonas looks around at our dog cages and there is no smile on his face. He looks up and then back at me. "We'll do it," he says.

"Who's we?" I ask. "You and me?"

"Nope," he says. "Me and Shake."

"Who's Shake?"

Jonas grins like his cat, Dog, after he's had tuna and a belly rub. He reaches his fingers into my cage as far as they can go and says, "Lean your head into my hands, Katey. I'm going to pray for you."

That sounds good to me so I lean my head over, ignoring the hairs that get yanked and hang loose from the metal bars. I feel his fingers on my scalp and his words wash over me like water. He prays for my body and then asks Jesus to open up my eyes so I can see the angels.

When he's done and I open my eyes I can't stop the squeal that pops out. The other girls shush me but I just stare. There are huge glowing angels with big swords and even bigger smiles standing all around the room. One beside each cage, two by the stairs, and one more beside Jonas. The angel stands big and pretty and his eyes are like blue waters. I'm even more surprised, though, to see the beautiful face of the woman in my dreams. Her spiky green hair and dark gray eyes give her away and I can't imagine anything prettier than her.

"Angels," I whisper. "Lots of them!"

Jonas pulls his fingers out of the cage and says, "I have so much to tell you, Katey. I've had the biggest adventure ever! And now you get to be part of it. Isn't that awesome?"

"Yeah," I say, "so can you get me out of here?"

My green-haired angel laughs and the sound is like bells and birds chirping and waves on the beach. She tells me her name is Thistle and says I should watch the lock on my cage. I do and I see that she stares at it with me. Then she opens her mouth and a sound comes out that is glass breaking on my mother's kitchen floor and metal bending and crumpling in the fender bender me and daddy were in last summer. The sound is big and exact and works like a key that pops the lock right off my cage. She helps me stand and then sweeps me up in a hug that surrounds me in light and beauty. I smell the ocean in her hair and flowers on her skin. Her beauty sinks into me, deep down into my bones, and even though my body still hurts, my heart feels happy.

When she sets me on my feet, Jonas is right there hugging me, too. Then he bends down to each of the girls and prays for God to open their eyes. One by one, they see. They open their eyes big and wide and look at the angels that have come to rescue them. They smile, they laugh, they cry and they are freed. But none of us are scared of the angels. We've had enough of being afraid.

The girls stand with their angels and everyone looks at Jonas and his big guy, Shake. They high-five each other and then Shake stands Jonas up on top of my cage and nods to one of the angels still standing at the bottom of the stairs. I'm not sure what's going to happen next, but I know who's about to come down the stairs.

Thistle takes my hand in hers and leans down to whisper in my ear. "It's alright, Katey. They can't hurt you anymore. Their time is up."

I watch as the angel bangs on the door at the top of the stairs so hard I think the door will fly right off its hinges. Then he stands in front of it and locks his huge arms across his chest. The door slams open and Ponytail Man is there holding his gun. He walks down the stairs right through the angel, swiping his hand in front of his face like he's walked into a spider's web. When he sees us all standing by our cages, he yells up to his partners to come help him. He uses terrible words and calls us all kinds of things. Then his eyes land on Jonas.

"Who are you?"

"Jonas."

"Did you sneak in?"

"Yep."

Ponytail Man laughs. "Free money walking through the door? It's my lucky day."

"I doubt that," Jonas says, and my breath catches in my too-tight chest because I see Ponytail Man point the gun at my best friend and scowl.

"Get in the cage, kid."

But Jonas does not. Instead, he says, "You have one last chance to do the right thing. King Jesus loves you. He hates what you've done, but he loves you. If you repent and turn to him right now, you'll be okay."

Ponytail Man yells again at the others to come down and hear the little preacher who broke into jail. Coca Cola Man and Hairy Bear Man come down behind Maestra. They all look at Jonas who repeats his message for all of them. They laugh and laugh and Ponytail Man starts toward Jonas. Fear fills me up and I want so much to crawl beneath Thistle's wings and hide myself, tiny and quiet, like a ladybug in a closed rose. But Jonas isn't done.

On top of my cage he raises his hands and asks Holy Spirit to open their eyes. They blink once, twice, and then they are all big eyes and open mouths and shouts of total shock. The angel they walked through looms above them with wings spread out so big and wide they cover the whole top of the basement and the stairs and block the doorway. Their guns are in their hands, waving, spinning, pointing this way and that, trying to decide which angel to shoot first.

Shake comes to stand in front of Jonas, who says quietly, "Shake, do it now."

Chapter Twenty-Nine

Amy followed behind R.P., Seamus and John. They ran across the field from one piece of rusted-out farming equipment or junked car to another. Finally they reached the barn and entered from behind. Seamus and R.P. watched the back door of the farmhouse from the shadows by the open double doors of the barn. Wings fluttered in the rafters overhead as a cold wind whistled through the hayloft. Amy held John back for a moment, wrapping her arms around his waist. Forty-eight hours ago she would have cut off her arms before allowing herself such a pleasure. Now, she reveled in it. She let him pull her in close until they touched from thigh to chest to her cheek resting in the hollow of his neck. She let her breath slide across his skin as she whispered, "I want to finish this, John. But I want you to promise me three things."

John buried his face in her hair. "Anything, Sweetheart. Just name it."

"First, I want you to take me and Jonas home so we can sleep the clock around."

He chuckled. "That's a great idea."

"Then I want you to come back to my house first thing tomorrow morning for breakfast with me and Jonas. I'll make a big one."

"With bacon? Gotta have lots of bacon."

"You bet. And buttermilk biscuits."

John sighed and she heard his stomach growl. "And what's the third thing?"

"I want that date night. Just you and me. Take me somewhere romantic."

"You got it, Amy. I'm all yours."

She could feel his pulse pounding just beneath her lips and without stopping to think about possible consequences, she placed one light kiss in the spot her breath had heated. John's palms cupped her face and brought her lips to his in a sweet, slow, deliberate kiss that sent jolts of electricity shooting through her veins. This is what it was meant to feel like, she thought. Peaceful and electrifying, comfortable and exciting. Before she lost herself completely in John's deepening kiss, she realized with sudden clarity that she didn't want to run away or end it before it could begin. She wanted her tomorrows to include John Yates.

They might have been happy to continue the kiss straight into tomorrow were it not for the rumble of laughter coming from the shadows near the front of the barn.

"Y'all about done?" R.P. asked.

Amy pulled away and was happy for the nighttime darkness hiding the blush she knew was creeping up her face.

John sighed. "You know, Ghost, you have the worst timing."

"No, brother, I think that honor goes to you. Why don't you guys try that again after we finish the job?"

John looked down at her. She couldn't see his face but she felt the warmth of his breath move against the curls on her forehead. "You're on," he said.

Amy knew her blush was scarlet and Seamus didn't help matters with a quiet catcalling whistle. All her embarrassment fled in the next moment, however, as a sound unlike anything she'd ever heard broke loose from the direction of the farmhouse. It was the roar of a lion, the chugging howl of a tornado barreling down, and the jarring explosion of rock against rock, all at a decibel that brought Amy to her knees. The earth around them shook with the force and strength of the sound emanating in crushing waves from the farmhouse. The rafters above groaned as the old barn shifted with its rattling foundation.

John sank to his knees beside her, unable to bear the weight of the sound any longer. But she noticed that R.P. and Seamus were running straight to the source of the sound, breaking in the door at the back of the farmhouse with a swift kick and attacking not with guns, but with God.

Slowly the sound died down and Amy hesitantly took her hands down from her ears, still ringing and popping. "What was that?"

Harbor and Ruckus helped them both to their feet. "That's Shake," Harbor said, "doing what he does best."

Amy and John followed their angels to the back door of the farmhouse, Ruckus clearing the doorway before allowing them to enter. The scuffed linoleum led to the kitchen, which was littered with beer cans, take-out food wrappers, and open boxes of cereal spilled across the counters. Lining the walls were empty gallon jugs of orange juice and pharmaceutical boxes of glass vials and syringes.

Bangs and thuds came from below them and suddenly a loud cheer erupted from a door to their left. This time Amy didn't wait for anyone to make sure the coast was clear. She barreled past John and down the stairs, peeking beneath the floor joists as she descended. Ten little girls cheered and hugged their warrior angels, some of whom had swept them up in the air, twirling them like she'd seen the angels do in the Children's Palace in Heaven. Then she saw Jonas, standing on top of a cage, arms raised in triumph, face split in an ear-to-ear grin.

She ran to her son and grabbed him in a hug so tight he finally said, "Mom, you're crushing me!"

She set him down and covered the top of his head with kisses before realizing that Katey stood next to her. She took in the little girl's blonde hair, dirty and limp, the scratches and bites on her skin, and the bruise on her pale face. Amy sank to her knees and held Katey against her, trying not to cry and failing.

"Katey, are you okay?"

"I am now, Ms. Amy."

"Are you sure? We've been trying so hard to get to you. I'm sorry we couldn't get here faster."

"It's okay," Katey said, looking at Thistle. "It's pretty awesome that you brought a bunch of angels with you."

Amy laughed, tucking Katey's blonde wisps behind her ear. "Yes, it is pretty awesome."

Katey looked over Amy's shoulder and asked, "What are you going to do with them?"

Amy turned to see three men and a woman held beneath the boots of four warrior angels, whose swords were drawn and held high, waiting for provocation. R.P. and Seamus picked up a handful of zip ties from the disheveled bed and handed them to John, who happily bound the hands and feet of the kidnappers and recited their Miranda rights.

"I think the police are going to take care of them, honey."

No sooner had Amy said the words than black boots appeared on the stairs, followed by the men who wore them and the guns they carried. With the appearance of the police, the angels turned to their girls and began whispering in their ears. Amy watched as Thistle spoke quickly and Katey nodded. Once they'd finished talking, the angels waved their hands in front of the children's eyes and stepped away. All but Katey and Jonas seemed to lose the ability to see the angels entirely. Amy wondered how long they would remember who had really rescued them from their captors. Forever or just until they were questioned?

An African American man with a Metro Nashville Police Department insignia on his polo stepped forward and clapped John on the back. "Off the grid, huh."

John stood up from kneeling beside his four arrested detainees and shook his hand. "You're late to the party, Chuck."

"You're a hard man to keep up with today."

John gave him a half smile and glanced at Amy. "True enough. You remember Amy and Jonas McEwan?"

Chuck walked around the bed, careful not to touch anything. "Nice to see you again, Ms. McEwan."

"Hi, Chuck."

John bent down in front of Katey and put his hand out to take hers. "Katey, I'm John. Are you alright?"

Katey looked at him and checked with Amy before talking. "I think so. But I don't feel good. I've had a lot of sleepy juice and I want to go home to my momma and daddy. Can you take me?"

John and Chuck exchanged a look. "Katey, you will definitely see your momma and daddy soon. I'll call them myself. But I need you to take a ride in the ambulance and go to the hospital, okay? There are some really good doctors who will make sure the sleepy juice didn't hurt you on the inside."

Katey chewed on the inside of her cheek. "I'd rather go home."

"I know," John said. "But it's really important for us to make sure they didn't hurt you too much."

"She hit me," Katey said. "When she made me watch the bad videos."

Chuck squatted down to her level then. "My name is Chuck, Katey. Will you tell me about all that stuff? So I can know everything that happened?"

"Can I see my momma?"

Chuck nodded. "Mr. John is going to call her while you talk to me and my little tape recorder. That okay?"

Katey agreed and John made the call. Jonas was pulled to the side to talk with another officer, as were each of the girls. Amy's vision clouded over not with tears, but with the face of her King. She closed her eyes and heard love and pride reflected in the timbre of his voice as it circulated like blood through her body. *You are mine, Amy, and you have done well. Your faith is like granite now and no one can take that from you. Well done, my sister, my bride.*

She felt the lion on her neck grow warm and just as deeply as she had felt his words rising in her spirit, she felt something more. Amy McEwan, servant of the Most High and warrior in the Army of the Lord, had just begun.

Chapter Thirty

After calling Angela and David Johnson and delivering the news of their daughter's safety, John helped load up each child in waiting ambulances and sent them off to Vanderbilt Children's Hospital for testing and evaluation. Next came the conversation John had been dreading since first stepping foot through the spiritual vortex that had taken him into the heart of the enemy's camp in Honduras. Had that only been earlier this morning?

Having set up a logistics command center on the hood of an unmarked black sedan, the chief of police had been directing evidence retrieval and interrogation for the last hour. Amy had gone with Jonas and Katey to the hospital where she would meet up with the Johnsons. Chuck stood with Chief Ryan Anderson and they both looked up as John approached.

"John Yates," Chief Anderson said, "just the man I've been waiting to see."

Yates took a deep breath. "Chief, I'd like the opportunity to explain my unusual actions today."

"Good."

"Is there some place a little more private we can talk?"

Chief Anderson raised a gray eyebrow. "You want me to hold your hand, too?"

John cracked a smile. "That won't be necessary, sir. Chuck can do that."

His partner rolled his eyes and fell into step with John and the chief as they walked toward the junked field outside the farm house. John laid the truth out before two of the men he most respected, knowing full well that they would likely not believe a word of it. As he spoke, neither man said a word and John was left wondering not only what they were thinking, but what possible disciplinary actions his boss was considering as John delivered his tale of time-altered intercontinental travel with dead men and supernatural battles fought alongside angels and demons.

When he wrapped up his story, Chief Anderson and Chuck Nichols stared him down, not saying a word. Finally the chief opened his mouth and John braced himself for the inevitable. But Chief Anderson was interrupted by R.P., appearing out of the shadows of the old Chevy farm truck stuck in the weeds beside them.

"He's explained everything as fully as he can," R.P. began, as if he had always been a part of the conversation, "but there's some intel he isn't aware of. I have orders to communicate this information to the three of you at this time."

The chief and Chuck both had their hands on their guns staring wide-eyed at R.P., taking in his black fatigues and the crowned lion sewn into the sleeve. John cleared his throat. "This is the guy I was telling you about. R.P. He used to be a Ranger before he, well, before he--."

"Died," R.P. supplied.

"Right," John said, running his hands through his hair. He decided if the chief's eyebrows shot up any higher, they would reach all the way back to his spine.

"You expect me," Chief Anderson began, "to believe this story as truth, and that the man standing before me is not really real."

"I'm real," R.P. said. "Go ahead and give me a shove."

Chuck glanced back and forth between his boss and John and then reached out a hand to shove R.P. back a step. "See?" R.P. said. "Very real. But also very much a current saint."

No one said a word and John felt sure the tension between them would crack his skull momentarily. So instead of trying to convince his boss, he just motioned to R.P. "So what's the intel you've got for us?"

R.P. waved his hand in the air and the holographic image of a woman appeared between them, suspended in space and rotating like John had seen the face of Kohlhaas do before their attack on his castle. Chuck and the chief jumped back a foot.

"What kind of device is that?" Chuck asked.

"Technically it's not a device," R.P. said. "It's an ability."

"Bull," the chief said.

R.P. quickly rolled up his sleeves and unbuttoned his collar. "See? No cameras, no projectors." He pointed at the image of the woman. "Here's what you need to know about her."

Chuck clicked on his tape recorder. John stared at the woman's face. She was beautiful. Tall, slender, well cared for. Her blonde hair hung straight just past her shoulders and she was dressed in a tan wrap-around dress. Her brown eyes, John noticed, were hardened like the creases bracketing her mouth.

"Amelia Knight is what she goes by in this country. But her given name is Ludmilla Klein. She is second in command to Kohlhaas and heads up the U.S. division of his organization. She is every bit as power hungry as he was and now that he has been eliminated, she is now in charge."

"The snake grew another head," John said.

"Yes," R.P. agreed. "She won't run things exactly like Kohlhaas, though. She isn't as lost to evil and madness as he was. She's searching and in her spirit, she is desperate. We hope to break the darkness from her. If we can't, she will have to make her choice and suffer the consequences as Boris Kohlhaas did. Either way, we have to find her."

Chief Anderson spoke. "Where is she?"

"She was supposed to be here," R.P. said. "But I've checked everything. There's no sign of her. No sign she came at all."

"I'll find out from the perps what they know," Chuck said.

The chief nodded. "Go."

R.P. waved his hand and Ludmilla Klein's image disappeared. He stared at the chief and placed one hand on his shoulder. John watched as R.P. leaned down and spoke quietly into Chief Anderson's ear. The man occasionally nodded and then R.P. stepped back and smiled at the man. Then he turned to John and stuck out his hand. "John, it's been a pleasure."

John took his hand and pulled him in for a hug. "I'm not saying goodbye to you, Ghost. I refuse."

R.P. let loose a rich, goofy laugh that brought a large smile to John's face. "I don't do goodbyes anymore," R.P. said. "So I'll see you around."

John and Chief Anderson watched R.P. walk across the field and disappear into what appeared as a quick flash of lightening. John turned to see his boss regarding him in silent scrutiny.

"Yates," he said, "this whole thing is bizarre. Completely unbelievable. First, I get a call from the NSA on behalf of freaking Interpol and shortly after, I see satellite imagery of my detective, bleeding, and being carried across an underworld lord's compound in Honduras by a key witness in an ongoing investigation when they're both supposed to be in Nashville. Next, no one can get a hold of my detective, not even his partner, with whom he is very rarely out of touch. Then I get some whacked out report, again from the NSA, of a link to some crazy blown up castle in Germany just before I get word that my rogue detective, in an amazing moment of clarity and brilliance, knows exactly where the victim is being held and gives us the precise address. I show up to see four tidily bound kidnappers and a room full of young girls happily released from their hell hole and my rogue detective telling me he's spent the day warping through time with angels and saints and fighting demons. Does that about cover it?"

John scrubbed the stubble on his chin and ran both hands through his hair again. "Pretty much, sir."

Chief Anderson sighed and looked out to the point at which R.P. had disappeared. "You know, I met Jesus not too long ago."

John dropped his hands. "You did?"

"Yes. Surprised?"

"A little. I didn't know, sir."

The chief shrugged. "I was raised an atheist. Never cared one way another about religion and all that hocus pocus stuff. But my wife, who I now know has been praying for me since she met me thirty years ago, has always been a believer. She took the kids to church while I worked all those years. Raised them up in it. Our boy, Nate, became a preacher."

Sudden recognition dawned for John. "Nate Anderson is your son? The pastor at Cross of Hope?"

The chief nodded. "Yeah. And I was there the night he had you come as a guest speaker. I sat in the back so you wouldn't see me. I didn't want him to know I was there, either. Something had changed in me, you know? I've watched you. You do your job well. You're smart and intuitive and you work around the clock when you have to. But do you know when you do your best work?"

"When?"

"When you stare out of the window and look at the parking lot. Your lips move. I've known all along that's when you pray. And do you know what happens after you stare at the parking lot and pray?"

"What?"

"The case breaks within twenty-four hours. Every time."

John felt like he'd been bowled over. But Chief Anderson wasn't finished. "I watched your prayers achieve results over and over again. So when Nate mentioned you were coming to speak, I decided to hear what you had to say."

The chief paused and looked John straight in the eyes. "I heard truth in your story, Yates. Truth from your time in the war and you experienced God by your side in the streets of Baghdad. Truth from the season of your life after you lost your wife and son and almost lost yourself. I know you. You speak truth. And after I heard all that, I drove around town and I thought about it all. Then I prayed. First time ever. And I asked Jesus to help me believe in him, to live inside me like you talked about."

John held his breath and waited for his boss to finish. "Everything changed," he said. "I changed. Because I knew you wouldn't lie. I took a gamble and I met Jesus. Really met him. And I can't believe I've lived all these years in the delusion that he wasn't real."

John nodded. "He is. And sir, I'm honored."

The chief waved his hand and cleared his throat. "I'll see you Monday morning, Yates."

The chief walked back to his field office laid out on the hood of his sedan and John stood under a tapestry of stars, marveling at Father God's ability to put plans into motion weeks, months, and years ahead of time that eventually culminated in the perfect placement of every piece of an outrageous, unbelievable, perfectly ordered series of events that had ended with a startling victory in every possible way.

Chapter Thirty-One

Amy and Jonas had gotten home shortly after midnight. After telling their side of the story to several incredulous officers from Nashville Metro Police and one particularly snide FBI agent, Jonas had been checked out by a pediatrician and declared perfectly fine. As badly as Amy wanted a hot bath, she wanted her bed even more. She carried a sleeping Jonas to his room, stripped him down and covered him up in his super hero sheets and blankets. Her eyes already closing, she fell into her own bed and slept until he jumped on top of her at ten the next morning.

"Mommy!" he squealed. "Wake up! It's late and I'm starving."

She groaned and rolled over, wishing she'd had the chance for two more hours of sleep. Then she remembered her breakfast plans. Would John come? She wondered. Would the light of day make their relationship seem weak and distorted outside of the intense circumstances from which it had been born?

Jonas poked her rib with his toes. "Are you hungry? 'Cause I'm hungry. Can we have bacon?"

She smiled and grabbed his toes, tickling his foot. "Bacon?" she teased as he wiggled and laughed. "Is that all I'm good for?"

Her cell phone chirped. It still sat on charge by her bed where she'd placed it Friday night. A new text message from John flashed on the screen. *Up yet?*

Her heart leaped and hope for the two of them flared. She responded. *Yes. Bring bacon. Lots of it.*

Be there in twenty.

After a speedy shower, Amy threw Jonas in the bathtub and started a pot of coffee. John arrived with two pounds of bacon and a bouquet of *Gerber* daisies. After a hello kiss that lasted until Jonas hollered to be washed up, breakfast was underway. Amy soaked up the sounds in her house, so very different from the previous weekend. Bacon sizzled in the skillet, Jonas laughed while John told silly knock-knock jokes, and Dog purred at her feet.

At the table she slathered Jonas' biscuit in grape jelly and filled John in on what had gone on at the hospital the night before. "I think they had pretty much concluded that most of the girls had minimal physical injuries. Their issues at this point are mainly psychological and emotional. The doctor told Angela Katey would probably be released sometime later today."

John chewed and swallowed. "You know, all things considered, that's really good news. Not perfect, but good."

"I agree."

Jonas pointed a piece of bacon at him. "You should have seen Katey when she saw her parents. She was so excited she jumped right through the air like *Spidey Girl* and her daddy caught her and twirled her around."

John smiled. "That makes me really happy."

They ate a few moments in silence and Amy had just taken a large mouthful of coffee when the air split open beside them and Harbor, Shake and Ruckus appeared, dwarfing her eat-in dining area and kitchen.

Choking on her coffee, Amy threw down her napkin. "You all have got to stop doing that! For crying out loud, knock on the door or something!"

They all smiled back at her, unoffended and unaffected by her words. Jonas gave Shake an enthusiastic high five and offered his angel a biscuit, which Shake politely refused. John tilted his chair back and regarded his angel with a half-smile.

"Something tells me this isn't a social call."

Ruckus and Harbor nodded, settling their hulking frames into relaxed stances, hands at rest on the hilts of their swords. "You're correct," Ruckus said.

"You know I'm off duty, right?" John teased. "Maybe you could come back tomorrow."

Amy looked at Harbor's kind and beautiful face, noticing that her dark violet eyes were hooded in furrowed brows. "What's going on?"

"We have found Ludmilla Klein," Harbor said.

"Who's that?" Amy asked. John filled her in on R.P.'s intel and Amy took another sip of coffee, grumbling around the rim about snakes growing two heads.

"Where is she and what can we do about it?" John asked.

"It's going to be tricky and we have to move fast," Ruckus said. "She is planning to take Katey once more. Today. Before she leaves the hospital."

Amy thunked her mug back on the table. "Why Katey? Why can't these people leave her alone?"

"Her father's recent success as a songwriter has enlarged his finances considerably," Harbor explained. "Once Andrew Dodson flagged him and targeted Katey, the snake focused in on them and Ludmilla wants both the money and the child. She is planning to kidnap her a second time and sell Katey to a bidder in Asia who is willing to pay double the original asking price. All the while she will milk David Johnson for every penny in ransom."

"This is disgusting," Amy whispered.

"Where is she?" Gone was the relaxed man in John. The firm, determined cop intent on getting the job done sat in her kitchen now.

"She's already at the hospital," Ruckus said. "We have to move fast."

John's phone rang in his pocket. He looked at the screen and glanced back at Amy. "I've got to take this first."

She nodded as he placed the call on speaker. "Good morning, Chief. What's going on?"

"Yates, you have completely turned my life upside-down."

"Sir?"

"There is an eight-foot angel standing in my living room telling me I should meet you at *Vanderbilt Children's*. Care to explain yourself?"

John smiled and looked at Ruckus, whose golden eyes glinted with laughter. "I'm about to head that way myself. We'll fill you in when we get there. Go with the angel, sir."

Chief Ryan Anderson was silent for a few breaths. "Do you have any idea how hard it is for me to stretch my faith this far?"

"Yes, sir. I do know."

The chief sighed. "Fine. I'll see you there."

John stood and pocketed his phone, ready to go. Amy stood also, but looked at Shake. "What about Jonas?" she asked. This time she didn't fear for his safety no matter what the King's plans for him were.

Shake winked at Jonas. "Quill is going to let me know if we're needed. Otherwise, we're going to hang out and work on our battle moves."

Amy smiled. "No real swords, okay? Not until he's at least twelve."

"Come on, Mom," Jonas complained. "Angels don't use fake swords. I need a real one, too."

Shake leaned over and said something to Jonas in a conspiratorial whisper. Her son grinned at her and waved goodbye. "It's okay, Mom. No swords this time. You can go now. I'll be fine here with Shake."

"Somehow I get the feeling I'm being shooed out of my own house."

Shake's turquoise eyes glowed like sunlight on sea when he smiled at her. "That's because you are. We have training to do." He winked again. "Now get outta here."

John grasped her hand and pulled her to his side as Ruckus and Harbor reopened the portal in her eat-in kitchen and stepped into the light.

Chapter Thirty-Two

Stepping out of the portal was like exiting a lightning bolt, John thought. His whole body thrummed with electrical energy. He felt like he could take a running jump to the top of Nashville's iconic *AT&T* "Batman" building with all the adrenaline pumping through his veins. Instead, he found himself tucked into a corner of the parking garage directly in front of the wide walkway leading into *Vanderbilt Children's Hospital*. His eyes swept the area and landed on his boss, quietly making his way across the garage beside a large angel with hair the color of burnished copper grazing the top of his muscled broad shoulders. His eyes, nearly the same color, focused intensely on Ruckus and Harbor.

Without preamble or introduction, the angel caught them up to speed. "We are in a precarious situation. Ludmilla arrived sometime early this morning and waited until shift change. She found a nurse who resembled her. Bethany Hanson was her name. Ludmilla executed her body and Bethany's spirit was immediately taken for her Homecoming. The body was stuffed in a supply closet. Bethany's angel led me to it earlier and Seamus is now arranging things so that someone can find it in the next couple of minutes."

Ruckus nodded. "Where is Ludmilla now?"

"She's posing as Bethany and gaining access to Katey Johnson with hospital clearance and credentials." The warrior angel nodded to Chief Anderson. "We agree she is planning to bring Katey here under the guise of escorting her to her family's vehicle. Only someone working for her will be waiting and she will take Katey with her at that time."

Chief Anderson spoke up. "We're going to interrupt her plans and arrest her instead."

John nodded. "Sounds easy enough."

Ruckus, Harbor and the other angel exchanged glances. "What?" John asked. "What aren't you telling us?"

Harbor looked around, her hand on the hilt of her sword. "The demonic presence in this place has increased."

Ruckus nodded. "Best to be on your guard. Hell is watching."

John looked at his chief, who looked at his warrior angel. "Kupari," he said, "I'm out of my element. You're going to have to tell me what to do."

John watched the massive angel lightly place a hand on his boss' shoulders. "I've always protected you," Kupari said. "Even when you did not believe. I'll not leave you now. Stay alert and remain beside me. We'll do this together."

John nodded, looking at Ruckus and remembering their battle in Kohlhaas' castle. He glanced at Harbor and Amy. He didn't know what all had occurred in the dungeon where the children had been held, but he had no doubt they could work together in much the same way.

For the next few minutes they stood to the side of the walkway, the angels invisible to passersby, John's arm draped across Amy's shoulders. For all intents and purposes, they appeared to be a group of family or friends waiting for the arrival or dismissal of a patient. Police sirens grew louder, stopping nearby, and an increase in security guard movement became apparent. John and his chief shared a knowing look. The body had been discovered, just as Seamus had planned.

"There she is," Amy said, tensing beneath John's arm. "There's Katey."

John zeroed in on the small blonde form quickly wheeled across the breezeway toward the curb. Without a word, the three of them moved to intercept Ludmilla and Katey, flanked by their guardian angels. John watched Ludmilla. She had changed into the dead nurse's pink scrubs and white tennis shoes. She'd even put on a white scrub jacket, complete with stethoscope hung around her neck, bouncing against the stolen ID badge. She'd pulled her bleach blonde hair back in a messy bun at her nape revealing a small black tattoo. As John got closer, he realized it was the same image he'd seen twice before: a scorpion encircled by a snake.

Chief Ryan Anderson removed his badge and opened his mouth to call out to Ludmilla when the air around them began to swirl in tornadic fury of light and shadow. It was like they had suddenly stepped into a vortex of shadows that howled and shrieked, pinching exposed skin and blowing hot, rancid air across their necks. The sensation lasted thirty seconds or less, but it was enough time for a navy blue sedan with tinted windows to pull up to the curb in front of Ludmilla and Katey.

John, dizzy from the surprise vortex, found his bearings just in time to see Ludmilla scoop Katey up in her arms and disappear into the passenger seat of the vehicle. Katey screamed out just as the door shut and the car sped off, tires squealing. Thistle lay flat against the concrete, two demons standing on top of her angelic body, their swords poised to hack against the joining of wings to body. John immediately raised his Glock to shoot out the tires on the retreating car, but there were people in his line of sight, still going to and from their vehicles, oblivious to the kidnapping that had just transpired in their midst.

Angela and David Johnson pulled to the curb, smiles on their faces, equally oblivious. Chief Anderson swore beneath his breath and looked at Kupari, who squared off against two demons guarding the retreat of the vehicle.

John growled in frustration. "Amy, explain what just happened to the Johnsons. Send them to the police officers right now. I'm calling Chuck."

"No time for Chuck," Ruckus interrupted. "Amy, you have twenty seconds with the Johnsons. Then we move."

Amy ran to the car, gesturing wildly as she quickly explained the situation. Harbor hovered over her, sword drawn and gaze fixed on the demons. More were coming from the shadows like wolves from the mist. Many growled curses in the guttural language of Hell. Some spat sizzling saliva at their angelic siblings, forever divided from them by the chasm evil created. John looked around, chastising himself for not reacting quicker and worried they would be outmatched and defeated in a matter of minutes.

But no sooner had the fear materialized within him than it dissipated in the warm flashes of light that blinked like strobe lights in every direction.

Two by two, Heaven sent its warriors into the fray, swords and arrows drawn, eyes locked on their gray, blistered counterparts. Within seconds, the citizens of Nashville waltzed between the hospital doors and their cars in the midst of swords crashing in ear-splitting metallic rings and demonic screams that made John's skin crawl. Soon there were more warriors clad in Heaven's crimson and gold armor than the blackened, foul demons who had been sent to protect Ludmilla's successful second kidnapping.

As the Johnsons ran toward the nearest security guard, Amy quickly joined John and Chief Anderson.

"We've got to get some cruisers and find them," Chief Anderson said. "I'll call it in."

Kupari laid one hand on his shoulder. "No. That won't work."

"I'm listening."

"Cars are too slow," Kupari explained. "Flying is faster."

"Flying," Chief Anderson repeated.

Amy's smile was immediate and radiant. She looked at Harbor. "Really? Can we?"

"Sounds good to me," Harbor said.

Ruckus looked at John. "You in?"

"Sure, but won't people see us? We aren't invisible to everybody like you guys."

Harbor smiled at Amy. "You can take care of that, right? Ask King Jesus to do it again."

Amy didn't need to be told twice. She closed her eyes and John knew the instant she locked her eyes on her King. Her face reflected such peace and joy that it made his breath catch in his chest. She began praying aloud, pouring out love and praise to Jesus as easily as she would have poured out the items on a grocery list. John felt himself drawn into her praise and closed his eyes, offering up his own. And then she said it. In simple, confident words she asked King Jesus for invisibility. The sudden sensation of warm water flowing over his head and down his body jolted John from his quiet moment of serenity. Chief Anderson looked just as surprised while Amy looked entirely delighted.

The angels, having soaked up the moment of prayer as well, seemed refreshed and ready for more warfare. Without a word, they moved behind the three they guarded so fiercely and faithfully, wrapped their arms around their torsos and hips, and leaped upward, wings giving one strong, graceful flap, then spread impossibly wide, sending the six of them careening just beneath the fluorescent bulbs of the parking garage, skimming the tops of a line of pickup trucks, then rising high and higher into the midday sun of February in downtown Nashville.

Katey – Part Eleven

Not again! This time it wasn't my fault and it's not D.D.'s either. I don't know who this woman is, but I don't think she's a nurse. And the guy driving the car is scary with his skull tattoos and gold teeth. I told them to pull over and let me out. I screamed and screamed until she wouldn't let me breathe anymore. Her hand clamped down over my neck so tight I had to stop.

But I'm not so scared. Not like before. Because now I know I'm not alone. There are angels. And God is really real! He knows where I am. He'll send help for me. I know he will. I just have to hang on and wait. And as soon as I see my beautiful angel's face, I'm running straight for her. Just let them try to stop me.

Chapter Thirty-Three

Over the campus of Vanderbilt and the trendy shops nearby Amy flew low and fast, secured by Harbor's strong grip. She let her eyes roam the streets below for the dark blue sedan with the tinted windows, but the speed at which they flew combined with the amount of dark cars they saw made it impossible to identify the right one. The wind bit cold and ferocious at her skin, making her teeth chatter. But she clamped her jaws together to stop the spasms and renewed her search for the car that held Katey.

She gasped as a surge of light directly to her right revealed a new form. Quill, shining with the light of Heaven and the noon sunlight appeared flying with them, his white air standing out like a flag in the wind.

He held up an onyx-colored hand and motioned them to the right. She remembered then Quill was in charge of intelligence. He would know right where to lead them. No doubt he had been communicating with R.P. during the first three phases of the battle to get Katey back. Now, it seemed he would be directly involved. She'd be willing to bet more than one angel stood over the Stone Table in the War Room watching this new wrinkle get smoothed out by yet another tussle between angelic and demonic forces.

As they tilted into the cold wind, the tattoo on Amy's neck grew warmer and in her spirit she could hear the drum cadences from the Throne Room beating a steady staccato rhythm layered in snares and djembes, bass drums and cymbals. The King's attention was focused on the here and now of their mission to rescue Katey once more and Amy knew Hell could send whomever they wanted. It wouldn't matter. There was no way King Jesus was going to let Katey out of his grasp.

They topped a line of apartment buildings along I-440 and Quill pointed straight down. Snaking in and out of the flow of traffic was the navy blue sedan. She looked at John, who flew with his eyes closed and his arms outstretched, completely surrendered to the moment in the arms of his angel. She recalled Sam's words to his dad. *No more sadness. Have more fun.* And John was doing it. He was living in the moment, trusting God with the details, flying. She stretched out her hand and grasped his. He opened his eyes and locked his gray eyes with hers as their angels began a steep dive down to the car for the attack.

She could hear demons screeching their curses, gaining ground behind them. Harbor looked over her shoulder and shifted Amy to the right, instructing her to wrap her left arm around the angel's waist. Amy did as instructed and watched as Harbor drew alongside Kupari. "Now!" she yelled, and Kupari deftly handed off Chief Anderson to Harbor's left arm, securing both of them in her strong embrace.

Kupari, his arms now free, closed the distance to the car in two seconds, flipping himself over five feet above the hood and landing with a crash on top of it. His feet dented in the front of the sedan and his massive hands clutched the sides of the windshield. As he peered in the glass, he let off a massive flash of coppery light, sending a shock wave of energy in every direction that made Amy's ears pop. With the flash the driver and Ludmilla had been given sight to see the angel attacking them and their terror was visible and audible as Harbor neared the vehicle, now squealing its tires and lurching across the expressway. Amy watched the driver let go of the wheel to cover his face while Ludmilla cursed the angel and grabbed for the wheel. Katey, completely delighted at the sight of the angel, grabbed the dashboard and cheered him on.

The car, completely out of control, weaved left and right, crossing the lanes of traffic and causing other vehicles to slam on their brakes and hug the guardrail or grass median. Kupari flapped his wings, using all his strength to guide the vehicle out of danger. As he did, the demons chasing them arrived on the scene. Harbor and Ruckus lightly set down Amy, Chief Anderson and John before flying to the left and right of Kupari, swords drawn, guarding him against the advancing blades of the demons sent to provide protection over Ludmilla's ambitions.

John and Chief Anderson set off at a dead run toward the vehicle, now straddling the highway. They both had their guns drawn as they neared the passenger side door. Amy had no clue how to help them take down Ludmilla and in a panic, she felt exposed and useless. Then the tattoo on her neck tingled and she remembered the monumental truth of belonging to the King. Her weapons were not physical. They transcended the boundaries between both worlds.

Amy took three steps forward, placing herself in the middle of I-440. Demons and angels circled overhead fighting with swords, fire and ice. More angels flew in, low and fast, kneeling on the side of the highway with arrows drawn, ready for a clear shot at a demon. The sounds of ice cracking and fire blazing, swords whistling and crashing filled the air and she joined it all with her voice, raising her words to a volume above the din of battle and calling out the name of her King: Jesus, Messiah, Warrior Man and Eternal God. She held up her arms and spoke into the air his authority, his ownership of all things temporal and everlasting, and declared him Victor. She praised him and thanked him and watched as John opened the car door. Chief Anderson, his gun trained on Ludmilla's head, suggested that she exit the vehicle and hand Katey over.

Ludmilla took in the battle of angels and demons above her head and watched, mouth agape, as Thistle flew straight for her, arms outstretched, a bright purple fireball in each palm aimed straight at her. Before Thistle could land on her feet, Ludmilla pushed Katey out of the door and planted her face on the asphalt.

Katey ran into Thistle's arms. The angel scooped her up and wrapped her wings around them both, protecting the girl from the spray of sparks and icicles falling from the battling angels and demons above them.

Once Ludmilla and the driver were both handcuffed, Chief Anderson walked to the police officers arriving on the scene in screaming cruisers and began directing the scene for them. They had no sight to see the truth of it and could only see the vehicles and the two kidnappers now cuffed and led by John to other waiting officers.

Amy's prayer ended and she watched as the demons, defeated once more, sank into the grates and shadows along the highway while the angels burst into brightness and disappeared back into the War Room of Heaven. As they did the drum beats from the Throne Room softened until they disappeared entirely, feathers on a breeze, and Amy swore that in the mixture of those cadences she heard Jonas' laughter. She looked around for his smiling face, but couldn't find him or Shake anywhere.

Ambulances arrived on the scene to collect Katey and treat any other injuries. Amy waved off the paramedics, assuring them she didn't have a scratch anywhere. Instead, she promised Katey she would check on her later and turned to find John leaning on the hood of a cruiser and smiling like a Hollywood star.

"I could get used to this," he said.

"Get used to which part? Flying or fighting alongside an army of angels?"

"Actually," he said, pulling her into his arms, "I was thinking I could get used to seeing you every time I turn around."

Tangling his hands in her red curls, he nipped her lips before deepening the kiss. She felt her heart rate skyrocket as she wrapped her arms around his neck, drawing him in even closer.

R.P.'s voice broke through the rising heat between them. "You guys have really got to pick a better place for all that."

Amy turned to him in surprise while John heaved a big sigh. "Ghost, you've got to work on your timing. It stinks."

"I told you I'd see you around."

"I'm busy right now."

Amy laughed at their banter and pulled out of John's embrace. "What are you doing here, R.P.? You missed the big show."

"I was watching. In fact, I had front row seats. Nice job to both of you."

"So what now?" Amy asked. "Katey is safe again. Ludmilla is in custody. The kidnapping ring is in shambles. You got something else in mind?"

R.P. smiled and placed his hands on their shoulders. "There's something I want to show you."

Chapter Thirty-Four

As much as John loved being a part of both physical and spiritual realities, it occurred to him that he was getting tired of being whisked back and forth across the dimensions through the electrifying, dizzying jolt of the portal. His heart pounded and he gripped Amy's hand as his vision cleared like mists in sunlight. He first became aware of the sweet smell of roses mixed with mint and pine floating past him on a warm breeze. Then his eyes focused on the sight before him and he fell to his knees. Rising as high as a skyscraper, the walls of New Jerusalem stood resolute in shimmering emerald, sapphire, topaz, chrysolite, and more. Above him a shofar blew loud and long, sending a trill of anticipation down his spine. One side of the gate before him, made of one solid, luminescent pearl opened as R.P. helped him to his feet and led him forward.

Amy bounced on the balls of her feet as she practically ran through the gates of Heaven, pulling John and R.P. with her. He remembered her excitement when she'd told him about her first visit, standing in her bedroom with tears rolling down her cheeks and Dog purring behind them as he stubbornly rejected her every word. He understood now why she wouldn't relent, why her faith had become stronger than his, why Jonas had been able to take on Katey's kidnappers without fear of consequences. They'd been here, in Heaven, with streets of gold gleaming beneath their feet, castles rising in glistening white around them, and the steady peal of thunder rumbling amidst the incredible symphony of music pouring out of the Throne Room in the central pinnacle of the city laid out before him.

John let his eyes roam across every architectural feat made of marble, gold, glass, and precious jewels. He soaked in the presence of his Heavenly Father, raising his hands toward the Room where his soul led him, allowing love in its fullest, purest form to consume him. He was Home.

Striding down the golden street before them were Ruckus and Harbor. The warrior angels had taken off their crimson and gold armor and now appeared relaxed in soft leather pants and white linen shirts. As they neared, Ruckus held up his hands and turned in a circle.

"Well, John, what do you think?"

John looked behind his angel at the elegant staircase rising to a second level of New Jerusalem, saints and angels coming and going in every direction with purpose and joy in every step and smile. "It's more than I could have ever imagined."

John looked down at Amy. "I'm sorry I didn't believe you at first. It's just like you said, except more. Words don't do it justice."

She smiled. "I know. It can't be captured with language. It's just so much bigger than words can express."

John looked back at Ruckus. "I assume we're not staying?"

"You assume correctly. It's not your Homecoming. But it is a very special day."

Ruckus winked and moved to the side. Two columns of figures had formed on either side of the street in front of John. They all wore the black fatigues of the saints in the battles they'd just fought. He'd seen them in action. They were good. Very good. Using warfare training and abilities gained in both the physical and the spiritual realms, they could hold their own against anything Hell spat at them. Surprised at their amassed, forceful presence, John let his gaze roam their faces and as he did, his heart began to pound. He recognized these saints. He knew them, or had known them, before their bodies had been killed. They were the infantry soldiers, the Navy SEALS, the Green Berets, the Rangers, the medics, the helicopter pilots he'd prayed with and sent Home. He'd mourned them for years, keeping steady in his mind's eye their final moments on Earth, so bloody and filled with so much pain. But that wasn't their present reality. The holes that had been in their bodies before were no longer there. They were whole, healthy, vibrant, and fully alive. They were the redeemed, the saints of Heaven.

John's legs shook as the grief he'd felt for years shattered into tiny pieces and blew away like sand in a breeze. One by one, they pulled him forward, hugging him, shaking his hand, clapping him on the back, thanking him for giving them support, peace, love, and words of hope in their final moments. He moved down the line, not missing a single one, as tears streamed down his face, releasing every last stronghold of torment, every last mental image of death from each of them. He was gifted with seeing the after, the post-death, the fully reborn version of the nightmares that had haunted him since the horrible moment of each of their deaths. By the time he came to the end of the line, John felt reborn as well. All the shadows in his soul had been replaced with warm light, fully illuminating what was now healed and whole within him.

At the end of the line stood R.P., grinning like the Cheshire Cat. He stuck out his hand to John and waited. As soon as their palms touched, John's vision clouded over with the final memory. He'd known this man. His was the worst one. He'd gone through the door first, his Ranger brothers had said. He always went in first. And always before, he'd come out in one piece. But this time, this day, he'd been gunned down as soon as the door opened. His brothers had finished the fight and gotten him back to the helicopter where John had been waiting, imbedded on the front lines as he normally was. His body was convulsing, his blood pouring all over John, trailing out of the open door of the chopper, glistening in the fading light of the sun. The gurgling sound of his last breaths had stayed with John ever since, a cemented reverberation in his worst nightmares and flashbacks. But John had held on. He didn't avert his eyes. He prayed over the sound of his breathing, over the sound of the chopper, over the sound of his brothers begging him to hold on for a little while longer. John prayed until the peace came and he knew the Ranger before him had made it Home.

When his vision cleared once more, he found himself held up in R.P.'s arms. "I didn't know," he said, his fist bumping the back of the solider turned saint. "All this time, through the whole thing, I didn't recognize you. I didn't know it was you."

R.P. squeezed him one last time and stepped back. "I didn't want you to know. I needed you to focus on what we had to accomplish. And you did, John. You did well. You made us all proud."

John looked him over from head to foot. "You're okay now? Really okay? Your injuries were so severe. Your death was so horrible."

R.P. nodded. "It was. But the moment was fleeting. I passed through it. It's like diving into the deep end of a pool. When you hit the bottom, it's dark and the pressure of the water is all around you. But you rise and break through the surface of the water. You breathe again and the pressure is gone. It's just not there anymore. Once I made it Home, everything that came before, every moment of pain, vanished. Those things can't exist in the presence of the Holy One."

John understood. He'd already experienced it here, in minute fashion, he knew, but he could understand in a way not possible with human limitations how vast and all-encompassing the healing love of God was. "Thank you," he said, "for opening my eyes to see you finally and allowing me to recognize everyone else." He paused and looked back at the two rows of soldier saints smiling at him. "This changes everything for me."

R.P. chuckled. "I'm so nowhere near done surprising you."

"Seriously? You've just about wiped me out here. There's more?"

"More than you could possibly imagine." R.P. crooked his finger in invitation to follow and Amy stepped in beside him, holding his hand and wiping away the tear streaks that matched his own. R.P. continued. "The two of you have the privilege of seeing something new in Heaven. Something just created."

He walked toward the staircase but instead of ascending the pink and gold hued marble, he circled around it and walked past a fountain. In its center was a massive crystal ball suspended by the force of water flowing up beneath, allowing the ball to roll and twist, water sluicing off in every direction so that the whole fountain, crystal and water and light, sparkled as if a million diamonds flowed instead of water. John and Amy followed R.P. past the fountain with Ruckus and Harbor, descending a set of curved stairs carved from the same ribboned marble. At the bottom they walked into a large cavern directly beneath a waterfall. The pounding rush of water was muted by a wall of green ferns and flowering vines of purple clematis and white wisteria that swayed in the mists from the voluminous cascades. Beneath them the floor was the rough white sandstone of the castles above and the arc of the circular cavern was filled with a series of holographic images. Thousands upon thousands of images, all in motion, glowed fully three-dimensional like the images R.P. had produced in Germany and again at the farmstead in north Nashville. A long glass stage stretched the full length of the cavern and Quill stood in the middle of it, his onyx skin glistening and his white hair bright and flowing between his furled iridescent wings. Two more angels stood with him on the stage, their combined concentration and focus on the images eclipsing everything else around them.

John's head turned at the sound of an eagle's cry within the fluid stroke of a harp's chords. His mouth dropped open as he took in the sight at the far side of the cavern. Twelve feet apart stood two golden altars, a giant flame leaping three feet high off each one. Inside the flames were two living creatures who did not burn with the fires. Instead, their existence was found within the flames they inhabited. The creatures had three sets of two eyes at the top, middle and bottom of their torsos. They were covered in gray and white feathers and their wings were stretched wide as they praised Father God chanting, "Holy, holy, holy is the Lord God Almighty, who was, and is, and is to come." They spoke the words in every language known to man and sang them like birds and musical instruments, breathing in the flames and releasing their worship as a sweet-smelling incense that rose above them, through the marble and jewels and gold above their heads, rising still to the Throne Room where the great *I am* heard and responded with himself.

John turned back to Quill who concentrated on the images and spoke first to the angel on his right, then to the one on his left. As he spoke, the angels waved their hands in the air and words appeared as letters and sound in an ephemeral script that glowed bright before fading. R.P. came to stand before John and Amy, his gaze intense.

"This," he said, "is the Hall of the Torchbearers."

Amy drew in a breath and tightened her grip on John's hand. "For Jonas," she said, "and Katey."

R.P. nodded. "And many others. You see, you are favored because you are living in the End Times. The King's return will be soon. These battles we fight are just skirmishes; previews, if you will, of what is to come. And as the days tick down and the darkness grows stronger, we too must grow in strength."

"How?" John asked.

"The Church must grow. The Bride must be pure. And the Torchbearers must be bright and plentiful. This place has been created especially for that purpose. Quill is Commander here. He sees the needs and instructs the Beta-Commanders who in turn send assignments to the War Room, to the Healers, to the Guardians, or to the Welcomers as needed."

"So this is like a second War Room?" Amy asked.

R.P. nodded. "Yes, specifically focused on the Torchbearers."

Harbor nudged her with an elbow. "You helped us see the need for this. It was your intercession and action that brought this place into being. Prayer changes everything, even Heaven."

Amy nudged her back, smiling. John looked around again. "This is amazing, R.P. Truly. But why did you want us to see it?"

R.P. grinned back. "You're my kind of guy, Yates. Always pressing for the bottom line." He stepped back and crossed his arms over his chest. "I'd like to tell you," he said, "but I can't."

"Why not?"

A voice rang out in a clear baritone that John recognized immediately. It was the voice that had created him, that had called Lazarus from the grave, and the voice of the One his heart longed for the most. "He can't tell you because I want to have that honor."

There was a smile tucked into the authority of the voice of the King and John turned around as R.P., Amy, Harbor and Ruckus all bowed on one knee. John faced Jesus and took in the warmth of his eyes, at once brown and gold and green and blue, focused intently on John's face, his eyes, his very core. John found himself on the floor, kissing sandaled feet, overwhelmed by love and adoration in a way he had never before experienced. He abandoned conscious thought and worshipped his King, fully recognizing himself in a sense of belonging he'd never grasped or known so intimately. He never wanted to leave this God-Man, this King of Kings.

Two hands rested on his shoulders and squeezed. "Please, John, stand and let me hold you."

He did as asked and King Jesus embraced him as a long lost brother, pouring into his body, mind, and soul a torrential flood of peace and love that consumed every panicked moment of fear, every incensed flare of anger, every roughened moment of sin in an all-encompassing touch that brought recreation, redemption, and total renewal. By the time King Jesus stepped back from John, he again felt reborn, a new man illuminated from the inside out in a way that darkness could never dominate or diminish again.

"John," the King said, "you make me so very proud and happy. You've done well, even when it was hard to believe the wild and crazy things I do in my kingdom." He leaned forward. "I like to do the unexpected, completely impossible things. They're the most fun."

He turned then and motioned everyone off their knees, picking Amy up and swinging her around in a hug that made her laugh and hold to him even tighter. He placed a hand on R.P.'s cheek and commended him for a job well done on Katey's rescue, and high-fived Ruckus and Harbor. He then stood back and breathed deep the scents of the green ferns and flowering vines floating in the clean, cool mist of the waterfall.

John watched the face of King Jesus, in awe of the regal authority that rested in every feature and jewel on his crown, while continuing to exude serenity and peace. John loved him, purely and deeply. He quieted his own breathing to hear the next words his King would speak. "This is a special place created for a special time in our kingdom's story. You are already a part of it." King Jesus pointed to an image and it sprang forward to rotate in front of them. "Look at what Jonas has been able to accomplish today with Shake."

John and Amy watched Jonas in the image, sitting in the floor of her living room. Shake sat beside him, watching and encouraging as Jonas, eyes closed, allowed his spirit to be aligned not only with the will of Heaven, but aligned specifically with the room they were standing in.

"What is he doing?" Amy asked.

"He is seeing what you see. Jonas is a Visionary, a Seer, a Prophet. He is cultivating a gift he has had since birth."

Amy's eyebrows furrowed. "I don't fully understand what that means for him."

King Jesus nodded and squeezed her hand. "It means he will call forth the things that are not so that they are. He will see past the physical and into the spiritual and his faith will be strong enough to build a bridge between the two. He will impart knowledge and healing, understanding and ability. These are the things his identity as a Torchbearer allow him."

"He's an intercessor," John said.

King Jesus nodded, his eyes shining with pride. "Yes. The fire in him will grow as he matures. It's going to be awesome."

John couldn't help but smile at King Jesus' excitement. His love for each Christian was full, huge, complete. "My sermons just got so much better."

King Jesus laughed. "They were already good, John."

"Thanks."

"Speaking of life as you've always known it," King Jesus continued, "I'd like you to leave behind what was before. I have something different in mind for the two of you."

Amy pulled her eyes from the image of Jonas and Shake and turned her attention to her King. "I don't want to go back to the status quo. I'm not even sure it's possible now."

"Good," he said. "I want more for you." King Jesus drew them closer to the glass stage behind Quill, who continued on with his job as if no one else was in the room. "All of the Torchbearers you see in these images were born into their identities. They were marked at conception."

"Marked," Amy said. "Like the tattoo you gave me?"

King Jesus smiled and nodded. "Yes, but their mark is between their shoulder blades. A single flame identifies them as a Torchbearer. Everyone in Heaven and Hell can see the mark. Humans do not have the vision for it unless we allow it for a specific purpose."

"For now we see in a mirror dimly, but then face to face. Now I know in part, but then I shall know just as I am fully known," John quoted.

"Yes!" King Jesus said. "Exactly. That is what it is like for humanity. But only for a little while longer."

"What do you want us to do?" Amy asked him.

"I want you to choose to be Torchbearers," he explained. "You weren't born to it, but you can choose it. You can be trained up into a higher plane. You have seen so much more than your brothers and sisters. Allow me to mark you as well so that you can carry this new knowledge back to them."

He paused and placed his hands on their shoulders. "But I caution you. It is a great responsibility. Torchbearers must seek me more because they require more sustenance from me. They require my presence and my Words in order to live fully in the Light they bear. Do you understand?"

"If we choose to be Torchbearers," John said, "we choose to have greater responsibility as Christians. We choose to carry you into dark places, putting ourselves in greater danger."

"Yes."

"But you will be with us," Amy said. "And the Army of the Lord will stand with us as well?"

R.P. stepped forward. "Yes, we will. I have been reassigned to the Hall of the Torchbearers. The saints of Heaven join the angels to stand with all Torchbearers. We stand down Hell and cover each one. You have my word, Amy. You will be protected."

John didn't need further assurance. He knelt before King Jesus. "I'm all in, Lord."

Amy knelt beside John. "Me, too." She lifted her face to her King. "Mark me as your Torchbearer, King Jesus."

The King placed a hand on each of their heads and breathed across their backs. John felt the mark enter his skin like a match struck along his spine. It burned brief and hot, making him wince before easing into a languid sense of peace and resolve that dropped into his soul like a stone into ocean waves, a thing of substance that remained after the heat had dissipated.

King Jesus helped them both to their feet, kissing each of them on their cheeks with an embrace of affection. "There's just one more thing," he whispered.

He placed his arm around John's shoulders and led him to the side, asking Amy to wait as he did so. Coming over to stand beside the wall of ferns and vines, the fine mist of the waterfall covered John's skin like diamonds. King Jesus stopped and turned John to face him fully.

"It has not escaped my attention that you feel more for Amy than just friendship."

John felt a blush staining his cheeks. He felt like he was sixteen again, showing up at Sandra Darnell's house to take her to the prom and meeting her father at the door. He didn't bother trying to hide a single emotion from his Lord. He couldn't even if he wanted to. "Yes, I do. I think I'm falling in love with her."

King Jesus smiled and squeezed John's shoulder. "I think so, too."

John looked down at his boots and back up into the gaze of love that never wavered. "You know that there's more, Lord."

King Jesus nodded, silent.

"I feel guilty for falling in love with her. For wanting another family with Amy and Jonas."

"Because of Sam and Candace," King Jesus stated.

John nodded, emotion swelling in his soul. King Jesus wrapped one arm around John's shoulders and squeezed, then took his other hand and parted the vines separating them from the water fall. John looked at the parted curtain of greenery and saw that a path led from the Hall of the Torchbearers down toward a pool of water. "Why don't you take a walk, John," King Jesus said. "There's someone who wants to talk to you."

John didn't look back. Instead he stepped out on the sandstone path cut between forsythia and lilacs, climbing roses and rhododendrons. The path curved around a tall palm tree and John stopped. At the end of the path was a pool rippling into a black sandy shore with the force from the cascades above. On the shore was a large onyx rock jutting atop the water and perched on the end of the rock was a boy. He knew who it was. Knew by the shape of his head and the color of his eyes, so much like his own.

The boy looked up and his eyes locked with John's. A grin split his face. "Daddy?"

John ran down the rest of the path, splashing through the water at the shoreline to get to his son. Sam jumped into his arms from his perch on the rock and John sank to his knees in the wet sand, holding his child, kissing his hair, his eyelids, his nose. He traced his fingers and toes, ran his hands over the creases in Sam's palms, and breathed deep the child's innocent scent. Years of sadness and anger melted away as Sam hugged him as tightly as he could, saying over and over, *Daddy*.

Not letting go, John finally led Sam back to the rock, sitting beside him and letting his legs dangle over the dark blue pool that caught their reflection and showed it back to him, the perfect picture his heart had desired to see for six long, lonely years. He looked down at Sam, who couldn't seem to take his eyes off his father for a single second. John cleared his throat and tried to find words, any words, to capture this moment and savor it until his final Homecoming.

"Sam," he began, "I've missed you. So very much. Do you know that?"

"Yes," Sam said. "Do you know that I've missed you, too?"

"Jonas told me he saw you. He gave me your message."

Sam's face lit up. "Jonas is cool. He's my friend." He paused and cocked his head to the side, reminding John of himself. "You know he's supposed to be my new brother, right?"

John felt like he'd been hit with a boulder in the chest. "Your brother?" he repeated.

Sam nodded. "Yes. I didn't tell Jonas because he doesn't know all the things that I know. But I'm happy about it. Excited, even. I want my family to grow."

John grappled with the bombshells of knowledge Sam was giving him hand over fist. "So you're okay with me dating Amy? Maybe marrying her? And being a father to Jonas also?"

"Yes. I want that for you. And so does mommy."

John's breath caught in his chest and he felt the emotion rise with the tears that pressed against his eyes. "How do you know, Sam? How do you know she's okay with me marrying someone else?"

"We talked about it. She knows everything, like I do. She wants you to be happy, Daddy. Just like us."

"Sam, my time with your mom was so short, sometimes it feels like it was just a dream."

"But we're real. And we love you. It was hard to see you so sad and angry for so long. We don't want that for you. Amy and Jonas bring smiles to your face and make your heart glad. That's important."

John ruffled his son's hair. "Because I need to have more fun?"

Sam laughed then, a big belly laugh that reminded John of his father's laughter. "Yeah, Dad. Way more fun."

John pulled his son tighter into his embrace, kissing the top of his head and imprinting the feel of his arms wrapped around his waist. He watched the image in the reflection in the water, trying to commit every touch, every word, every sound in every syllable to memory.

"Sam," John said, "what if I don't want to leave you? What if I want to stay?"

Sam pulled away and shook his head. "You can't, Daddy. I know who you are. I know what you're meant to do. It's important work and you can't ignore it. They need you in the darkness. You carry the Light they need to see King Jesus."

John swallowed, trying and failing to control his emotion. "I'm going to miss you so much, son. Every day."

"I'll miss you, too, Daddy. But I'll be here, waiting. And you need to remember that I'm happy here. Really happy. It's hard to be away from you, but nothing is ever bad for me here. I'm never sick. I'm never in pain.

I'm never in danger. It's okay to miss me, but don't get swallowed up by it. Find your happy and your fun instead."

John pulled his son into his lap and rocked him as he would have had he had the chance in Sam's infancy. He held his son's warm, healthy body and felt his heart beating inside his chest, strong and steady. He trailed kisses along his hairline and reveled in the touch of Sam's hand as he traced the contours of his father's face.

All too soon, Sam pulled away and John felt the smile on his son's face before he saw it. He turned and watched King Jesus near the pool's edge with Amy at his side. John wiped the tears from his face as she wiped her own, and stood up on the rock beside Sam, who squeezed his father's hand and looked up at him with a smile.

"It's almost time for you to go back."

"I know, son. I'm going to be brave like you and find my happy and my fun."

Sam's smile widened and he wrapped his arms around his father's waist once more. "I'm proud of you, Daddy."

John's voice broke under the weight of his emotion. "I'm proud of you, too, Sam."

He kissed his son one last time on the crown of his head and watched as Sam slid down the side of the rock and hugged both Amy and King Jesus before following a path behind another wall of ferns and flowering vines. Before he disappeared he turned back to John and waved. "I'll be waiting for you, Daddy. See you at Homecoming."

John nodded. "I love you."

"I love you, too." Sam turned and disappeared behind the wall of greenery and John braced himself on his knees, breathing deeply and trying to wrap his mind around the precious moments he'd just had with his son.

Amy stepped forward and placed her hand on his shoulder. John grabbed her around the waist and hugged her tightly, vowing to himself that he would do just as Sam had said, wooing her and allowing their love to grow so that one day soon, his family would grow.

King Jesus closed the distance between them, his sandaled feet splashing in the water coming in small, dark waves against the shoreline. He wrapped both of them in his arms, placing a kiss on each of their foreheads. His touch was a balm to John's shredded emotions. The topsy-turvy rollercoaster of elation and sadness came to a standstill with the warmth of the King's breath against his skin. Heaven's love flooded into John, bringing not just peace for the moment, but a renewed sense of his purpose as a result of the God-Man with whom he was joined from the inside out, to whom he had pledged his allegiance and obedience. With that rejuvenated purpose, came a different kind of peace. One that eclipsed momentary emotion and took root, a Redwood into fertile soil, providing a canopy that stretched across both dimensions and allowed him not just life, but abundant life.

He felt Amy's thumb softly circling the black Celtic cross tattoo above his thumb joint and he breathed deep the floral scents around them, now clinging to the strands of her red hair.

King Jesus stepped back. "It's time, Torchbearers. Time to return to the world you know. But for a greater purpose and with greater resources than before."

"I don't want to leave you, Jesus," Amy said. "I'm afraid to be out of your presence."

"You won't ever face that. You're mine, Amy. You live within me and I live within you. There is no darkness so great, no demon so foul, no fear so terrible that I will ever leave you or turn away from you. I am yours and you are mine."

Amy nodded her agreement and King Jesus turned to John. "You must step up into a great role of leadership among the Torchbearers. They will be drawn to you. Keep coming to me. Every day. I am a well that does not run dry and as long as you drink from me, you'll be able to keep up the pace and do the job that needs doing."

"I'll do it. I promise."

King Jesus smiled. "I know you will."

He led them further into the pool, the dark blue glassy surface of the water lapping against their knees, then their thighs, and finally to their waists when King Jesus stopped. When he faced them again, John saw a twinkle in his eye and remembered that Sam wasn't the only one in Heaven who liked to have fun.

"Princess Amy and Prince John," King Jesus said, "go forth in peace."

John and Amy looked at each other and back at him.

"How?" Amy asked.

The King's eyes danced with amusement. "Dive deep."

"Dive deep. Into this water?" John asked.

"Yes. When you resurface, you'll be with Shake and Jonas."

"You really do like unexpected adventures, don't you?"

King Jesus smiled again and placed his index finger against John's temple. "You know that I do. Now go have one."

Amy intertwined her fingers with John's as they both took a deep breath and sank down into the water. As they sank the sandy bottom gave way and they kicked their legs as a light burst in front of them. The water was warm and the light, a kaleidoscope of colors and starbursts, drew them forward. As they neared the brightness of the portal home, John heard the voice of his King filling the pool around him, closing in like a second skin around his consciousness. It was as if the King had placed his mouth against the surface of the water and filled each molecule with the sound of his voice. *Call my Torchbearers*, he said. *Call them out of their dream states, their busy lives, their apathy, and their ignorance. Call them in every language from all parts of the world. Reveal me to them. Ignite them with the fire of my presence. Then send them out into the darkest places and light the world on fire.*

THE END

Made in the USA
Lexington, KY
02 August 2017